NECESSARY ENDS

The Novels of Stanley Middleton

A Short Answer
Harris's Requiem
A Serious Woman
The Just Exchange
Two's Company
Him They Compelled
Terms of Reference
The Golden Evening
Wages of Virtue
Apple of the Eye
Brazen Prison
Cold Gradations
A Man Made of Smoke
Holiday
Distractions
Still Waters
Ends and Means
Two Brothers
In a Strange Land
The Other Side
Blind Understanding
Entry into Jerusalem
The Daysman
Valley of Decision
An After-Dinner's Sleep
After a Fashion
Recovery
Vacant Places
Changes and Chances
Beginning to End
A Place to Stand
Married Past Redemption
Catalysts
Toward the Sea
Live and Learn
Brief Hours
Against the Dark

NECESSARY ENDS

Stanley
Middleton

HUTCHINSON
London

First published in the United Kingdom in 1999 by Hutchinson

Random House UK Limited
20 Vauxhall Bridge Road, London SW1V 2SA

Random House Australia (Pty) Limited
20 Alfred Street, Milsons Point, Sydney,
New South Wales 2061, Australia

Random House New Zealand Limited
18 Poland Road, Glenfield
Auckland 10, New Zealand

Random House South Africa (Pty) Limited
Endulini, 5a Jubilee Road, Parktown 2193, South Africa

Random House UK Limited Reg. No. 954009

A CIP catalogue record for this book is available from the British Library

Papers used by Random House UK Limited are natural, recyclable
products made from wood grown in sustainable forests.
The manufacturing processes conform to the environmental
regulations of the country of origin

ISBN 0 09 180069 2

Typeset by SX Composing DTP, Rayleigh, Essex
Printed and bound in Great Britain by
Creative Print and Design Wales, Ebbw Vale

> 'tis but the time
> And drawing days out that men stand upon.
> *Julius Caesar*: William Shakespeare

> Lights becoming darks, boys, waiting for the end.
> 'Just a Smack at Auden': William Empson

> . . . death, a necessary end
> will come when it will come.
> *Julius Caesar*: William Shakespeare

> These fragments I have shored against my ruins.
> *The Waste Land*: 'What the Thunder Said': T.S. Eliot

I

The old man squinted at the sunshine dazzling through the branches and leaves of limes and sycamores. He breathed deeply, groaned in contentment. The August weather blazed hot as he stood at his door, on the veranda at the front of his spacious bungalow, and he stretched his arms before tackling the three steps down to the garden path. He would not need his jacket he decided, but he carefully smoothed the rolled-back sleeves of his shirt before he set off. At the gate he turned right, away from the village, with its shop, pub and church, its newer houses.

Samuel Martin was in no hurry.

This summer afternoon, a Friday, he felt pleased with himself. He had put the vacuum cleaner round the whole house, cleaned bath and lavatories, cooked himself a large one-course dinner, pork chop, potatoes and runner-beans, and after a nap had cleaned the sitting room windows. Now the rest of the day was his own, and he'd walk down to the sea. He felt rather weary, but that would not stop his constitutional. He did not usually spend so much of his time in cleaning; once a week sufficed, and Friday was as good as any other day. 'I'm a man of habit,' he told people occasionally when they tried to tempt him out on a day set aside for some domestic duty. 'Of good habits.'

The road along which he walked was not altogether straight, but had a verge, grass mainly but with cow-parsley here and there, so that he could walk along, facing the traffic without fear. Not that there would be many cars at this time, ten minutes to four. Holiday-makers would have made for the beach either early or after lunch and would not consider returning for at least another two hours.

A car approached; Martin stepped aside. The driver raised a flat hand in greeting or thanks. The vicar, he decided. Sam had not spoken to the clergyman during the nine months he had lived here, and had not attended any church service or function arranged by the Anglicans. Neither had he patronised the other end of the village where crouched a small nonconformist chapel, but they held services only every second Sunday morning, or so he had gathered. But the vicar would know who he was. Everybody knew everything about everybody, so they claimed.

The road ran between walls and high hedges. The few houses built alongside the road stood well back from it, and were gracious, substantial places with wide gardens, grounds almost. Sam could not put a name to all the occupants, but he knew who they were in the sense that he could recognize their appearance. Mr Rolls, he called one man, who drove his Silver Shadow smoothly along the road noticing no one. On the other hand the same man, in shirt sleeves and yellow waistcoat and jodhpurs, working in the borders alongside his drive, would raise a hand, call out a greeting.

Footsteps behind caused Samuel Martin to turn. A young man in a track-suit top and shorts jogged up level and as he passed said, not breathlessly,

'Lovely afternoon.'

'Not too hot? For running?'

'No. Pleasant.' The voice came from a retreating back, as the runner did not turn his head. A visitor. 'Plenty of shade.'

At the end of the road, just past the riding school, he turned down a narrower lane, between high straggling hedges, and made his hot way towards the sea. He crossed a stream, standing for a moment on the squat bridge to watch the ducks before he strode on. Hedges and front gates gave out, and on the left a small new building, a public lavatory, encroached almost onto the tarmacadam, its bricks still red and its entrances scrubbed and disinfected. Sam used the urinal. 'Like royalty,' he told people, 'I never pass a convenience.' Someone must drive round each morning and clean the place out. On the other side of the road a copse darkened his path.

Now he was out on a golf course, a links. A sandy path, then a wooden, then earth again showed the way up and down to the sea. A group of four golfers approached at right angles, but he saw and heard no flying balls. One of the men, golf bag on a trailer, out wider than the rest, spoke, remarking on the weather.

'Not too much wind?' Sam asked.

'No. Specially compared with yesterday.'

'Hard work, was it?'

'I'll say.'

The player tramped on, clearly pleased. Samuel watched him reach his ball, select his club, and strike for the green, though he could not judge how successfully. He could hear the cheerful voices of the other golfers. Now he crossed the fairway; on either side marshes, clumps of bushes and vegetation blotted with occasional thin paths and small sheets of water catching the sun stretched ugly, darkly monochrome. Notices at the edge of the path warned him to keep off: this was a bird sanctuary. The flatness rose to a hillock of dunes and beyond that lay beach and sea. The higher land was cut through by his path, and as he walked forward he noticed a small figure approaching him with stiff, irresolute steps. A child, a little girl made a slow way towards him.

He waited.

'Hello,' he said when the child was within a few yards.

'Hello,' she answered. Both had now stopped.

'Are you all on your own?' Clearly she was.

'I'm lost,' she said. The voice sounded clear, steady, and the face though unsmiling showed no signs of fear.

Sam had no idea of the age of the child. He guessed five, but had no standards of comparison. Fair haired and with a pale complexion, the girl wore a simple sun-frock, yellowish, with a small-belted waist and a pair of soft shoes. The legs were sandy and lightly brown, the kneecaps blacker.

'Who are you with?' he asked.

'My mummy and my daddy.'

'Anyone else?'

'Benny. He's my brother. He's three.'

'Were you playing together?'

'Yes. But I decided to have a walk.'

'On the beach?'

'Yes.' The word mocked the simplicity of his enquiry.

'And then you couldn't find them?'

'Yes.'

This seemed slightly unlikely to him, for although the beach was wide, long and cut through with long pools, even at this time of year the number of people on it would be limited. A dozen, or twenty at most, families, he guessed, occupied themselves behind their wind-breaks, on their spread towels or folding chairs.

'Why are you coming down here?' he asked. 'If your parents are on the sands?'

3

'This is the way we came in, I think. They may have come up here looking for me.'

The child spoke with such clarity that he now considered that his estimate of her age was too low. Her eyes looked straight into his and the pale, pretty face was set, unmarked by grief, bland perhaps with shock.

'And your name is?' he asked.

'Emma Craig.'

'And do you know your address?'

Emma immediately rattled off the number, the street name, the town, Grantham, Lincs and then the postcode.

'Phone number?' he asked.

She gave it without hesitation. Clearly she'd been well drilled.

'I tell you what,' Sam Martin said. 'We'll go together to the beach, and if your parents aren't there, I'll ring the police with my mobile phone. I don't usually carry it about with me when I'm out for a walk, but today for some reason I did.' He looked down. 'Let's get back to the seaside, shall we?'

As they set off he put out his left hand to hold hers. The girl ignored it, but walked on looking straight ahead. Perhaps she had been warned against intimacies with strange men. They passed a wooden hut, presumably a store-place for the keepers of the bird sanctuary, or the green attendants, and beyond the dunes a concrete structure which had puzzled him from his first day. He could see no use for it; perhaps it was all that was left of some wartime building. It did not look like a pill-box or the base for a gun-turret.

'Which way were you when you went for a walk?' he asked.

The child pointed westwards.

'What colour was your mother wearing?'

'Red.'

'We should be able to spot that easily enough,' he said.

They reached the highest point of the path before it descended, in part sparred concrete now, to the beach.

'Which way were they?' he asked again. A second time she pointed westwards.

'Yes. Let's have a good look from here.'

As he expected, there was a scatter of people about, the majority near to the opening in the dunes, though four or five individual groups had moved much further down the beach. All were too far away to disturb the silence unduly, though a diminished shriek from three children and a commanding father trying not very successfully to fly a kite distantly cut the air.

'Can you see anything of them?' Martin asked.

The child shook her head.

'Let me lift you up. You'll be higher and see more.'

Emma held out her arms. He lifted her, held her without trouble.

'Can you see anything?'

Silence, and then a tiny explosion of pleasure.

'It's Mummy and Benny,' she shouted and jiggled in his arms. 'I can see them.'

He peered in the direction she pointed. Two figures, one larger, one small made their slow, black way. He could not make out whether the bigger one wore a red dress.

'Are you sure?' he asked.

'It's Mummy. I know.'

'Give her a call then.'

The child shouted, but the advancing figures neither stopped nor paid attention. Obviously they heard nothing, were too far away.

'Are you sure?' he asked again. His eyes scoured the beach. 'Give 'em another call.' The child tried, without result.

'Keep your eye on them,' he ordered. 'We'll go to meet them. Shall I give you a donkey-ride or will you walk?'

'Walk.'

He let her down to earth, and sang 'O, light as a feather was she' and they descended to the flatness of the beach. The sea stretched, first in narrow, long, standing pools, then in its completeness, gold and wrinkling silver. Once on the flat sand he looked again for the couple. They had disappeared. A pang of acute disappointment stabbed. He could not have been mistaken. They may not have been Emma's mother and brother, but they had been walking there. He had seen them. Not the child only; his eyes, not altogether trustworthy now, had noted them. Had he deceived himself to comfort the child?

'Can you still see them?' he asked.

'I can.' The child pointed with confidence. He hoped her right.

'Lead on, then.'

The girl set off in a stumbling run, he following. Suddenly he saw the couple again as Emma pointed. It was as if they'd

5

appeared from the pools and dark sand. Emma waited for him to catch up. The going was not easy underfoot.

'Is that your Mummy?' he asked.

'Yes.'

They took further steps head down. When he looked up the couple were still in sight, and possibly the larger wore red.

'Let's give 'em a shout. What shall we call?'

'Mummy,' she answered at once, authoritatively.

'Ready, then. One, two, three . . . Mummy.'

The approaching two had heard and looked. The mother waved with her free hand. Emma burst forward ahead of him, arms flailing. All the family were running. Samuel Martin kept up his sober walk, but smiling now. Emma called out again. The woman let loose the small boy's hand to rush forward both arms wide to embrace her daughter. Then she turned and snatched Ben into the circle. She kissed both children in a delirium, asking, 'Where were you, Emma? Where did you go?' then panting, 'We lost you. You went out of sight.' Mother and daughter both wept, and the look of surprise on the boy's face spread. Ben stepped back like a miniature adult to gape at the reunion. In the end it was Emma who restored order.

'This man found me,' she said.

Her mother snatched the girl up in a frenzy of hugging before she faced the rescuer.

'Where was she?'

'I was looking for you,' Emma said.

'She was up this end,' Martin said. 'She was just walking off the sands in case you'd gone back to the car.'

'Car? Up here? It's not on the sands.' She spoke without conviction, in search of some suitable expression of her mingled torture and joy. A pretty young woman, barely thirty, with fair hair, a red and white dress, and the same sandy shade to her legs as Emma's. She wore sandals; her arms were brown and a bright streak of tears shone on her face like a snail-trace.

'Thank you,' she said. 'Thank you. We thought she was gone.' Not yet in control of herself, the mother, in a dance which involved the touching and drawing in of her children, staggered about a few square metres of sand, back, forwards, sideways, then into a stoppage, a stasis, an eye of the storm, to check that her offspring were with her and available still. Recovering, more settled now, she thanked Martin again with breathless uncer-

6

tainty. 'It's kind of you. We thought we'd lost her.'

'Where's Daddy?' Emma asked. Her voice had reason about it, called them all to order.

'He went the other way to search,' the mother answered. All turned in that direction. 'It's a pity there's not a phone-box about or I could ring him on his mobile.'

'Let's use Robin Hood's bugle,' the old man said to the children. He took his instrument from its case, raised its aerial and passed it to the mother. She tapped with a jerky violence. The three watched. A male voice. The woman rushed the phone to her ear.

'Daddy,' she said. 'Is that you? We've found her. Up by the car park end.'

They heard the man's voice again, but could not make out what he said.

'A gentleman who helped Em to find me has lent me his phone. It's fortunate, isn't it?'

Again a long speech to which the mother listened, nodding her head. She did not interrupt him, but took it all in. Not until he'd finished did she speak.

'Right,' she said. 'We'll make our way back to the car. We can't go too quickly with Ben. We'll wait for you there.' Another burst of male monologue which she cut off with, 'Yes we're all perfectly well. See you soon.'

'He's coming back. We'll go to the car.'

'I should like to have spoken to Daddy,' Emma said.

'Oh, I'm sorry, darling. I should have thought.'

She handed the phone to Samuel Martin and he hid it in its case.

'I'll straighten my baldric,' he said to Emma.

'What's that?'

'The string over my shoulder.' He ran his thumb rapidly under it. 'I'll walk back with you all,' he said, 'to the car park.'

'Thank you,' Mrs Craig said. 'My husband won't be long. He's very used to running and quick walking.' She checked on the group and their possessions, and they set off, at Ben's laboured pace, over the dark sand.

They did the first part of the march, along the beach and up the path to the gap in the dunes, in silence, and Martin judged it to be best. Mrs Craig held the hands of both children, while Samuel carried her bags. The mother, he could see, had not yet

7

recovered from the trauma of loss. She made for the car with a fixity of intent, almost as if she expected further catastrophe should she turn aside from her purpose. She did not exactly drag on the children's arms, but they went forward at a pace that kept Ben near to trotting. She issued no instructions, neither encouraged nor reproved; he guessed, he could not see, that her mouth was still set, thin-lipped. The shoulders, awkwardly held, had no relaxation in them and bespoke the terror of those desperate earlier minutes when the child had disappeared. They crossed the golf course and walked out to the trees, the lane.

When they arrived, shoes full of sand, outside the public convenience, she asked, 'Anybody for a wee?'

Both children refused.

'You'd better go. I don't want to get to the car, and then have you asking to come back here. I know you two.' The edge of temper in her voice seemed unnecessary; she had not yet resumed control.

'I'll look after the kit,' Martin said.

Mrs Craig swept the children in. As soon as they returned, he offered to carry the bags to the car. Emma, wandering again, shrilly shouted,

'Here's Daddy.'

A black figure now crossed the golf course at a smart pace. The man seemed all angles and projections. He carried, in a kind of clumsy conjuring trick, all the rest of their accoutrements: bags, blankets, wind-break, bucket and spade. He wore three hats, one on another; mother's, Emma's, his own. That he kept a hold on so much and so firmly seemed a little miracle, but he accomplished all this at a sharp pace.

Emma called out to her father; he shouted back, voice muffled, but with no slackening of his progress forward. They waited. When he arrived they could see that he was dripping with sweat. His face reminded Martin of a boxer's, after a violent contest in an overheated sports stadium.

'Phew.' He blew breath comically out. 'That was hard work.' He looked down at his daughter. The angry red of his face contrasted with her paleness. 'You all right, Miss?'

'Yes, thank you.'

'Oh, God.' More play with the handkerchief. 'What did you go wandering off like that for?'

'I didn't think I'd gone far, so far, and then I couldn't find you.'

'I warned you about going off on your own. You're not old enough.'

'I'm eight.'

'Ted, this is Mr Martin who helped us find her,' Mrs Craig intervened, pacifically. He could not remember giving her his name at any time. He must have done so. His name and address were taped to his phone.

Craig looked him over carefully for the first time.

'Thanks very much. We'd just begun to wonder if all was all right, you know.' He turned to his wife. 'There's something to be said for mobile phones.' He turned back to Martin. 'We're on holiday here for a fortnight.'

Samuel Martin explained where he lived, gave them his address, invited them to call on him if they felt like it.

'Are you a native?' Craig asked.

'No. I came down for good in January. A friend, acquaintance perhaps, was selling his bungalow, and knew I was looking for something of that size. He had it for a holiday home. It's fairly large. Four bedrooms. I use one for a studio.'

'Studio?'

'I do watercolours. In an amateurish way.'

'Is this good painting country?' Mrs Craig asked.

The husband had placed his burdens together at the side of the road. The children had squatted, each separately, on bags, and were occupied with rest, not much interested in the adults and their conversation.

'It's pleasant. There's more than enough for me. And I've a car so I can travel round if I'm bored.'

'Are you a professional?' Craig asked, suspiciously.

'No. By no means. Apart from lessons in the lower forms at school, I've had no instruction at all. I've read a book or two, and looked at the odd programme on TV.'

'Are there not,' Mr Craig asked solemnly, 'painting classes to be had?'

'I suppose so. There were plenty in Beechnall where I came from. And in King's Lynn and Norwich and Hunstanton, I guess. But I've never patronised them.'

'Patronised?' Craig asked sarcastically. Martin stared at him in an awkward silence.

'This may sound arrogant to you . . .' Sam broke off.

'Not at all.' The mother.

'I thought, perhaps wrongly, that the teachers would be giving me useful tips, short cuts, and I didn't want them. I wanted to stumble on and find out for myself what I could do.'

'"I did it my way",' Craig said.

Martin gave no answer. Mrs Craig looked about her as if to collect her belongings and family together before her husband and the old man clashed.

'But, surely, when you read your books or watch these artists on TV, they all give you their suggestions, their methods, their tricks of the trade.' Craig again, modestly socratic.

'Oh, yes,' Martin answered, 'and I don't mind that. And the reason I don't is that they don't interfere. If I went to a teacher, he'd say, however politely or tactfully, "I don't think I'd tackle it like that" or "The perspective's not quite right, is it?" or "I think you could get a greater spread of colour there". That sort of thing is what I don't want.'

'Why not?'

'I fear, and remember, that I'm an amateur dauber, no more than that. And that before very long I'd be a pale imitator of the teacher or the classical masters he admired.'

'That's how they learned in the old days, as apprentices in the master-painter's studio. Copying at first, then being allowed to add some unimportant detail to one of the master's pictures, but in the master's style. There'd be no stress on originality.'

'There isn't in my case. I've not yet arrived at anything that could be called a consistent style. But we're boring the children to death.'

'Are we, Emma?'

'In a way.' The child answered with diplomacy.

Her father laughed and began collecting his baggage. When he'd arranged it manageably he said,

'That's very interesting to me. I'd like to talk to you again.'

'I'll carry the bags to the car,' Martin answered. 'You have my address. Or at least your wife has.' He dictated it once more, and the party set off for the last few yards into a tarmacadam car park among trees. There they dropped their loads.

'Give us that address again,' Craig said.

'What's the best time to find you at home?' Mrs Craig asked.

The family wished him good-bye, thanked him, the children politest of all. Martin waved at the car as they passed him a few minutes later. He walked with a jauntier step, singing to himself.

II

Two mornings later Mrs Craig rang Martin to ask if they could call in on him on their way down to his beach.

'About ten?' she asked.

'I'll be in.'

The family arrived without fuss. He had left the gate open, and at one moment the morning silence ruled outside, next the scrunch of gravel and the ferocity of his doorbell disturbed him, and there the Craigs stood in respectful but smiling order, as if for a photograph, children in front of their parents. They entered, and grouped themselves again, this time in his sitting room. Now Emma stepped forward, and presented him with a small parcel topped by a silver star.

'Thank you for finding me,' she said, handing it over.

'Oh, not at all. That was nothing.' He weighed the parcel in his broad left hand. 'What is it?'

'Guess,' the child said.

'It's not a matchbox.'

'No. Bigger.'

At this Ben crowed with laughter, as if at some joke of his own.

'It's not a shoe box either.'

'In between.'

'Betwixt and between,' Martin said. 'But what's in the middle-sized box?'

'Guess.'

'Three bars of soap,' he said immediately. They all laughed at that, Martin loudest.

'Better. Sweeter.'

'Honey?' he tried.

'No.' Emma encapsulated encouragement into the one syllable.

'Suck,' Ben said. 'Suck.' He made noises of salivation and lip-smacking.

'Sweeties,' Martin said.

12

'What sort?' from inexorable examiner Emma.

'Chocolates? Caramels? Fudge?' She shook her head at each unsuccessful guess. 'You'll have to let me into the secret.'

'Allsorts,' Ben screamed, swelling with excitement.

'There, he's told you now,' Emma said, grown-up.

'We'd better try them then.'

Very neatly he removed the bow, the star, the wrapping paper with its distinctive silver horse-shoes, and then the cover of the packet. He opened its lid and split the bag, holding the sweets out for Ben, the youngest, to choose. The childish fingers hovered in a hesitation of delight.

'Hurry up, Ben,' his mother ordered, 'or Mr Martin will think you don't want one.'

The child looked at Martin in dismay. The old man nodded encouragement, but did not contradict Mrs Craig with words. Ben chose; size counted with him. He put the sweet into his mouth and pulled it out to examine it again.

'Ben.'

Emma made her choice, as did the parents, and finally Martin.

'Thank you very much,' he said. 'It's very kind of you.'

'The least we could do,' Mrs Craig replied. She wet with her tongue a small piece of lace handkerchief and applied it with vigour to Ben's mouth. The boy squirmed, and cried out.

Next the host offered them drinks of lemonade, 'home-made and sweet', but these were refused. Instead the mother asked if they might be shown round the garden. Martin ushered them out. Neither parent knew much about horticulture, but the children were extremely well-behaved and kept to the paths. They played a subdued version of tag, hiding behind their mother's skirts, but never stepped on or near a plant.

'You've trained them well,' Martin congratulated her.

'That's my parents. Grandad Allen goes spare if they as much as put a foot on his soil.'

'He's a keen gardener, is he?'

'Vegetables. Potatoes. Beans. Peas. Cabbages. Sprouts.'

'Strawberries and raspberries.' Emma added her mite of information.

'Apples, pears and luscious plums.' Mother topped her.

'Gooseberries.'

'And rhubarb,' Father said. They all, Ben included, pulled sour faces.

'When I was a boy, my mother used to put a spoonful or two of sugar in a square of brown paper and I'd dip my rhubarb in it,' Sam said.

'Did you like it?' Emma asked, screwing up her mouth.

'I must have done.'

'Would you like it now?'

'I don't think so. It's about seventy-five years since I tried it.' They laughed.

'You're exaggerating,' Mrs Craig said.

'Exaggerating what?' he asked.

'Your age.'

'I'm eighty-one.'

The children flew squealing down the path, flapping their arms, shouting,

'Butterflies! We're butterflies!'

'I should have guessed you were early sixties at most,' the mother said. 'What do you think, Ted?'

'No more than that,' he answered.

'That's flattering,' the old man answered. 'It feels otherwise.'

They completed the tour of the garden rapidly, as the children wanted to get down to the beach. The two received another licorice allsort, and did not need to be reminded to thank the giver. Ben, Samuel noticed, carefully copied his elder sister.

'My husband would like to call in on you one day in the evening,' Mrs Craig said. She, last in the car, was standing in the drive still. 'When the children are in bed, I prefer to put my feet up, but Edward goes out for a walk, or a drink. He's never long, but we both enjoy this bit of time on our own.' She laughed, very short and drily. 'That's what marriage is like. Or at least ours. Have you ever been married?'

'Twice,' Martin answered.

'I shouldn't have asked that.'

'Oh, I don't mind.'

'May he come to see you, then? In the evening, at a time convenient to you?'

'Right. Give me a ring, and I'll tell you if I'm free.'

'Thank you.'

She scrambled into the car in some embarrassment, he thought, clipped in her seat belt. All four waved as Craig backed the car out, quickly, with robust, neat skill.

Martin wondered what the man wanted to see him about. Had

he and his wife discussed this? Why had Craig not raised the matter himself? He didn't seem lacking in self-confidence. Edward Craig would be no more than thirty-five, but got his wife to do his dirty work for him. He laughed at the crude expression. What did Craig do for a living? Why would he want to visit an eighty-one-year-old whom he barely knew? Sam Martin yawned, put his questions aside and turned back, climbing up, into his bungalow.

This was a free period. He tried to organize his life: three mornings a week painting, one cleaning, one shopping, one nothing arranged, all easy, and last, Sunday, wasting time with the pile of newspapers. In the afternoon he completed or continued the morning's toil and took some exercise, a short walk, it depended on the weather. In the evening he listened to music, or read, strolled in summer, visited the pub perhaps once a fortnight. Last December, immediately after his preliminary arrival, he had attended a 'show' in the parish hall, a comic football match one Saturday afternoon against the next village, and the church school's nativity play. None had been to his taste; all showed an amateurism that demonstrated lack of either leadership or constant practice, but he blamed himself for his lukewarm appreciation. He was an old curmudgeon, and daily growing worse. He made himself look the word up in the OED. Earliest usage 1577. Origin unknown. A guess that 'cur' had been 'cor', and the result a concealer or hoarder of corn. Mudgeon equals méchant? Not very likely. A touch of the avaricious about early meanings. That didn't apply to the pound or two he paid for tickets or gave to collections or spent on home-made cakes and coffee. He went grumpily upstairs to his sketch-books, his photographs and then to one of the '*16 fogli*', *Carta per Acquerello*, already taped to one of his drawing boards.

He served himself with a boiled egg sandwich while he listened to the One O'Clock News on the BBC. He fell asleep deeply for a quarter of an hour before the weather forecast, but had washed his plate, mug, spoon, knife and saucepan and was ready for art by two o'clock. He lost himself for ninety minutes, felt thoroughly disappointed with what he had done, and tiredly dazed. He'd try again after tea.

He walked out through the village, called in the shop for a block of ice-cream and a Battenburg cake, listened as he waited to two women discussing a burglary at one of the larger houses. The policeman investigating had told one of them, the indignant victim, that he was pretty sure in his mind who had done the crime, but that there would be no clues. The thief was crafty, wore gloves, and there was nothing that the force could do about it.

'So you leave them with my video and music centre?' the householder, a retired Vice-Admiral's wife, had objected.

'We shall go to see him. We shall have a warrant. We shall search the place. But your stuff will have been flogged off last night in a pub, or hidden in some derelict barn wrapped in waterproof.'

'Why do you bother going?'

'We hope it frightens him. He's sixteen. If he knows he's known to us he's more likely to be put off. If they get jobs, most of the young criminals are going straight by the time they're twenty-five. Moreover, it annoys his father, who's as big a twister as his son, and he'll be roaring at me that I'm pestering and harassing honest men instead of defending the public from muggers and rapists and murderers and paedophiles.'

'And my video?'

'It may turn up. One of these days. Especially if you've marked it with one of those infra-red pencils. And it's possible that one of these visits we'll find they've been careless or over-confident and left the stolen goods about the house, and then we've got 'em.'

'Otherwise you wait another nine years until he's twenty-five and in work?'

'And married. Yes, Ma'am.'

'And do you find that satisfactory?' the aggrieved lady demanded.

'No more than you, Ma'am. But it's not an altogether satisfactory world.'

This dialogue was delivered by the Admiral's wife in a reduced but confident quarter-deck voice. When the two women had disappeared from the shop still talking, though this time about the depredations of a gardener the other had hired to trim her lawns, the shopkeeper sidled up to Martin and said, 'I'd as soon consider stealing the crown jewels as breaking in to Mrs St John's house. She'd think no more of letting fly at you with a shotgun than of swatting a fly on her window-pane.'

'Oh,' said Martin, non-committally.

'She knows her mind.' The shopkeeper leaned forward. 'And everybody else's.'

Sam made his purchases and walked out. As he passed the two ladies, still mezzo forte in the street, he ironically raised his hat. They stared, hen-eyed, at him and responded mutedly.

The next evening he visited the pub with Edward Craig by arrangement. He did not enjoy himself, finding the occasion dead. They drank two half-pints, discussed paintings, not easily, painfully, neither man willing to upset the other.

Craig said one or two things about his work; he was a teacher at a junior school and claimed to get along with the job quite easily.

'Yes,' he admitted, 'yes, I suppose things are different from fifty years ago.'

'Better or worse?'

'Better on the whole, I'd guess. It depends on the criteria you choose.'

'I was at school seventy years ago, and the teachers were knowledgeable.'

'In what way?'

'They could spell, for instance, and do arithmetic. The old days of apprenticeship teachers had gone. All these had passed the matriculation. That was the Rubicon in those days. Five solid School Cert. subjects. English, including literature, Maths, a foreign language, a science and one other of your choice, all taken together, and no certificate given if you hadn't passed all five.'

'That might cut out some talented people.'

'It undoubtedly did. But those who became teachers, and they had often done what we called Higher Schools before they went to university or college, were educationally well-grounded. And remember there was a recession. Industry threw out its research scientists, couldn't afford them, and a job like teaching was a job for life. The senior teachers worked on in the classroom until retirement. Young teachers, middle-career teachers all worked alongside them. A blend of experience and young enthusiasm.'

'Are you sure?'

'If by that you're suggesting that I think all was perfect, I don't. But there were a majority of people in the profession who were well-qualified, who by and large wanted to be there, who

17

were respected in society for what they did. And they came from the top ten per cent of the intelligence range.'

The argument dragged on, neither convincing the other. Martin suddenly saw himself in Craig's eyes as a masculine equivalent of Mrs Admiral St John. The two men finished their drinks, stood up and said they must go, neither demurring. They walked off in opposite directions, Craig with rapid steps, Martin more hesitantly. Sam stopped now and again, to lean against a wall, not tipsy, but dazed by this inconclusive interlude. He could not understand why he, his own man, had agreed to this meeting with a stranger less than half his age. In recalling their argument he saw that Craig, a teacher, was not prepared to admit that the system today was inferior to that in Martin's schooldays. The classes were larger then, but, Sam argued, the teachers nowadays had thrown away that advantage by dividing their pupils into small groups, or even trying to teach individually. That demanded practitioners of the highest order, not the run-of-the-mill majority that every section of humanity provided. Craig had suggested that his colleagues needed to know more than those learned energetic men who had chased Sam Martin through his years at the grammar school.

'IT,' Craig had offered.

'Information Technology,' Martin had scoffed. 'You couldn't expect the masters who taught me to know about that. The modern computer wasn't invented. But they knew a foreign language or two, the literature of this country and of classical Greece and Rome, something of the Bible, modern history. And they wouldn't have got a place teaching in a secondary school unless they had some strong sporting or outside activity to offer.'

'Science?' Craig had sarcastically inquired. 'What about science?'

'Evolution, relativity, quantum mechanics, all had seen their great practitioners by the time I reached grammar school.'

'But they didn't appear on your syllabus? You did classical physics even if that was to be the subject you wished to study after you'd left school?'

'They split the atom in the Thirties. The papers were full of it. I guess the grounding the schools gave prepared people to understand new science better than the political correctness you and your friends hawk round. The Thirties seemed a time of enormous expansion of knowledge to me.'

18

'You were lucky. Ninety-odd per cent of the population weren't in the grammar schools. By your own admission.'

So they had chipped away at each other's arguments, not exactly losing their tempers but close to it. Craig treated Martin with more respect than the older man showed to him, or so it appeared in retrospect, and now in the street, of a summer evening when it was still light, Martin regretted this, and stopped from time to time to shake his head with embarrassment at his own rudeness.

He should not have turned out. Today he was fit for no company but his own.

That morning he had received from a former colleague, Jeremy Sands, a card announcing the death of Sands' wife. Jennifer would not yet have reached seventy. He remembered the first occasion Jeremy had brought his new wife in to an office party. She was prettier than Sam Martin had expected. That must have been typical of him, then. He'd written Jeremy off already: medium-sized, moderately handsome, hardly top-rate material, but decent, loyal, attentive, a perfect underling. And Samuel Martin had expected a wife to match, all neatness and compliance, not making a show of herself, shy, but understanding the hierarchical nature of the office and approving of it.

Instead of the shy spouse, Sands (Sam had never been sure that the man would marry, or even of his sexual orientation) had now in his early thirties introduced this beautiful young woman to his colleagues as his wife. Martin at that time was nursing Joan, his own wife, through an illness that proved in the end terminal. It meant he expended money, he could afford it, on experts to look after the invalid and the children. Joan was able still to come downstairs for part of the day, but she was listless, thin, sallow-cheeked, only rousing herself to voice complaints. Martin had not altogether played fair by her, he decided now. If some snag came up at work, he'd stay behind and sort it out when he could very well have left it to the next morning. But it was better than being at the beck and call of an ailing wife, who took her pain and weakness out on him.

He had not realized how near death she was. The doctors had spoken of a remission of the cancer, if not of a cure, when she had died suddenly of a heart attack. The woman who came in to provide the early evening meal for the children had heard a thump, called upstairs, received no answer, and had found Joan sprawled on the bathroom floor. Martin, called back from his office, had arrived at the same time as his wife's doctor, a thoroughly conscientious woman (who had probably missed her lunch to call in immediately), had confirmed that Joan was dead.

'It is a good way to go, Mr Martin,' she had said.

'I'd thought she was getting better,' he argued, uncomfortably.

'So she was. The consultants were pleased with the way the cancer was responding to treatment. But blood clots are often a concomitant of cancers. It's as if the body won't allow itself to suffer unduly, has the drastic remedy already to hand.'

He had looked hard at the doctor, at her permed grey hair, her bony hands, her eyes which barely seemed to blink. She seemed serious.

'She has suffered, certainly,' he said.

'Yes. And I think we don't know how much, however sympathetic we may consider ourselves.'

He thought he knew. That beautiful, vivacious, shapely girl he had courted during the war had been reduced in the last two years, either by the disease or the treatment, to a yellow, lethargic bag of bones. She had been quite unrecognizably different from the Joan he had danced with, whom he had left behind, married and pregnant, when he'd been posted abroad, from the brilliant mature mother, looking not a day older on his return, who welcomed him with such reassured joy.

'Is there anything I can do for you, Mr Martin? This is likely to hit you hard. Perhaps not altogether immediately.'

'No, thank you. You're very kind.'

The grey eyes stared into his, at his old-fashioned phraseology, his lack of comprehension.

'The children are at school, are they? You'll have to break it to them.'

'Mrs Terman usually collects them. I'll do it today.'

John, his son, had been scared of him when he returned from the war, but Joan had introduced them, brought them together, taught the two-year-old child to love and respect his father, that big uniformed stranger who'd pushed his demanding way into the home. Soon Joan, untroubled and immediately pregnant again, had taught her two males to be playmates, shown Sam how to dispense love, and John to receive it. Not seven years later she was dead.

With the announcement of Jennifer Sands' death again taken from its envelope, he condemned himself for his treatment of Joan. They had had fewer than eleven years as a married couple, three years with him abroad in North Africa and Italy, and two at the end when the cancer had ravaged her. But her six years as a complete wife had been amazing. Six years and she had done miracles. And yet at the end he'd lacked kindness, seen Joan's illness as a deficiency, a delinquency even, her opportunity to care for him, the children, the home being neglected. He realized that this was untrue, but wished he had been like other men of his age, with a wife who supported him, gave him the necessary time to show ambition, to make money. Then he could, as his colleagues did, reward her with gifts, with powers of free spending, expensive holidays, her heart's expressed desires. But she had shrunk into illness.

Now when he ran it over in his mind he was not proud of himself. How must Joan have felt when the doctors had diagnosed the killing cancer? They had fought, as she had fought, worked, experimented with the latest drugs, the most up-to-date machines. If anything, he decided, they had hastened her death by a few months, killed her with their scientific kindnesses. She was an intelligent woman, not much given to self-deception. How must she have felt when she was given two years to live? She would have understood, in spite of her weakness, nausea and pain, what responsibilities she had to relinquish, what anticipation of the future success of her husband and children which now meant so little because she could play no part either in its preparation or celebration. The final illness had changed her character for the worse, and now he was not surprised. Her eleven years had been full. Jennifer Sands had enjoyed something like forty-five years. He took out his writing materials and sketched a note of condolence to Jeremy, the bereaved husband; he had not seen the man for fifteen years so that he had little to say. They had exchanged Christmas cards; the Sands had been invited to Sam's second wedding, but they had been away on a flying visit to the United States.

As he carried the rewritten letter to the pillar-box outside the post office he remembered the stricken faces of his children, John and Frances, as he had told them of their mother's death. He'd picked them up from school, but decided to delay the announcement until they had reached home. At the door, he had taken their hands, led them to the drawing room, sat them on the settee, himself in the middle, and solemnly broken the news. Nine years old and six. Children should not be asked to bear such grief so early in life. All three had shed tears; he had hugged Frances. John had stood straight-backed by then (school had begun to instil British stoicism), but the tears coursed silently down his face. They had attended the funeral, and their presence had comforted him, and to the best of his understanding had not suffered permanent damage from their early deprivation.

Both of his children led fulfilled lives, as far as he knew. John was a rich barrister, a QC, who resided in Chelsea. Frances, his little Fran, lived in California with her husband, a well-to-do writer who worked in the film industry, a proud lady in a free American way, upstanding, mistress of all she surveyed. John had two boys, Fran a boy and two girls, but contact with these and their parents was intermittent. Had Joan lived or Meriel stayed there would have been regular celebration of birthdays, visits, frequent phone calls, holidays taken in common. Instead Sam would now have to work hard to tell the age of his grandchildren. There had been no overt quarrels, no deliberate neglect; Sam had been busy, then lost at his second wife's desertion, and opportunities for family reunions never even considered. Frances had several times been over with her children without making any attempt to see, or even phone, her father. He had last met her three years ago at the celebration of John's fiftieth birthday. They had been friendly enough, talked twice at length when she described her life in America, but to all intents and purposes they had been strangers. They had made no specious promises about writing or visiting; they had enjoyed their time together in an undemonstrative way and that had been that.

When two years after Joan's death he had married Meriel Rhys-Davies he had been half afraid that he was making a fool of himself. The girl at twenty-two had been seventeen years his junior, lively, well-read, affectionate, and to his surprise, genuinely fond of him. He had married in haste, out of uncertainty, but it had worked well. The children had taken to their stepmother, and she had learnt to handle them with loving tact, even strictness. They still kept in touch. Frances had called Meriel Mummy fairly soon (New Mummy), though the correct John had always used her first name, Meriel. There had been no children of the second marriage, and on the whole, he now

22

considered, he had been relieved. The fault lay in her womb, but she took no great steps to find out if the condition could be remedied. She had John and Fran, and they sufficed. The marriage had lasted, happily as most, for some twenty-five years, when Meriel, bold as brass, had suddenly on the eve of his retirement and quite out of character, announced that she had fallen in love with Thomas Walker, a man he barely knew, and that she intended to live with him in Stamford. Within a week she had cleared out from his home all the things she considered important to her. At the time, he had been deeply immersed in the alterations and readjustments to the firm that his retirement entailed. She was away with all her goods and chattels before he realized what had happened. It had seemed wrong, unlikely, ill-conceived then, beyond all rational processes, the action of a very practical madwoman. He could not forget that two nights before she had come out with her announcement they had made love together, eminently satisfactorily, in his view. He wondered later if that had been some sort of test, which he had failed.

Sam Martin did not contest the divorce. In his last year the firm, hauliers and road transport, had received two competing offers to buy the business out. This negotiation occupied him fully; Meriel's solicitors were neither rapacious nor aggressive, perhaps on her instructions, since Thomas Walker was extremely well-to-do. Once the decree absolute was pronounced, Sam heard little more of his ex-wife, not even at second or third hand from people with whom she had been very close when she lived in Beechnall with him. Occasionally he had read in the Sunday papers reviews of children's books she had written. She had published several, perhaps twenty, small booklets for younger readers, but these seemed to him of little importance. The publications were lavishly, often beautifully, illustrated, while Meriel provided perhaps four or five lines of print to each page. This seemed of no account; any mother with anything like a decent education and an ounce of imagination could produce such a text. His wife's skill lay in the fact that she knew the people who published these pieces, ephemeral and trivial as they were, and could thus get her mediocrity of words accepted rather than those of the other equally qualified hundreds who sent in their tales for the nursery. Meriel had occasionally said a word or two about her writing, and though he had listened and feigned interest, there was nothing worth questioning her about. What she did was roughly the intellectual equal of the domestic tasks she performed every day, and no one in his right mind would question her about which vacuum cleaner she used or from which tap she drew water for mopping the hall or brushing down the patio or the yard.

He had thus no idea how carefully she wrote these sentences about flowers or fairies or animals. Did she put down exactly what she meant at first typing, or did she spend much time writing and rewriting? These stories would be read out, he guessed, to children incapable of reading for themselves, but he did not know whether Meriel tried her words out aloud. She had left him a pile; all had been signed by her, some of the earlier ones had been dedicated to John and Frances, but they were kept, carefully wrapped, in a cupboard. The operative word was 'kept'; they were still here, in this house, sixteen years after her departure. He had imagined at the time that she would have taken them away with her other property, but she had not done so. He did not know why. Neither had he, on the other hand, consigned them to the dustbin. He never looked at them. On the infrequent visits of children to his house, John's for instance, he did not fetch them out for their entertainment. They remained in the darkness of a locked cupboard, not to be used but neither to be destroyed.

He had been surprised therefore, some year or two after his divorce, to read extremely favourable reports of two books she had written. These were unlike the stuff she had done at home, but were full-sized hardbacks, intended as far as he could deduce from the reviews for teenagers. Ten years ago he had seen her photograph in *The Times* on the presentation to her of a prize for young people's fiction. The novel was called *In Ecstasy* and clearly did not deal with either elves or cuddly animals. She still wrote, he saw, under the name of Meriel Martin. The accompanying article said little about her private life, but gave her address as Wendle Hall, Wendle, Lincolnshire. He had no notion whether this was the name of a village or whether she or Walker, if she was still with him, had acquired a country seat. He found a village Wendle in his road atlas, but he did not discover any manor house there. On his regular visits to the public library in Beechnall he had rooted out copies of her books in the children's section, and twice he had seen a copy of *In Ecstasy* on the adult shelves. There was a recognizable photograph on the flap of the dust-cover, but little about the woman herself, except that she lived quietly in rural Lincolnshire. He did not do more than flick through the pages, and could not therefore decide whether the title referred to sexual or religious exaltation or to the drug he read about often enough in the newspapers. The vocabulary, to judge from the first page or two and the last, was adult, and the ending uncomfortable, if not downright pessimistic. He did not take the novel home, and to his puzzlement walked out of the library that morning having borrowed nothing. He couldn't understand his behaviour; it did not annoy or distress him to think that Meriel had written a book worthy of adult readers; he was pleased rather than otherwise. And yet he'd gone home bookless. It did not make sense. He had not felt angry; he had experienced no sort of extreme of emotion, but he had deprived himself of a pleasure, acted in a way he could not account for. The second time he did not even touch the book, but shuffled past. He had concluded, without much conviction, that he had not yet recovered from the divorce.

He frowned into the darkness of the summer's midnight, more unsure by the minute.

III

Two days later Mrs Craig telephoned him.

'Karen Craig,' she announced herself. He had not known her first name. 'This may annoy you, I'm afraid.' She waited.

'Go on,' he grunted. 'Try me.'

'Ted said how much he enjoyed talking to you the other night in the pub. And he suggested that . . .' She stopped. He did not help her out. 'He suggested that perhaps I might like to accompany you to the pub one evening. Or,' she giggled nervously, 'you might like to go with me. He'd stop in and look after the children.' She gabbled the last sentence. 'I know it seems a bit forward on my part.'

He thought as much, but did not say so.

'When he came home he was full of it. You'd been talking about education, he said, and he thought you were full of bright ideas. You didn't approve entirely of modern methods, but then he doesn't, either.'

'He defended them.'

'He likes nothing better than an argument. But he really made it sound interesting, and I told him he had all the fun, while I had to sit at home. He then said that I should ring you and suggest that we had an hour together.'

'And an argument?'

'A chat, anyway. I said I couldn't do that. He told me that if it was what I wanted to do, then I should give you a ring. If it was what I really wanted to do.'

'And do you?' he asked.

'I suppose I do.' She sounded less confident again.

'Why not come here? It's only ten minutes away. I'll walk you back if it's dark, which it won't be. Or in any case. You can tell me what you like to drink, and I'll see it's here. What is it? G. and T.?'

'Lager and lime, actually. That's what I used to have. Not that we ever go out drinking these days. You can't with small

26

children, can you?'

'This evening,' he said.

'You mean, come this evening?'

'Why not?'

They fixed the time. Nine o'clock on the dot. The children would be in bed, if not asleep. No, Ted would know how to deal with them; he always made a point of reading to them if he was at home. He was a good husband, a caring father.

Karen Craig arrived one minute before time, slightly flushed from her walk. He poured out her drink; he'd taken instruction from the landlord at lunch time. She sipped and expressed satisfaction. She had dressed carefully in a cream dress with a stylish light-blue raincoat, unbuttoned. She wore no tights; her shoes looked sensible but matched the coat, her hair, carefully done, seemed naturally curly.

'I felt embarrassed,' she said, 'asking you for an invitation.'

'I felt flattered. Not many eighty-year-olds have pretty ladies asking to meet them. I suppose I shouldn't use the word "lady". I don't understand political correctness. "Woman" is slightly pejorative to me, though "womanly" is good.'

He raised his weak whisky in a silent gesture of greeting.

She smiled back, and his spirits rose.

They took a swift turn round the garden before it was too dark. When they returned she sat more comfortably as she described her usual domestic chores. She looked forward to September when Ben would spend the morning in a nursery class. What she most looked forward to, she claimed, was the quarter of an hour she'd have to herself with a cup of coffee when she'd got back home from delivering the children. She laughed at herself. 'It won't be all that marvellous,' she said. 'I'll soon get used to it.'

Karen spoke interestingly, he thought, making it all clear. She had been a teacher, but did not regret the change of rôle. 'I think that parents should give their children full support at home at least until they begin school.'

'Not always possible,' he objected.

'No. I admit that. We've managed. It depends on your priorities. Ted was twenty-nine when Emma was born. We never had a very expensive car, or exotic holidays. When I think about it now, it was as if we were preparing for a family. I wouldn't have said so, at the time, but that's how it appears now.'

She sipped at her drink, barely wetting her lips, he thought.

'And your husband teaches?'

'Yes, like me in a junior school, but he's just been appointed to his first headship. He's lucky. It's a good school with a good record in a middle-class catchment area. The parents are keen. They want their money's worth, but they put effort in themselves.'

'He never mentioned he was a headmaster.'

'No? I'm surprised. It's at the forefront of his mind all the time. He's looking forward to making a start. And an impression.'

'He's full of good ideas, is he?'

'Yes, I'm sure he is. But he's a diplomat. That's why he got the job. He won't go rushing in changing everything, until he's had a good look round.'

'He'll be a success, you think?' Sam asked.

'One doesn't know with a completely new situation. But, yes, I think so.'

She sat quite at ease, legs crossed at the neat ankles, hands primly in her lap, head slightly to one side as if about to query something he said. Sam Martin took enormous pleasure in her company, in the voice, in the quietly expressed opinions, the friendliness, the open nature of her smile, in her appearance. She was a good-looking woman, but exhibited no great pride in her beauty, made no play with it. Karen sat modestly, enjoying the conversation, set free from her usual occupation, but quietly relaxing, all within reason. Sam had not felt a happiness such as this for some years.

She began to question him on how he spent his day. He explained his rota, said why he thought it sensible to work to such a plan.

'Have you always been like that?' she asked.

'The man of habit?' He laughed out loud at himself. 'Yes, to some extent. But at work something always came up, and then it was a question of making your choice.'

He explained briefly to her the nature of his business, a national-international haulage concern. After the war he had put the business, begun by his father, back on a firm foundation, locally at first. He had been lucky that at this period he had met and then taken into partnership Morris Isaacs, an accountant, a man of ideas. Morris had terrified Sam at first with the breadth of his schemes, the depth of his borrowings, but they had succeeded. They bought up firms, established other depots, appointed efficient managers. Sam himself began to think as boldly as Morris. His partner smiled at the change, but often incorporated Sam's ideas into his own schemes for he realized that Sam knew the nature of the business, what customers wanted, what drivers could be asked to do, what was worth paying money for, where to economise.

Sam said little about his own skills to Karen. He praised Morris Isaacs. It had been hard work for them both, and when Sam approached sixty-five he had made no bones about his wish to retire. He told Morris who thought, then smiled and said, 'Say nothing for a week or month or so, will you?' Within a fortnight two American and one German company had sent in experts to scrutinize the firm. It became clear to Sam that Morris had for some time been at least preparing himself to sell the business. This he did, to advantage. Sam was left a rich man. Morris, though a year older than Sam, had agreed to stay on for a year, perhaps longer, as managing director. Sam's divorce was over. Meriel had married Tom Walker. John and Frances had settled with their families. Retirement loomed and attracted.

Sam, this bright summer's night, remembered the time. The loss of Meriel had wounded his *amour-propre*, but his grief and anger were intermittent. He'd been called in, once the firm had been sold off, for consultancies. He would have done the work for nothing, out of interest, but Morris would have none of that. He'd been summoned to New York, twice, and to Pittsburgh by the American firm who'd taken over. He'd enjoyed being quizzed about the European side of the business, but considered his presence there an unnecessary expense. He gave such value as he could for their money, and occasionally noticed that he'd opened their eyes. All this, and the investment of the enormous wealth, for so he saw it, which poured in, kept his spirits high. Meriel had gone; he lived alone in the same house; he lived frugally and he took up painting.

Karen demanded to see his work.

He showed her two examples on the wall of the drawing room in which they were sitting. Both had plain gold frames.

'Do you do the mounting and framing yourself?' she asked.

'Yes. I could do that before I came to paint.'

'How did that happen?'

'One of the children gave me the equipment for a Christmas

29

present. My wife, my second wife Meriel, would have put them up to it. We took a great number of photographs at the time, and I framed some.'

'Couldn't you buy standard-size frames?' Karen asked. 'We do.'

'Oh, yes. But I learnt how to do it for myself.'

'Are you good with your hands?'

'Yes. Moderately.'

The two pictures, a seascape and a square-towered church, were lifted down from the wall.

'This is not exactly the best light for looking at pictures,' he said.

'No. But these are good.'

'Perhaps it suits my style when you can't see them properly.'

'You're too modest,' she said. 'You can draw, for a start. And those cumulus clouds, they seem real. That must be hard, because they're always changing.'

'I can take photographs. And since I began on watercolours I spend quite a lot of time just staring at clouds. They've got to appear natural, but they have to fit in, make an important part of the whole composition. When Turner was a boy he used to paint skies and sell them to young ladies. They'd then do their own pictures under his clouds.'

'They'd ruin it all, wouldn't they?'

'They weren't in Turner's class for sure. But a good number of them had had lessons, and could manage quite well. You look at some of Queen Victoria's efforts. She wasn't without talent.'

'And you spend a lot of your time at it?'

'Yes. Especially in summer when the days are long. I don't like painting by artificial light.'

'But the picture will be seen by artificial light?'

'I suppose so.'

He led her across to his 'painting room', he said he dared not call it a 'studio', an annexe newly built on the north side of the building. The place was bare except for two tables on one of which was a half-finished picture, a Norfolk seascape, the wide sky dominating. He had put on all the lights. On one wall stood a set of unpainted shelves.

'I want to try to get things in an ordered way,' he said, 'so that I can lay my hands on anything I want immediately. That's important because painting is something where I can't depend on

30

habit. I never quite know what's happening, what I'll do next, what the effect of the brush-stroke will be.'

'And is that good?'

'I'm not sure. Perhaps it is. It keeps me occupied for the present. How long the craze will last I don't know. It's all a mystery. Perhaps in a few months I shall come to the conclusion that I shall never make much of a fist of it, and give it up altogether.'

'Is that likely?'

'I don't know. I hope not. It really is filling in my time to advantage.'

'It's a quarter past ten. Ted'll think I've got lost.'

Martin switched off the painting room lights. She finished her lager and lime as he fetched her coat. They set off together down the village street, still chatting.

'Sometimes I think I ought to travel,' he said.

'Broadens the scope of the painting?'

'It may do. I went to Paris to look at pictures. And then I tried it again a couple of months later. It did me good. I've been staring at pictures in museums pretty well all my life, but now I was out to learn. I'm going again in September.'

'My word,' she said laughing. 'You're serious.'

She took his arm as she described Emma's attempts at art. They stepped out with some speed so that when they arrived at her front gate he was breathless. The sky revealed stars here, was less hidden by branches.

'That's been a lovely evening,' she said. 'It really was a big change.'

The front door of the house was flung open and two outside bulbs illuminated the end of the path. Edward Craig appeared.

'Here are the dirty stop-outs,' Sam said, loudly.

Craig came down the front steps.

'I didn't expect you yet.' They could see him smiling, in holiday mood. 'I didn't think you'd talk yourself out until midnight.'

'Old folks go to bed early,' Sam answered. 'They look forward to it. It's sad really, because often they don't sleep well when they get there.'

'Can't you read?' Karen asked.

'Yes. To an extent. But one needs light. And the position often pains you or leaves you stiff.'

'Haven't you got a telly in your bedroom?' Ted Craig inquired.

'I've not sunk so low.'

They all laughed, socially, standing together on the path, at the beginning of shadow.

'Are the children asleep?' Karen asked.

'Yes. They went upstairs for bath and bed without a murmur.'

'They must have been tired.'

Sam Martin envied these exchanged sentences. They represented the lives, the shared existence, of four disparate people. He had nothing of this. To be truthful he did not remember its equivalent when Joan was alive and John and Frances small. He'd been too busy, too involved, to pause and examine short sentences.

He invited the Craigs for lunch. They could drive up from the beach, have an hour in his company and then disappear again.

'Leaving you with the washing-up,' Karen said.

'I don't mind. It passes the time. That's half my trouble.'

'Only half?' she asked.

'Yes. The other half that niggles is the thought that the grave's pretty near, and I therefore ought to spend what bit of time's left profitably, learning to make a decent job of my watercolours, improving my ideas and my technique all the time.'

'Won't our visit interfere with that?' Karen, again.

'No. I don't mind a slight change, a half-day off now and again. As long as it doesn't happen too often. It's an important part of the process. To stop, deliberately, and do other things.'

'Doesn't that happen every day? Or night? When you go to bed, for instance?' Edward queried.

'Well, no. The importance seems to lie in the fact that I deliberately take the time off, know I'm doing it.'

'Is that when you get your ideas?' Edward asked.

'Not that I've particularly noticed. No. It's the decision to break off. If I did it more than once then I'd be upset, guilty. When you get old you lose energy, and let things drift. But when I give myself a half-day I feel I'm on top of my weakness.'

They parted. Karen said she would telephone to talk about food the children would enjoy. Edward shook Sam's hand to thank him. Karen kissed him lightly on one cheek, and skipped indoors as Emma might have done.

As Sam walked back along the village street, where many

windows still shone, some uncurtained, he felt pleased with his evening. Karen had held his arm and he was flattered. It had been in no way sexual, and yet not meaninglessly friendly. The young woman wanted to know him, took pleasure in his company. He breathed as deeply as he could of the air of a moonless night, and knew that life meant something. The Rolls-Royce man, out walking his two labradors, stopped and said it had been a beautiful day.

'Yes, I think so.'

'Aren't you sure?' Rolls-Royce asked facetiously.

'I am. But that's unusual for me. To be quite sure of anything.'

'Ummh.' Silver Shadow nodded brusquely as if certainty had been unfairly removed from his life. He signalled the dogs forward. They obeyed. The steel tips of his ox-blood golf shoes hit the road with a confidence of sound. Sam smiled.

IV

Lunch with the Craigs proved a success. After Karen had spoken to Sam about the children's favourite dishes, he had spent an interesting morning getting things right. The family arrived from the beach at one, and ate hungrily. He was rewarded to see the children leaving almost clean plates, and the sugar pigs he distributed after the meal excited the visitors. Father Edward said he hadn't seen these confections since he was a boy, had thought they had disappeared with so many of his childhood delights.

'You'd think he was about eighty, the way he talks,' Karen mocked.

'He's thirty-seven,' Emma said. She appeared to take in adult conversation while engrossed in a game, this time solitaire.

'That's old, isn't it?' Sam Martin said to her.

'In a way,' she answered, and again immersed herself in her puzzle.

Sam refused to let the adults help him with the post-prandial chores, so that the house was clear by two fifteen. He washed the dishes slowly, stacked them neatly away, cleaned bowl and sink. He felt very tired; he had chosen a meal well within his range, but the cooking and serving had wearied him. He helped himself to a second sugar pig, and settled into an armchair. Outside the sky stretched immaculately blue, as sunshine blazed. In spite of fatigue he could not sleep. His legs itched; he scratched himself quite ferociously, turned to Radio 3 for comfort. An orchestra created noises, he could describe the performance in no other way, discord which without being loud grated on him. What he needed was youthful Mozart full of delicate drive and that would have lifted him, allowed him to drop off to sleep. This stuff had neither melody, nor harmony, nor understandable rhythms, but staggered and rested without sense. Annoyed, he remembered that he had not bought a *Radio Times* and so could not look up the composer of this cacophony. He had not been to the village shop that morning, on account of his kitchen duties, and so had not bought a *Times* which sometimes gave composers' names in their radio announcements: Haydn, Messaien, Martinu. None of them. He fell awkwardly asleep.

He woke at a loss. He had little idea where he was. He had been dreaming, and the remnant he recalled showed him a girl he had known in school seventy-odd years ago. Blond straight hair; light eyes; delicate. Audrey. He could not recall her second name. Abbott, Ainsworth, Healey, Hunt. The harder he thought the more diffused the figure became. Their dream-dealings had not been unhappy. The transaction had been more intense than, say, shopping or sweeping the floor, but it had not entailed sex or murder or deep deceit. Neither he nor she had been old, in their twenties, perhaps, pleased with each other, talking about . . . he could not remember.

All this puzzled him. He had not seen Audrey Whatever since the infant school when he had appeared with her in a playlet at the front of Miss Jones's class. He had been the Pope who saw the slave-children in the market-place at Rome and who had said, when told they were from Angle-land, 'Not Angles, but Angels'. And he had been instructed to touch Audrey's head with saintly, inquiring fingers. He could not recollect her reaction to his hand on her scalp, merely the eyes lifted towards him. Whether she looked up at Pope Gregory on instruction or out of interest in Samuel Martin he could not remember. This was not a rehearsal for some public occasion; they did it once, perhaps to illustrate St Augustine's conversion of England, not exactly a thrilling topic for six-year-olds, but in those days pupils did as they were bidden and accepted whatever crumbs of learning they were offered. Besides the techniques had worked; seventy-five years later he still brought the lesson to mind. They knew their craft, those old teachers. *Non Angli sed Angeli.*

Audrey had remained in his class for a year or two and had then disappeared, though whether in his mind or in actuality he could not now say. He had seen no more of her, he'd claim, after the junior school, and certainly not in his adult life. And yet in the dream he had immediately recognized the young woman as the fair child, the little Angle he had touched.

Perhaps the blond hair of Emma and Ben, or of their mother, had stirred this out-of-the-way corner of his brain. Emma would now be just a year or two older than Audrey then. The dream had been in no way unpleasant. The lady who had been Audrey had

35

held a conversation with him in the dream, over a trestle-table, out-of-doors. What they had discussed he could not remember. She had worn a white dress and a white hat, with the brim turned up at the front. How he had known her as the Audrey of his childhood he could not conceive, but known her he had.

Sam sat for a moment in his chair. These days when he woke from a casual nap, it took time to recover his wits. He tried to put two and two easily together, and failed utterly. Audrey would be over eighty now, if she were still living. He wished he knew, but realized he asked the impossible. All through his long life people had vanished, had dropped out; girls he had loved and touched, men who had been friends, respected colleagues. It was, doubtless, his own fault for cutting himself off from his roots and coming to live out here. But it had been as bad when he was still in his old home. He dragged himself upwards to his feet, groaning slightly. His shoes, he noticed, were highly polished. Age had not taken from him all sense of what was proper. He shuffled out to the kitchen, and swilled hands and face under the cold tap. He splashed water onto his hair and carefully parted and combed it. He nodded at his image in the kitchen-mirror; he was himself.

He decided he'd take a short walk along the street, call in at the shop, buy a newspaper and next week's *Radio Times*.

For a moment he wondered if that was what they called it these days. *TV Times*? Determined, he found his way over to the cubby-hole where he kept old papers. He found a copy. *Radio Times* still. He felt relief that he had been right. The whole world had not been altered. He laughed at himself, ran cold water over his dusty hands again, checked that he was carrying his wallet, locked and bolted the back door, made for the hall, where he took down a Panama hat from the stand, double-locked the front, managed the steps and from the garden-gate made sure that all the visible windows were fastened. Satisfied, he made his way along the street.

The weather was perfect for holidays, but it did not suit him. When he moved out from the shadow of the big trees, the sun seemed to burn through his alpaca jacket and shirt in spite of a breeze which shifted the odd cumulus cloud. Once in the shade he was more comfortable; this was deck-chair weather. The wind riffled the high leaves. There was no traffic. He felt better. This was a good time of the year, when he could idle through warm evenings reading or listening to the Proms. He must not forget his *Radio Times*, because these days the BBC produced a number of modern works, uncomfortable stuff. The audiences did not seem to mind, clapped with enthusiasm after some random musical foolishness that would have turned the cat's milk sour, but he on his own found nothing to applaud.

He turned a corner and came upon a woman ten yards ahead, hanging on to a gatepost. He recognized her at once; she was the Admiral's wife's shopping companion. He could not put a name to her, but that was not surprising; he often found difficulty these days in putting a name to somebody he'd known all his life. He debated with himself what she was doing on the wide grass verge clinging to a post. Perhaps she felt unwell. Again he hesitated, then stepped towards her. Preserving the proprieties he raised his Panama.

'I beg your pardon, madam, but are you quite all right?'

She turned her head towards him. The face was ashen, lips thin and bloodless. She appeared to be summing him up, even in her distress.

'I suddenly felt dizzy,' she said, in a trembling voice.

'Would you like to sit down?' Sam said. 'I'll go along to the house here and ask for a glass of water and the loan of a chair.'

'Oh, no. Don't do that. I haven't . . .' She broke off. He waited for the completion of the sentence, but she ventured nothing further.

'Have you far to go?' Sam asked.

'No.' She seemed to be trying to recall the exact coordinates of her destination. 'No. I live three doors up.' She pointed. That would be sixty or seventy yards, he estimated.

'If I gave you my arm, could you manage it?' he asked. 'It will all be in the shade.'

'In a minute.'

She turned her head away from him and slumped onto the post. He stood away from her, awaiting recovery. It seemed long enough before she straightened slightly, and glanced towards him.

'Take my arm,' he said. 'And we'll see how we shape.'

Martin picked up a shopping receptacle which was lying on the grass. Her handbag was slung by a strap across her shoulder still.

'Take your time,' he said. 'There's no rush.'

The two moved slightly; both swayed but managed a step or two.

'How's that?' They stood for a moment then she nodded. 'Right?'

They made a few yards forward, stopped, then after a word of encouragement pushed on again. He spoke most of the time, short phrases of cheer as to a child. She did not answer, but put one foot in stoical fear before the other. It seemed an inordinate length of time before they reached her gate.

'Is this it?' he asked, recovering his own breath. She nodded. 'Let's have a little rest.'

She drew herself up but made no effort to detach her arm from his. Her complexion seemed ghastly still, and she trembled.

'It's very hot today,' he said, making time for her next effort. 'The sooner we get you indoors and out of the sun the better. Is there anybody at home?'

'No.' That was her first word since they started their short journey.

'Are you ready?'

Again she nodded, and he opened the gate. They made the twenty-five yards to her portico and front door without a stop. The house stood at an angle to the drive. She fidgeted in her shoulder bag for keys; this took so long he thought she'd never succeed. In the end she handed a small bunch to him, but he had to decide which to use. He was lucky at the second try; she had released his arm, and stood with her back to one of the pillars of the portico. Now he turned, hooked his arm through hers and led her forward. She made no complaint.

The hall into which they stepped was cool and wide with a straight spindle-staircase running up the middle. At the top this divided and occupied the whole length of the back wall. The place was darkish after the sun's dazzle, lit by small panes on either side of the door, and three long windows with stained glass edges above the portico on the front wall. These were partly covered by blinds. The floor was uncarpeted and to one side stood a darkly polished wooden table, with two chairs. Two landscapes, an eighteenth-century family portrait and a large gilded mirror doubly enormous with an elaborate frame of curled, intertwining leaves, fruit and stems hung on the walls. He found, once his eyes were accustomed to the light, a peaceful, ordered, tasteful, uncluttered place.

'Which way?' he asked.

'Left, please.'

They moved out of the hall into a windowed corridor, hung with three watercolours which he would have liked to examine, but their progress continued at a stately pace. The woman, he ought to recall her name but could not, now walked steadily though not allowing him to release her arm.

They reached a spacious, sun-soaked kitchen where she made for a table and pulling out a chair without difficulty sat down. She pointed towards one of the windows.

'Do you mind closing the blind,' she asked. He did as requested. 'Would you bring me a glass of water, if you please? You'll find a glass in that cupboard.' She pointed. He marched across. By the time he had completed the task, she had produced two tablets which she held in the palm of her left hand. She drank, swallowed, not without difficulty, sipped, swallowed again. Now she replaced the glass on the table.

'Thank you.' She inclined her grey, beautiful but artificial, curls towards him. 'Thank you. This surprised me. Perhaps it was hotter outside than I had been led to believe.'

He agreed with her, politely offering trivial information about the temperatures.

'You must follow the forecasts on TV,' she said.

'I look at them, certainly.'

'They aren't always right, are they?'

'Near enough.'

The small exchange seemed to stimulate her. She sipped again from her glass, efficiently but ladylike.

'I'm sorry,' she said, having replaced her glass, 'but I don't seem to, to,' she hesitated, 'recall your name.'

'Martin. Samuel Martin.'

'You live here?'

'Yes. At "Avalon", the bungalow up the road.' He indicated the direction with a curt jab.

'You know my name?'

'No. I'm sorry, but I don't. I ought to.' His voice faded sociably away.

'Mine is Jeffreys. Alice Jeffreys.' She paused, smiled prettily, herself again. 'I think I've seen you about the village.'

'I've seen you,' he said, 'shopping with the Admiral's wife.'

'Hilda St John.' Mrs Jeffreys fiddled with her wedding and

two engagement rings. 'Would it be too much to ask you to make us both a cup of coffee? That is, if you'd like one.'

She issued further instructions on the whereabouts of instant coffee, cups, milk, a kettle. (There were, he noticed, three.) While he was occupied with his task, she left her seat and found a tin of chocolate biscuits. She issued further orders about the coffee which was to be sugarless and not too milky. Mrs Jeffreys' voice had recovered its strength, far-back, posh. She spoke imperiously, knew her mind.

When he was seated by her at the table with coffee she said, without preamble.

'Hilda St John's got her work cut out.'

He waited, eyes fixed on her.

'Clement's beginning to lose his marbles.' She sniffed as if at her own phraseology. 'Some sort of dementia, senile dementia.'

'Is he old?'

'Seventy-five. Not old by today's standards. She's younger. Ten years or so. About my age.'

'Has it incapacitated him totally?'

'Well, no. Not altogether. He can attempt to dress himself. He'll make mistakes; with buttons, that sort of thing, y'know. He can eat fairly respectably, if the meal is simple. But his memory has almost totally gone. He knows he's an admiral, but I suppose he's been called that for years.'

'Has the trouble been going on for long?' Martin asked.

'Yes. Some time now. He became very forgetful, and he showed other oddnesses. It's all become very much worse in the last year or two. I feel sorry for her. Everything falls on her. She has to do it all.'

'Don't they get help?'

'A cleaning woman. And just recently they've had a nurse in to bath him and so on. When they first came here he was a very striking, handsome man. Not now.' She drew breath in, 'Hilda's pretty well organized, I'll give her that.'

'Have they a family?'

'Yes. Two daughters. Both married. Both abroad.'

'Do they come over?'

'The American one was here earlier this year. She came with her children. But they're too far away to do more than make phone calls, which they do, frequently. Hilda's on her own. But she's managed so far.'

40

'But?'

Alice Jeffreys' face expressed her contempt for his word.

'The time will come when he has to go away. Into a nursing home. They'll be able to afford it, but not if she keeps her present home. And she'll resent having to leave. It's a nice place, and full of good things they've picked up in their travels round the world. She has excellent taste. I'll give her that. And she has status of sorts here. Not quite the lady of a manor, but not far off. The Admiral's wife. Not too far removed.'

'And that's important to her.'

'She'd say it wasn't, but we all like to be somebody. Clement retired rather early from the Navy, and so didn't get his Knighthood. I've never quite made out why, or what he did. Intelligence, something like that. Secret service. Oh, I don't know; I'm making it up.'

Mrs Jeffreys had finished her coffee, and now stood.

'I shall have to get on,' she said. Her voice rang normally strong. Sam drained the last of his coffee. He removed both cups to the draining-board.

'Thanks,' she said, rather absently, as if she was gathering her wits. 'And thank you for helping me home. I don't know what came over me. Perhaps it's this very hot weather.'

She led him out of the kitchen, along the corridor, and paused at the front door, where she held up her face to be kissed. He bent, touched her left cheek lightly with his lips; she pulled him to her. He started back with surprise. Her face registered mild pleasure, but she was once more the lady of the house showing out a casual visitor.

'Thank you,' she said again.

'You must call in on me,' he invited. 'I'm in the telephone-book. S. J. Martin.'

'Yes,' she answered, but vaguely. 'Yes.'

She opened the door and he was outside amongst the flowers, lavatera, Japanese anemones, a flare of phlox. The door closed quickly behind him, and he made for the road, smiling to himself. He could, he imagined, still feel the touch of her soft lips on his. Why had she kissed him thus? Was it some old local custom? He doubted it. Her good turn for the week, cheering some octogenarian with an unexpected embrace? He felt livelier for it, initiated into some mystery beyond expectation. She was the last person he'd think of when it came to such generosity.

She and Mrs Admiral St John were on a par. Women in their sixties, used to a superior place in the hierarchy of this small village, not given to eccentric gestures, cleanly, self-regarding, well-dressed, liable to step back from the mundane, at least in public, from the averagely unusual. She had kissed his lips. Perhaps the attack, heat-stroke, dizziness, blood-pressure had suddenly revealed her weakness to herself or to him.

He turned back to 'Avalon' and tea, much pleased with life.

He prepared a sheet of paper on his drawing board that evening, looked over sketches and photographs, did not change his mind over the nature of his painting. Next morning once he'd made a start he'd vacillate. He wished this was not so, that he knew exactly how to proceed, but he could not hope for the impossible. He laid out sketches and photographs, compared them with the wide sheet of empty paper in its frame of masking tape, felt a satisfaction. 'A challenge,' he said out loud. He hated the word, catch-word. These days everything challenged everybody. Wait until they reached his age.

The telephone rang. Edward Craig asking him to join him at the Plough in half an hour's time.

'No, thanks,' Sam answered. 'I've got my glad rags off and I don't want to turn out again. I'll tell you what. I've a crate of ale that needs breaking into. Just come up here. I'll be glad of your company.'

When Craig arrived, Sam asked him if he'd prefer to sit outside in the garden. Ted knitted his brows.

'What about you?' he asked.

'Indoors for me.'

'Indoors. I'm glad you said that. Karen's all for the patio. And the children. But once I get out there, every wasp, fly or mosquito homes straight in on me.'

They sat in the studio, the coolest of the rooms. A trickle of breeze found its way through the open windows.

'See you've got your work set out,' Craig said, pointing at the board. 'First thing tomorrow?'

'All being well.'

'What if you don't feel like it?'

'I shall still make a start. I don't believe in pandering to myself and my whims. If I make a mess of it I can always throw it away.'

'Is that often?'

'Not often enough,' Sam Martin answered. 'I'm too easy on myself. I see the difficulties I've tried to cope with, and perhaps that makes me more self-indulgent, critically speaking, than I ought to be.'

They discussed one or two pictures in a folder. Though Craig screwed up his eyes, put his head on one side, hummed and hawed, he'd no real interest in painting.

'Do you have pictures on the wall at home?' Sam asked.

'Yes. I like them.'

'Who chooses them? You or Karen?'

'Karen, usually.'

'And how will you get on in your new school? Won't you be responsible for choosing pictures? Or have they acquired plenty already?'

Sam found to his surprise that Edward Craig was vague about what was on the walls of his new domain, though he'd been there a dozen times. Edward clearly realized that this, in Sam's eyes, implied a fault, but dismissed the criticism cheerfully enough.

'There's usually somebody there who'll know something about it. If not, I'll rope Karen in. I can't be expected to know everything. I'm a practical man. And important though pictures and music may be my job is to see that they can all read, do elementary arithmetic, and know their way about a computer.'

'What about history or geography? Even more important, science?'

'We have to do 'em all. The national curriculum demands them. But they'll only be touched on. That's why I shall need to make sure that Maths and English are hammered in.'

Certainly Sam liked the sound of practicality about Craig's words. How strict he would be, how insistent in overcoming apathy or objections on the part of his staff Sam could not guess. There was about him an air of efficiency; he remembered Edward's easy carrying of all that lumber at their first meeting.

They talked about the weather. At the bottom of the garden of the bungalow which the Craigs had rented, their landlord had installed a largish caravan. This had been taken by a middle-aged couple who, for the first time for some years, were holidaying on their own without their children. The Haywards.

'They were keen. They were going to enjoy themselves.' They'd made this clear to the Craigs on the first day they had met. They'd a daughter, nineteen, a great slummock, who'd gone

43

to the Costa del Sol with her boyfriend, and a son, seventeen, cycling through France. 'We can just please ourselves,' the man had said. 'Be as idle or energetic as we think fit.'

It appeared, however, that the hot weather had ruined their plans. The Craigs could not understand this. From what the two had said they'd spent the past half-dozen years in Spain or Majorca, grilling themselves. When Edward mentioned this Tom Hayward had replied,

'We were ready for it. There was a swimming pool right to hand. We were in and out of it all day.'

'There's the sea here,' Ted objected.

'There was the sea there, but we didn't go in it. Here it's shallow, and mucky, and cold and if the notices are to be believed the bloody fierce currents'll sweep you off your feet and land your corpse in Norway or Germany or Holland before you know where you are.'

'And many of the Mediterranean hotels have air-conditioning now,' Mrs Hayward said. 'Not all, but many. This caravan's like a furnace before the day's out. We can't sleep; we drink too much; we don't feel like meals; we eat in between.'

'We're either suffering from indigestion or a hangover.'

At first the complaints had been humorously phrased, but as the sun grew hotter the Craigs could hear their neighbours' quarrels. They made no attempt to lower their voices.

'What do they row about?' Sam asked.

'Anything and everything. Where they're to spend the day. What to eat. Why they chose this place.'

Karen, in the goodness of her heart, had invited them in to dinner one evening. They'd sat in the coolest room with a couple of fans ruffling Sandra Hayward's holiday perm. Instructed not to dress up, Mrs Hayward had worn what looked like a sea-through nightie over a bikini. Her husband had sported khaki shorts and an Oasis T-shirt. Both beetroot-red of face, they said how cool it was, and how comfortable. They had provided the wine, and drank most of it. They had laughed at themselves. Later, about midnight, Edward Craig had looked out of the back-bedroom window and seen Hayward, apparently stark naked, wandering round his caravan beating the ground with a stick.

'What was he doing?' Karen demanded.

'Hunting snakes.'

'Did he say anything?'

'Silent as the grave.'

Craig told this and other anecdotes with real verve. Sam could see that he was an accomplished teacher. When he announced the successes of his school at assembly, or castigated wrong-doers, or read and explained some moral tale he'd not easily lose the interest of his audience. Sam enjoyed their hour and a half, and insisted on walking back with the visitor. A light on in one of the upper rooms indicated that Mrs Craig had already retired. The pair, like schoolboys up to mischief, crept round to the side of the house to listen for sounds of discord from the caravan. They met only silence.

'Worn out,' Sam said.

'Or murdered each other.'

They shook hands, and parted laughingly, Martin saluting militarily.

Next morning Sam calling in, rather late, at the village shop for his newspaper, noticed on his way there that the Craigs' car had gone and on his return a fiery-faced couple were driving off. The Haywards, he presumed.

He ran his own car into his already stifling garage and noticed a tall man hesitating at the open front gate.

'Mr Martin?'

Sam walked towards the stranger who had asked his question in a dark, southern voice.

'Yes.'

The man advanced. He wore an excellent charcoal-grey suit, white shirt with silk tie and polished black shoes. His grey hair lay straight, neatly parted.

'My name is Jeffreys, John Jeffreys. You were very kind to my wife the other morning when she was feeling unwell.'

'Come in.' He led Jeffreys indoors. 'I ought to have called in to see if she was recovering.'

'She's fine. It was one-off. She's never had anything like it before. I insisted that she drove out to the surgery to see what the doctor had to say. He blamed the sun. It's been so much stronger than usual. And Alice had been out in the garden, dead-heading, before she set out for the street. We oldies have to be careful, he said.'

'Your wife doesn't qualify as old in my book.'

'No. She's sixty-one, and pretty fit. I'm sixty-four and I still

45

go to work. Not every day, but at least twice a week.'

Sam did not mention his own age, but offered Jeffreys a drink which was refused.

'There is one other thing. The St Johns' house has been broken into, and the burglars beat up the Admiral.'

'Is he all right?'

'I don't know about that. They pushed or threw him down a flight of stairs after they'd set about him.'

'He's not well, is he? Even before this lot?'

'No. To put it plainly he's gone gaga, and never leaves the house. He's a good few years older than I am, and not very steady on his feet. He was unconscious when they wheeled him off to hospital. Not that he'd remember much, I guess.'

'When did all this happen?'

'In the early hours.'

'I walked past the house a few minutes ago and didn't see anything untoward.'

'The police are inside now. Fingerprinting and trying to get out of Hilda what's missing.'

'Didn't she see anything? Didn't they attack her?'

'That's the odd thing,' Jeffreys answered. 'Apparently the Admiral was wandering about the house. He often does, I believe, when he can't sleep. She saw the intruders attack him and she hid herself away. They weren't in the place more than fifteen minutes. Or so she says. She was incoherent, really. Not surprising. She rang 999 for ambulance and police, and came and knocked us up.'

'What time was this?'

'Early hours. Two o'clock perhaps. I went back with her to see if we could do anything for the Admiral. He was out, unconscious at the bottom of the stairs, and his head was bleeding but he was breathing.'

'Were the police and ambulance long?'

'It seemed it. Perhaps twenty minutes. It felt longer. But they were good when they did arrive. I think they said he'd have to go to Norwich by the look of it. They connected him to a drip and all the rest. They thought nothing was broken, though they couldn't be sure.'

Jeffreys completed his tale, made a deduction or two, said he must be hurrying back as Mrs St John was with them until a sister from Cheltenham could get over.

'You won't have had much sleep,' Sam said.

'None at all.'

'Can I help?'

'Well. My wife and I had promised to drive over to Sheringham this afternoon. We've promised an old cousin of hers some things for a church sale she's holding. It'll do Alice good to get out of the house. And she'll tell the story to Dorinda, I expect. But she won't leave Hilda. She has to stay at home in case the police want to look round again to check something. If you could sit with Hilda while we're out it would be to everybody's advantage. It must be a man, Alice thinks; she can't leave Hilda alone or with a female companion.'

'I wouldn't make much of a showing against burglars. And I don't know Mrs St John. What would she think?'

'She'd do as Alice suggests. May I use your phone?'

Jeffreys rang his wife who said she'd make the introductions and arrangements.

'Can you be here by two? We'll be back by four thirty, at least.' The length of their outing expanded. 'It's most considerate of you, Mr Martin. It means Alice can go out with her mind at ease.'

Sam Martin turned up on time. The Jeffreys' Rover stood in the drive.

'I'll take you round,' Alice said. She was dressed for the visit. 'Hilda won't be very congenial company, I'm afraid. But if she can drop off for half an hour or so it'll do her good. I'll show you where the phone is. She'll be sleeping with us tonight. I've insisted on that.'

She led Sam round, rang the bell but walked straight in.

Hilda St John sat by the hearth in the sitting room. The fireplace was lavishly full with an arrangement of laurel leaves. She rose to greet Sam Martin, shook his hand, and thanked him for his kindness in sitting with her. These things were not easily borne at her age. She said she had made another enquiry at the hospital when she had learnt her husband's condition was stable, and that they could visit this evening. When she finished, and her voice was steady though lacking its quarter-deck ferocity, her lips and hands were trembling.

'Don't worry. We'll run you down this evening.' Alice Jeffreys tucked her friend up neatly in a large tartan blanket. 'Mr Martin will see to it that you're all right.'

The Jeffreys left. Sam heard their car drive off. Mrs St John had closed her eyes.

He took out the book he had brought. The one he had chosen, *The Heroes* by Charles Kingsley, he had snatched up in a hurry; he had never read it and had no idea what it was about. It had been lying flat on the top of a row of books, a small volume, fit for his pocket, its dust cover neat in unobtrusive green and brown: the Nelson Classics. That would have to do.

Sam glanced over at Mrs St John. Her eyes were closed still, but the face showed nothing of repose.

'Is there anything I can get you?' he asked quietly.

He received no answer, not a twitch of lips. He returned to his book.

It was dedicated to Kingsley's children, Rose, Maurice and Mary, 'a little present of old Greek Fairy Tales'. Over the page he read an apology to the few scholars who might come across this 'hasty *jeu d'esprit*' and be annoyed by his inconsistent spelling of Greek names. Oh, important, learned readers. He himself would not be incommoded or annoyed on this score. He started on the preface, addressed to 'dear children'. Here an old-fashioned clergyman spoke (gently asserting Christian belief), about the Greeks, the Hellenes. One of the great glories of their language was that it was the medium chosen, presumably by God or Providence, to convey the truths of the New Testament all over Europe. He remembered the classical master at his grammar school dismissing the language of the Gospels and Epistles to the Lower Sixth as 'puppy Greek'. Ah, well. Sam noted the date of this preface: Advent 1855. The father-clergyman-educator would be thirty-six. He hadn't published *The Water Babies*, but had only twenty years to live. Sam wondered why he was bothering his head about these matters, why he was slightly angry, why put out that only the boys would be allowed to learn Greek. Nowadays the girls were likely to be in a majority amongst the few hundred left studying classical languages in the schools. It did not matter to Sam one way or another. Here he sat annoying himself over a book written very nearly a hundred and fifty years ago. He'd brought the wretched thing along to pass the time, not to irritate himself with. He sighed, looked over towards Mrs St John.

The woman was sitting bolt-upright. She was wrapped still in Mrs Jeffreys' protective blanket, but her eyes were wide open.

The expression on her face, in the eyes, was one of malice, of hatred. She did not seem to be staring at him, but the face was set, ugly-hard, a basilisk, a Medusa. (He had noticed that the subject of Story I in Kingsley was Perseus.)

'Are you all right?' he asked.

She did not appear to notice that he'd spoken.

'Can I get you anything?' he asked, slightly louder. 'A drink?'

She seemed to stir; the eyes flickered.

'Could you fetch me a glass of water, please?' The request was polite, mildly delivered. She inclined her head, in the direction of the kitchen, he guessed. He went out, found his way and her glass, and returned. He stood at her side. Her claw-like hands came from within the blanket. They were uglier than the face, brown-spotted, lined, twisted with arthritis. Mrs St John took a sip, then a second. Before handing the glass back to him she made a murmur of thanks. As he received it from her, he looked about, at a loss for a place to put it down. Once he'd seen it safe and doing no damage to the polished surfaces, he asked again,

'Can I get you anything else?'

She seemed not to understand.

'A biscuit? A hot drink?'

'No, thank you.'

He was surprised to see tears rolling down the ravaged face. Her expression of undisguised hatred had not changed, seemed to lack all connection with the large globules which ran, then dripped separately off.

She motioned him to his chair. He obeyed. Neither moved. Her tears dried. She closed her wrinkled eyes, appeared to sleep. He returned to *The Heroes*, to Perseus on the island of Seriphos.

He glanced at his watch. Time barely moved. The names in his book seemed odd, unmemorable in his present state of mind. Acrisius, Proetus, Dictys, Polydectes. He toiled on, not un-interested, but having to force his way along the lines of excellent print. His head dropped and he fell asleep.

When he woke, he found himself at a loss and looked about for guidance. The large room with its pictures, plants, heavy furniture seemed portentous, darkish with blinds drawn against the sun. His book had fallen from his hands and lay open, face-downward, between his feet. When this happened, as it frequently did, the jerk or the thud on the floor usually awakened him. Sam looked across to Mrs St John. Still upright, though now with her head on one side, she slept. Her breathing sounded noisy, not quite a snore, but less inhibited than she would consciously have allowed. The mouth hung open, with speckles of saliva at the corner. She would dislike his seeing her thus, he decided. He placed his book safely on the table beside him, composed himself, and fell asleep again. At home he would have struggled up to keep his eyes open.

This time on his awakening he noticed that Mrs St John was staring at him.

'You've been to sleep,' she said.

'Yes,' he answered pacifically. 'I usually have a nod after lunch.'

He sat higher in his chair. In spite of the blinds he could now see the room perfectly well. The furniture, the pictures, the objets d'art were all well chosen. He could detect no signs of either burglary or struggle. Woodwork gleamed even in this subdued light; pictures hung straight on the wall; statuettes had been placed to advantage by someone who knew what she was about.

The air in the room smelt stuffy, unduly hot. Mrs St John writhed in her chair and switched on a quite powerful fan. He was grateful for the cool current, but the fan was noisy.

'Thank you,' he said.

'Oh,' she answered. 'I thought you were asleep again.'

'Can I get you anything?' he asked. 'A cup of tea?'

'No, thank you. Don't worry yourself. Just sit still. My husband rushed about all his life, never took a minute's rest. Now he's beaten up by criminals. And they attacked him from behind.'

'So that he wouldn't be able to identify them?'

'If they had approached him head-on, he wouldn't have been able to recognize them again. His memory's gone.'

'I'm sorry. Are the police optimistic?'

'They didn't say so. They dabbled about with their powder. And looked at the locks and scratches on doors and windows.'

'Did they think it was a professional job, or amateurs?'

'They didn't say.'

'Is your husband all right physically?'

'He's unconscious. He's broken a leg and a wrist. He's badly cut about the head and he's terribly bruised, all over his body.'

'I'm sorry.'

'He's not a young man, you know.'

'How old is he? If I may ask.'

'Seventy-two. Beyond his three-score and ten.'

'But not as old as I am.'

'Oh.'

The monosyllable dismissed him. She had no interest in his age, or his boasting about it. Her voice had just sufficient strength to defeat the whirring of the fan. He was surprised how still she sat, how little the malevolent expression on her face changed, how tightly her hands were clenched.

'Has he not recovered consciousness?'

'No.'

'Not at all?'

'No. He is in a poor way.'

'He's a man of strong constitution, I take it?' Sam wondered why he posed this question.

'In his youth, he was very strong. But for the last ten years he's been an invalid. If he could have anything wrong with him, he did. And this last three or four years he's taken no exercise. He's shaky. A walk to the bottom of the garden would be beyond him even on his better days.'

'I'm sorry.'

'So am I. And with this physical decrepitude, there has been mental deterioration. Dementia. You understand?'

'Alzheimer's?'

'That's one form of dementia. Not his. But something like that.'

'This must be a great worry to you?'

'It's like looking after a child, except he has an adult body. I can't manhandle him as I could a child. Not that I'm sure I could do that these days, but you know what I mean.'

'Do you get help?'

'Yes.'

'That's good.'

He felt more at his ease now, except that her facial expression and her pose did not change, did nothing to encourage questions. It was as if he was addressing an idol or totem, an expressionless, carved Buddha. She never looked directly at him, and though her voice was low, much less hectoring than when he heard it in the street, it lacked warmth.

51

'The Jeffreys will run you to the hospital this evening?' he asked.

'Yes. To Norwich. They've moved my husband there for some reason. More beds. Or to put him in intensive care.'

'I see. If it happens you need to go somewhere and they can't help, don't be afraid to call on me. I'll be glad to ferry you about.'

'I shall be able to drive myself. I've done all the driving this last few years. But John Jeffreys thought I shouldn't today. I've been up more than half the night.'

'Very sensible. They seem a very nice couple.'

'Yes. I suppose they are. Alice and I don't always see eye to eye.' She did not expand.

'And it is to be expected?'

'We are much the same age. At one period we even attended the same school for a year, though we don't remember each other. You would, or rather one would, expect us to have more in common than in fact we have.'

Sam felt himself dismissed by the change of pronoun.

'We can't all be alike,' he said, pacifically.

'Don't get reading all sorts of things into what I've said. Alice and I disagree about some matters. End of sentence.'

'Unimportant?'

'I didn't say so. You seem inclined to deduce meanings which don't exist.'

'I'm sorry.'

'I'm not myself,' Hilda St John said. 'I'm on edge. Any minute the telephone might ring to inform me that Clement has died.'

He sighed loudly, taken aback by her thought.

'I keep going over the scenario in my mind,' she said. The phraseology struck Sam as awkward, unbecoming. 'If Clement dies it will be very much easier for me, physically, in my day-to-day life.'

'I see.' He spoke doubtfully.

'On the other hand there will be drawbacks. There will be no advantage in living in a house of this size, even if I could afford to do so. That means I shall have to uproot myself, sell off or give away a great number of my possessions and then look round for a suitable small place in which to live.'

Sam listened, uncertain whether to encourage her with

questions or to allow her her own way with her ideas. At present she seemed loquacious, even on a day when her husband was likely to die, and she had barely slept.

'Where that will be, in which part of the country, I haven't even the ghost of a notion yet. But it's worth running these ideas over, even vaguely. Then when I have to make my mind up for real I shan't be quite unprepared. I'm not sure that in these circumstances . . .'

The telephone rang. Both started. By the time Sam had stumbled to his feet, Mrs St John had thrown her blanket aside and was making for the receiver.

Sam Martin sat, crouched rather, in the quiet room, admiring Hilda St John's firm step. For all she knew this could have been the message telling her that her husband had died, but she had walked out steadily, looking neither right nor left. He heard the murmur of her voice some distance away, but could not gather even the gist or tone of her answers. He heard her replace the phone, though she did not immediately return.

When she returned he stood; that seemed proper.

'I've put the kettle on,' she said. He bowed his head in thanks. She found her way back to her chair, but did not sit down. 'That was the police. They have arrested a man, and are looking for another.'

'That was quick.'

'Well, the Superintendent said that they'd had a little bit of luck. "We don't always, but this time we have."' She mimicked the policeman's Anglian brogue.

'What was that?'

'He didn't say. He said it was "early days yet".' Again the bucolic drawl. 'I didn't press him. He seemed a decent man. He enquired about my husband. He had no need to, but he did. He'd be in touch again, he said, but he thought I ought to know the development.'

'That's good,' Sam answered.

She stared at him without friendliness.

'I'll make the tea,' she announced.

'Can I not do it?' he asked.

'No. It will only complicate a simple process. How do you like your tea. Milk?'

'Very weak, please. With milk; no sugar.'

'Like me.'

53

She stumped from the room.

Sam sat again to stare about the place. Order prevailed. Perhaps the burglars had not penetrated so far into the house, though this was the main room nearest to the front door. Maybe they had entered through the back premises, or even upstairs. At the least they had gone up to the second floor, if only to throw the somnambulating Admiral down. Where had Mrs St John been? In bed? Up but hiding? He did not know. If only she had been more attractive he would have admired her more. She knew her mind; she stoically followed the way she had chosen. Though her life, such as it was, had been smashed last night, she kept a brave face in front of him.

She appeared with the tea-tray.

'The cup that cheers,' he said, unthinking.

'I hope you're right.'

They drank together, but the pause had robbed her of fluency.

At about four thirty, John Jeffreys came in. They'd start, he ordered, for Norwich at quarter to six. And. Alice had said she must spend the night with them. The bed was already made up. Hilda St John tried to argue, but seemed glad to yield. She passed on her snippet of police news. She thanked both men, and they walked out together.

'We rang the hospital,' Jeffreys confided. 'They wouldn't say much as we're not relatives, but he's very ill. They hadn't much hope. But we'll take her over. You never know.'

V

Next day about eleven thirty Mrs Jeffreys telephoned Sam Martin.

'Bad news. The admiral died this morning. We heard about half an hour ago. Suddenly. We're going to have an early lunch and go over to Norwich to do the paperwork.'

'How does she seem?'

'Remarkably composed, really. She's well organized, and is phoning relatives. John thought it a good idea to let her get on with it, that it would give her something to do.'

'She seemed yesterday to be steeling herself for it.'

'I guess that's so. She's always had to look out for herself. He was often away. Though he had a dry-land job. Or, at least, since I've known them. Since they've lived here. That was before we came.'

'Is there anything I can do?'

'I don't think so. Once they've set off for Norwich I'll perhaps give you another ring.'

'I'm sorry about all this.'

'Yes, it's sad. It will change her life about. In some ways for the better. The admiral was never an easy man to get on with even when he was right in the head. Very handsome. Looked the part. But awkward, obsessed. Everything had to be just right and if it wasn't he'd play up. He'd bawl his wife out as if she was a servant or a sailor in front of strangers. It wouldn't have suited me.'

'Your husband's more accommodating, is he?'

'We all have our little ways, and he's no exception.'

She rang off. He enjoyed talking to Alice Jeffreys. Life glowed from her. He wished he knew more like her. The conversation had interrupted his morning's painting and he worked on until two thirty when he ate a cheese sandwich. Mrs Jeffreys had not, to his disappointment, rung with further demands. He made his way down to the beach, hoping to meet

55

the Craig family, but they were nowhere to be seen. Probably they'd taken a run into Hunstanton or Wells, Kings Lynn or Sheringham to shop before they went home on Saturday. He hoped they would meet again, though he did not know why. The parents were pleasant and the children well-behaved and pretty, but that seemed little enough reason to court their full-time attention. Perhaps he was becoming lonely. He was that already, he decided, walking round the roads to peer into gardens or windows minutely to share part of the humdrum life of others. Pathetic man. He'd plenty to do while at least he had a good part of his health and strength. After his turn along the beach where human temperament was on display, he turned sadly back home.

Two days later he had just reached the gate of 'Avalon' from shopping when somebody shouted his name. He looked up from his morning melancholy to the rapidly approaching figure of Alice Jeffreys.

'I was just coming to call on you,' she shouted. He voiced his pleasure.

He showed her into the drawing room, feeling smug that the place looked not only tidy but even beautiful in late August sunshine. Yes, Mrs Jeffreys agreed, she'd enjoy a cup of tea. He made smartly for the kitchen.

When he returned she was on her feet in front of one of his watercolours.

'I take it you did this?' she said.

'Yes.'

'You're very good.'

'That's kind of you, but I don't think it's true.'

'And why not?' She swept back to her chair as if annoyed by his contradiction.

'Because though I sometimes make a decent shot at what I'm trying to do, I can't always be certain. Sometimes I paint stuff I'm thoroughly ashamed of, depressed by. A decent artist ought always to achieve a certain standard of competence, but I can't, even now after I've been at it so long.' He carried her tea across. She held it graciously.

'Why is that?' she asked. 'Surely some scenes, subjects suit you better than others. That's to be expected. Or perhaps you aren't satisfied, ever, with repeating the same successful pictures over and over again. I've read that Cézanne was often dis-satisfied with what he was attempting, to such an extent that he'd attack and violently destroy his canvas. That may have been a matter of temperament, of course. He seemed uncertain of so much.'

'In his youth he'd put his pictures out for judgement to accepted authorities, and they dismissed them as worthless. I keep mine to myself.'

She chose a chocolate biscuit, and placing the cup on the small table leaned back, ready for his lecture. Instead he asked about Mrs St John.

'She's doing well, really. She's a brave woman. Stoical. I imagine this last year or two at home have been pretty hellish. She's out this afternoon again with my husband, making further arrangements, shopping. She'll enjoy that. It must be years since she was able to do things in her own way.'

'Your husband is most kind to ferry her about.'

'Oh, John'll enjoy it, too.' She looked at him. He saw how attractive she would have been as a young woman. 'He gets bored. And he's always been fond of Hilda. He sees her as, oh, a superior type.'

'Superior?'

'A bit higher in the social scale than the rest of us.' Alice laughed. 'Even above her husband. Her father was a lord. The third Baron Stannard.' The name meant nothing to the listener. 'So she's an honourable.'

'And your husband likes that?'

'All the world loves a lord. Don't you?'

'I can't say,' Sam answered, 'that it's a subject to which I've given much of my attention.'

'Oh, dear. That has put me in my place.' She laughed, perhaps at herself. 'You had an hour or two with her the day after the trouble. How did she impress you?'

'The poor woman must have been in shock as well as tired out.'

'That means she didn't make a favourable impression.'

'She was waiting,' Sam said, 'all the time for a call to tell her that her husband had died. Not the most favourable of circumstances. She just sat. Her facial expression didn't seem to change, whatever she said.'

'Did you think she was beautiful? Attractive in any way?'

'No.'

'The opposite?'

57

'That would be nearer.'

'Yes. And yet John is drawn to her, has been pretty well since we first knew her.'

'And is the attraction reciprocal?'

She repeated his last word mockingly.

'Yes. She returns his admiration.'

'And you don't mind?' He wished at once that he had not asked this.

'No. Not now. My husband's always been a ladies' man. One woman at a time was never enough for him. I resented it, and bitterly, when I was younger. But now. Well, he's older, and more sensible, tactful. And his libido's running down. He can meet Hilda nowadays without touching her. He's just as attentive when they meet, but he's not searching all the time for opportunities to get close, if you understand me. They've committed adultery? You want to ask me that. I'm absolutely convinced of it. I've no precise proof. I didn't see them with my own eyes. And John would never admit it openly. He's too much of a gentleman. He wouldn't want to hurt my feelings. Or hers. You think this is all very unsatisfactory, don't you?'

'Well. I don't want . . .'

'You think, in the first place, that I shouldn't have told you. We hardly know each other, and here I am confessing, revealing my husband's sins for all I'm worth. You don't think that's right, do you?'

'I'm an old man.'

'What's that got to do with it?'

'I'm easily flattered. An attractive woman, years my junior, pours out her troubles. I like it far too much to be passing moral judgements on you.'

'What's it like being old?' The tone of voice was comical, throw-away.

'I'm one of the lucky ones, but I still don't like it. People die all the time. Old friends drop off like flies. Not the feeble ones. Those I expected to outlive me by years. Every week. Boys I was at school with. In the army. Relatives. It's frightening in that it seems so regular and frequent.'

'May I ask how old you are?' Alice said.

'Eighty-one.'

'I don't believe it. You don't look anywhere near that.'

'Flattery, again. I've got all my hair. And I'm not too wrinkled

58

or fat. But I feel my age. Not in the aches and pains. I'm fortunate there. Some poor souls of my age are crippled with arthritis or can't sit down sharply without breaking a bone. No, it's not physically, but in my head. The world seems to have left me behind. There's so much I don't know. And events I remember quite clearly are to many of the middle-aged people I meet as distant as 1066 or 55 BC. That's terrifying. All that time has gone, slipped away, disappeared. Things that happened more than seventy years ago are as vivid as yesterday's or last year's affairs. I've been left behind.'

'But you can do things.'

'Such as?'

'Look after yourself, cook and clean. Paint your pictures. Walk or drive out.'

'How long will it last?'

'By the look of you ten, fifteen years.'

'If I think back fifteen years it's as nothing.'

'Yes, but you've got to live this fifteen one slow day at a time.'

Alice's face was red, as if she had taken violent exercise in the last few minutes. Perhaps arguing with him troubled her.

'The worst thing is that there's nothing to look forward to.'

'Do you mean "death"? Just death?' She disregarded taboos, obliquely.

'I wasn't thinking about that. I don't often. Not seriously. When I feel some ache or pain or nausea I wonder if it's the beginning of the end. And hearing about some friend's death makes me wonder. But I'm well enough not to be too overcome. I sometimes do try to imagine what form my final exam will take. I don't really mind dying, I think. Don't get me wrong, I don't want it to happen. Not yet. If there is a worry it's the manner. I'd hate to die after a long, debilitating, crippling illness, in squalor, without hope, incontinent, nauseated, reduced to groans or shrieks, utterly dependent on others.'

'I see that,' she said. 'So would everybody.'

He waved a hand impatiently at her, unwilling to be interrupted.

'When you're young,' his voice crackled with his eagerness to talk, 'there's always something to excite one. One imagines. Looks ahead. Holidays, for instance. Travel. Something in the paper catches your interest. You book for concerts. A letter

59

drops through the door with good news, or different news. Now one day's very like another. I'm dependent now on the weather for stimulation.'

Alice laughed.

'I've come in to see you,' she said.

'Yes, and that's beautiful. I don't understand why you bother. You're an attractive woman who can pick and choose. Why you come to visit me I don't know.'

'You underrate yourself. I am enjoying every minute of this.' She leaned towards him. 'I don't go round complaining to every man I meet about my husband.'

'No.'

'No, that's right. But you seem sensible, have a sympathetic face, are amenable to reason.'

'I don't think so.' He jerked his head upwards. 'Are you happy, would you say?'

'I can put up with life.' She spoke with an easy grace. 'Life in this village is not the most exciting in the world. But we have two good holidays a year. I have a week or more away with my sister in London. We chase about. John and I aren't falling over one another every day of the week. I've plenty to be thankful for.'

'But you're not satisfied.'

'No. It's all slowing down. But that's beside the point. What I really came to tell you was that the Admiral's funeral is probably a fortnight today, dependent on the coroner's office.'

'Here?'

'Yes. At the church. Can you make it?'

'Yes.'

'Good. Hilda would appreciate it. She'd also like you to go up to the house afterwards. The service is one of remembrance, if that's what they call it. There'll be a cremation beforehand for family only. And then we're all due at church two o'clock. Do you like funerals?'

'Not much.'

'Nor I.' Alice seemed thoughtful. 'There'll be a biggish turn-out, I guess. Daughter coming from the States. Naval people and the like. And Hilda's friends. She'll have a caterer in so you'll get a cup of tea and a bun.'

'Flowers?'

'Family only. Donations to the Alzheimer's Society and

60

Cancer Research. I'll give you the details if you like.'

'Cancer? Had he cancer, then?'

'It appears so from the post mortem. I thought I'd give you plenty of notice. There may be alterations.'

She bent and kissed him. She clutched the cloth of his coat-sleeves. He smelt her delicate perfume, enjoyed the softness of a breast. She laughed.

'I nearly forgot to tell you about the funeral arrangements. That's not like me.'

Alice led the way to the door where she kissed him again, though more perfunctorily. He shuffled back to the sitting room, and, dazed, sat in the scented chair she had vacated.

VI

Sam Martin, in fashionable dark grey with black tie, arrived in good time for the memorial service; even so the church seemed full so that he had to sidle in along a row and crush himself against a pillar. It was cool inside the nave, and the organist played 'I know that my Redeemer liveth' and capped that with what Sam took to be Bach.

The family entered to music. 'Jesu, Joy of Man's Desiring'. No coffin, no braying clergyman. A quiet group, mainly female, some in black but not all, stepped sedately up the aisle. No one, as far as Sam could see, wore uniform. He knew few people amongst those immediately round him, almost all of whom were middle aged with carefully waved or parted hair. The pillar blocked those on the south side of the church from view.

The vicar announced, rather parsonically, why they were there. Sam wondered if there were strangers, aliens even, in the congregation who had no idea why they had, in the clergyman's words, 'gathered together'. Wasn't that in the marriage service? He could not remember. They weren't 'dearly beloved'. He did clearly recall that phrase. By the time he had unconvincingly pursued the barren topic, they were on their feet singing 'The King of Love my Shepherd is'. He was surprised how much of the hymn he retained from his days in the junior school choir. He saw the headmaster of the school querying his pupils about the word 'perverse'. His eyeglasses had flashed with sarcastic brightness, and the black hairs on the backs of his well-washed hands had threatened as he had pointed at one hobbledehoy.

'Ah, Wallace. Had I asked you the meaning of "foolish" you doubtless could have enlightened me, even provided me with a few examples of foolishness taken from your own behaviour this very day. But are you perverse, would you say?'

The lad had hung his head. Had he stared straight back at the master, it would not have been long before 'insolence' had been added to 'perversity' and 'foolishness'. Wallace knew enough to improvise an appearance of shame or humility in the face of learning.

'It derives, comes, from a Latin verb, to turn, *vertere*, and *per* – wrongly. To turn wrongly. Deliberately to choose a wrong course in spite of advice to the contrary. You have been shown the right way, but have turned in another direction. We have turnèd every one to his own way. It is not because you did not know. You did. You had been instructed, clearly, without ambiguity, and yet you went elsewhere. Do you understand that, Wallace?'

'Yes, sir.'

Sam asked himself why this scene presented itself. He should have been concentrating on the hymn and its occasion. They were now advancing through death's dark vale, and the organist had reduced his volume with the result that the singing had become lifeless, sloppily quiet, with a vaguer rise and fall. One could hear the vicar bawling at the front, trying vainly to rally his troops. The organist opened up on the spreading of a table. Sam could not remember the headmaster, 'Knocker' Turner, asking for, or offering, any explanation of 'Thy unction grace bestoweth'. One short piece of interpretation a day was sufficient for his ignorant charges. Turner had no illusions. Walking through the schoolyard in his patent-leather shoes he might well pause by the luckless Wallace and demand the meaning of 'perverse'. If the right answer appeared, a brief word of congratulation was offered as the teacher walked away. But if, more often than not, a wrong answer or none was forthcoming, Turner waited for a crowd of sycophantic gawpers to gather round, then provided the correct interpretation. 'And do not forget,' he'd say. 'Or next time I make enquiry of you, you may not find me in quite so philanthropic a mood.' They all dropped their eyes in case he chose them to furnish the meaning of 'philanthropic'.

The congregation reseated itself. The vicar read from St John's Gospel telling them not to let their hearts be troubled. The faces round Sam showed no overt signs of either cheerfulness or distress at this encouragement; they were here on a solemn occasion and they would act with decorum. 'In my Father's house are many mansions; if it were not so I would have told you.' He pondered on 'mansions'; they'd all have their castles, manor houses, country seats; he doubted that. Probably this was a mistranslation. Sam could not say, was in fact pleased that he was unable to set his own mind at rest. Would old Turner have known?

He could not understand why he felt so fractious, in so carping a mood. He was here as a very new resident of the village to pay respect to one of the best-known inhabitants, to demonstrate sympathy to the daughter of a lord. The vicar had now launched into an account of Admiral St John's life. He had been destined from boyhood for the Navy. Missing active service in the War, he had still found a life of adventure. He had seen action in Eastern waters, at Suez, in the Falklands. He had been a valued member of an Antarctic expedition. As a young man he had taken part in international races as a mile-runner. Tall, handsome, upright, brave, looking every inch the sailor he was, he had demonstrated both his diplomatic skills and formidably high intelligence in administrative work. Here the vicar became vague about the nature of the Admiral's duties, but had a luminous certainty that whatever the man was called on to do he did it with all his might, and brought it to a triumphant conclusion. It had been suggested to him, here the voice rose to a fierce plangency that suddenly fell away, by those who knew the man best that the Admiral might well have finished his career at the very top of his chosen profession, had he enjoyed even moderate good luck and better health. Even so . . .

Here the vicar paused, glanced lordly over the heads of his listeners, before allowing his own to droop. The Admiral in the last few years had suffered much illness, but with the loving support of his wife of almost forty years he had faced his afflictions with a bravery equalling, if not exceeding that of his earlier days. He had looked disability straight in the eye, accepted his lot, trusted in his Lord. Each Sunday morning he had attended church until he was unable to do so, and had never lost his faith. The vicar here rolled his trunk, peered into a far corner and said that during the seven years he had been incumbent here he had been privileged, the exact word, to talk man to man with his parishioner. And a privilege it had been. At first the Admiral had been strong, firm, prompt of decision, but as his burden of infirmity increased with the years he had lost none of the bravery, none of the integrity. The strength had gone, but the spirit remained. If any man could claim with St Paul that he had fought a good fight, had finished his course, had kept the faith, that man was Clement Aidan George St John. In a low mutter he

64

consigned the sailor's soul to the protection of Him who had calmed the Galilean storm. In a stronger voice he announced that they would sing the dead man's favourite hymn: 'Eternal Father, strong to save/Whose arm doth bind the restless wave'. The congregation stumbled to its feet and did the Admiral hearty justice.

The loud singing cheered Sam. He remembered that he had received that morning a letter from Karen Craig thanking him for his kindness to them. She apologized that she had been remiss in writing but they had been desperately busy. Not only had Emma to be driven to school, but Ben had now started mornings in the nursery where he throve, demonstrated his social skills. No sooner had these two settled than the parents had set about buying a new, larger house. Edward had been excellent here, utterly efficient, but it was typical of him to combine his first term as a headmaster with the difficulties of a house-purchase. She wouldn't exactly say he'd deliberately organized this, but . . . She supposed this thoroughly suitable messuage had appeared on the market and Edward was going bald-headed for it. The metaphor amused; the husband's hair was thick, with an over-hanging lock in the front like a poet's. She enclosed a photograph of the four of them, taken by Sam in his garden on their camera, and one of himself with Emma and her mother. These delighted him, unaccountably.

The congregation had been invited to stand while the organist played through Elgar's *Nimrod*. They then sat with some overt manifestations of relief in a period of silence until the organist, on a signal from the vicar, let fly at Henry Purcell's *Trumpet Tune and Air*. The mourning family paid no heed to the sharp military rhythm but drifted out in their own time, pensive but relieved. The congregation, as if under instruction, made its way out of the church from the front. This was clearly not their first funeral or memorial service.

Outside the sun shone, with clouds that moved almost smartly. On the large open space by the south door people gathered in dark groups, smiling now, not afraid to raise their voices. Mrs St John and her daughters stood in the porch by the door and, black-gloved, shook hands with members of the congregation as each emerged from the nave. This, to some small extent, held progress up, but the Admiral's wife did not countenance long passages of conversation. When Sam Martin's turn to be

65

received arrived, he took Mrs St John's hand, bowed his head and said nothing. She said she hoped to see him at the house. He passed on to the daughters, not even offering his name.

He stood alone, in the shadow of a sycamore tree, kicking with one foot at the ground. He looked round for John and Alice Jeffreys, but they were nowhere about. The Rolls Royce man, marching across the space as if it was a barrack-square, acknowledged Sam with a raised finger. The old chap who helped Sam with his garden nodded bucolically. People shook hands and conversation seemed almost frenzied, with heads fiercely waged and gestures frenetic. Sam felt himself an outcast. It would be worse once he reached the St Johns' house; he would be cramped, but still unacknowledged. Some man laughed, over-loud, to his right. Sam could not make out who it was.

'Oh, hello. What are you doing here?'

The voice struck familiarly, but he could not believe his ears. He turned to the woman who now stood to his left in the sunshine. Meriel.

'I live here.'

He could barely get the words from his clogged throat. This was his ex-wife.

They stood in untoward silence. Sam had no idea of what to say. Not that he particularly wished to speak. He glanced diffidently at her.

Meriel, as far as he could make out in the brightness, had hardly changed. Her clothes were more sober than he remembered, and she wore a fashionable black hat. A faint smile flitted across her face, welcoming him perhaps. She seemed, as she always had, much in command of the situation, neat, beautifully turned out, confident. Certainly she looked no older. He made a calculation. She would be sixty-three or -four, but to his ancient eyes she appeared no more than forty. Perhaps everybody looked young to him. Meriel. He found himself trembling. He had thus far been enjoying the service, looking on from his side-line at the manner in which the family, the parson, friends, colleagues, acquaintances, the organist, the caretaker, the villagers had paid their respects to the Admiral. These observances and his obser-vation of them had kept him on his toes, his memory and imagination constantly at work. 'Knocker' Turner, Willy Wallace, boatswains' whistles, brass buttons, those in peril on the sea, had all whirled about the select, subdued atmosphere of the church. But amongst all this he had not spent one second's thought on Meriel. His ex-wife had been in no way, however indirectly, connected with the world of retired sailors. To tell the truth Joan's, his first wife's, funeral had barely been recalled. He felt slightly ashamed at this neglect.

He looked again at Meriel.

She stood perfectly still, at ease, waiting for him to offer some social gesture, or perhaps make his attitude to her clear. She in no way feared the outcome. She had caught sight of him, recognized him (it was sixteen or seventeen years since their last bad-tempered meeting, in a solicitor's office), and had walked across out of curiosity, mischief, sense of occasion. God knew; he didn't. Had he dismissed her, turned away from her, she would have accepted it, made another unfavourable judgement on him, and walked off, a competent woman, elegant, sufficiently sure of herself to be snubbed and yet instantly recover.

'It's a very beautiful day,' he said.

That seemed about as stupid as possible, but neutral, committing him to nothing.

'Yes,' she answered. 'It's a pity Clement's not here to appreciate it. Are you keeping well?'

'Thank you, yes. I can't grumble. Given my age and circum-stances. And you?'

'Very well indeed.'

'Your husband?'

She took a sharp side-step, and stared at him. There followed a short silence. Her eyes narrowed.

'Tom died two years ago.'

'I'm sorry. I hadn't heard.'

Her face betrayed a flicker of puzzlement or incredulity. Sam himself was taken aback. He ought to have known. His children, her step-children, kept in touch with her. Or so he believed. They wrote letters to him and telephoned, if infrequently now their own children were grown-up and away. They must have mentioned Tom Walker's death, at some time. He could not recall their doing so, and he was certain that he would have remembered, because he would have felt basely, it's true, a kind of triumph. After all these years, he would have, however wrongly, claimed that he had done better than his rival, had beaten death off more efficiently. Walker wouldn't have been anything like his age. He had been older than Meriel, but only by

67

five or six years. When Sam Martin had married the twenty-three-year-old Meriel Rhys-Davies he had been nearly forty, seventeen years her senior.

'Yes,' Meriel said. 'A heart attack on holiday.'

'Abroad?'

'Yes. Norway.'

'I'm sorry,' he said, again. It did not matter to him. 'Had he been ill for some time?'

'Well, yes. I suppose so.'

He wondered if the conversation troubled her. It did not appear so. Sam had no intention of adding to her hurt. Even when he remembered, as he did now, her cool announcement after twenty-six years of marriage that she was about to leave him, to live with Thomas Walker, a man he barely knew, on whom he had never wasted a thought. At the time, having almost reached sixty-five, Sam had been about to give up his strict day-to-day routine at the Beechnall headquarters of his company, and had been planning holidays, cruises for the delectation of his wife. She'd supported him well, cared for her step-children, and now she'd be rewarded with a life of travel in luxury. Perhaps that had been the trouble. At the age of forty-seven she had decided to take up with another man. The shock had sickened him. After twenty-six years he had taken her for granted, a reliable, useful, handsome omnipresent piece of furniture. He'd met this Walker a time or two, found him acceptable, companionable even, if shy. A widowed lawyer from a wealthy land-owning family he made no great demands on anybody, seemed always on the edge of any group or activity, and yet this shadowy figure must have been conducting an affair with Meriel, and had convinced her, or been convinced by her, that she should leave her husband. Sam Martin's pride had been lacerated, and Meriel's calm announcement of her future plans had piled insult on savage hurt.

'Do you know the St Johns well?' she was asking now.

'Not really. I doubt if I ever spoke a word to the Admiral.'

'Oh?'

'I've been here only since the end of last year, and he's hardly left the house during that time.'

'Why did you come to the village?'

'To find a smaller place, but with a studio to paint in.'

'Paint?' He found her tone ironical.

'Watercolours,' he answered, flatly.

'Do you exhibit at all?'

'No.'

'Yes,' she said. 'Clement declined with startling speed, really. Just a few years ago he was a striking man, full of energy.'

'So I hear.'

'You had sold our Beechnall house, I suppose?'

He did not recall zig-zag changes of topic like this from Meriel. They may have been a result of her embarrassment. 'Our', indeed.

'No. I let it.'

'Oh?' Again the pretty, interrogative monosyllable.

'I may not have been suited down here. Old men like me don't take easily to change, and if I found I had made an error of judgement then I could have gone back to Pelham Road.'

'It was a beautiful house. Too large for one elderly man, I imagine. Do you know, I often thought I'd like to look at it again, but since I left there I've hardly been back to Beechnall. Not half-a-dozen times, I guess.'

'Are you at the same address?' he asked.

'More or less. I've left the Hall. George, Tom's son by his first marriage, lives there. He's been farming the estate for years now. I live quite close, in the village. He's very efficient is George. Likes the country life. He always has. Went to agricultural college and now manages the place.'

'Has he children?'

'Yes. Three.'

'Do they visit you?'

'Oh, yes. I see them often. I go up to the hall. And their mother comes down with the younger ones.'

'How old are they?'

'The oldest is nine. The youngest fifteen months.'

'Step-grandchildren,' he said, drily. Then relenting, 'Does life in the country suit you?'

'I find plenty to occupy myself.'

As Sam stared down at his highly-polished shoes, sudden shadows broke into his empty meditation. Alice and John Jeffreys had appeared, crunching over the gravel.

'Am I interrupting anything?' Alice almost shouted, confident that she was not. 'John, may I introduce you to Lady Walker? My husband, John Jeffreys.' John shook Meriel's hand, said he was sorry to meet her on such an occasion. Alice would have none of this, cheerfully instructing him to enjoy the sunshine. She then turned her attention to Sam, asking Meriel:

'I take it you know Mr Martin?'

'I do,' Meriel's voice sounded subdued after Alice's, but exactly right for the occasion, giving nothing away. Alice loomed tall over Meriel, but appeared uncomfortable, feeling the necessity for action.

'Hilda sent me across to tell people that it's time we started back for home. Have you a car here, Lady Walker?'

'It's in the village, outside the house.'

Sam was surprised at Meriel's title; he'd no idea that Tom had been either knighted or ennobled. The fact that Alice addressed her thus meant, he guessed, in these free and easy days, that the two women had met for the first time this morning and for a short time only. Sam sighed. Now that Alice had interrupted, he resented it. Before her appearance, he had found the interview with Meriel slow, difficult, uncertain.

'We'll all walk along together, if you don't mind,' Alice said. 'I've passed the message on.' She obviously had noticed nothing out of the way. The two women set off together. The men fell in behind.

Alice and Meriel made the quicker progress.

'What's the name of the, the . . .?' Jeffreys pointed at Meriel's back.

'Walker.'

'Oh, yes. Yes. Walker.' He smacked his lips. 'Very smartly dressed. It's not everybody who can appear fashionable on every sort of occasion. And she looks extremely well in mourning clothes. Yet I don't suppose she attends all that number of funerals. What do you think?'

'I have recently had to attend more funerals than I'd have chosen. As you get older more and more of your acquaintances die.'

'Until you reach the age when they're all gone,' Jeffreys said, surprising Sam.

'You're mourning the next generation then.'

'I can see there's no cheering you up.'

They were out now on the road. Jeffreys stopped them again so that he could light a small cigar.

'Alice doesn't like me smoking indoors. Even in somebody

70

else's home.' As he put the match to the cheroot, Sam watched other mourners getting into their cars or strolling towards the house in the dappled sunshine. 'Good turn-out,' Jeffreys said, inhaling deeply, expelling a blue expansive cloud. He would not move until this first piece of ritual was accomplished.

'He'd be well known,' Sam said.

'Hereabouts, yes.'

'Popular?'

'Hard to say. He's been ill, cooped up indoors for so long. He'd gone ga-ga, you know.'

'But only recently.'

'The last few years.'

Alice and Meriel had stopped to look back for them. Jeffreys blew a defiant smoke-barrage in their direction, and then waved a large left hand, first finger extended, towards them, presumably indicating from his broad smile that all was well, that they need not worry on his account. In this street of heavy forest-trees the ladies turned to walk their two last hundred yards.

'Don't rush,' Jeffreys ordered. 'I'm going to finish this before I go in. Have you never smoked?'

'Yes. At one time. When I was younger. Everybody did.'

'Clement St John didn't. And look where it got him. And he wasn't much older than I am. Seven years, perhaps. It's nothing.'

Sam did not answer, found himself disliking Jeffreys. The man was well-dressed, in a light-grey suit, white shirt with stiffish collar and black tie, but his shining shoes were indecently large.

'I hardly saw him and we lived next door. I used to drop in since I retired to see if I could do anything for Hilda. And he'd just be sitting there. He'd just about acknowledge your "good morning", and that was that.'

'Sad?'

Jeffreys started at the word, jerking his head back, then nodding.

'I don't think I should have liked him in his prime. All the women said how handsome he was, and how intelligent, but he was a selfish sod in my view, and gave Hilda a pretty nasty time, from what I hear.'

They had now reached the garden gate where the two women waited, chatting.

'I suppose you want to finish that thing?' Alice asked her husband, pointing to the cigar.

'Economy, economy. Waste not, want not.'

'And get cancer in the process.'

'They sound like lines from a poem,' Meriel said. Jeffreys let out a great bellow of laughter.

'I'll wait,' Alice said, 'if Lady Walker doesn't mind.'

'No. It's lovely out here.'

Others passed them, greeting them, before going along the path to the house. Jeffreys finished his cigar, douted it on a stone, and threw it into the hedge bottom.

'Ecologically correct,' he said, laughing aloud again.

In the foyer Hilda St John and her daughters waited. This time they shook hands and kissed and did not limit conversation, so that a small queue formed. When the Jeffreys and Meriel and Martin found themselves in place, the mourning ladies made much of John Jeffreys, kissing, patting him, even laughing. They exchanged views on the service, said how delighted they were that Meriel could come, and told her how helpful Alice had been. They all seemed not uncheerful, but when Sam Martin's turn came round, the three shook his hand and Mrs St John said she was so glad that he could spend his time on them. He did not reply beyond a polite murmur of acquiescence, and walked across to the tables. The caterers were in place, and in uniform, issuing, or directing guests toward food. Sam took a cup of coffee, and stood solitary for a moment before following two other men into the large drawing room.

There again he stood, as he had expected, on his own. He could look out into the brightness of the garden. He collected a second cup of coffee, and two sausage rolls. He ate these slowly, to pass the time, speaking to no one but the jobbing gardener who said how well the grass was growing this year, and how much more of his time he had to spend on mowing.

'They like it,' he said. 'Lovely green instead of brown and bare patches.'

'I think I do.'

After half an hour Mrs St John came across to say a word, as did the American daughter. He noticed at the far side of the room Jeffreys was animatedly talking to Meriel. Alice seemed not much in evidence, as if she did some valuable administrative work in the background. What this was he could not guess. Perhaps she'd gone home for a quiet five minutes or a gin-and-tonic.

72

A good number of guests had moved out into the garden, where the talk sounded light-hearted. They had forgotten the death, the funeral, the years of suffering and embarrassment. Now they had paid their solemn tributes of attendance, of flowers, of letters or contributions to a named cause and were celebrating their survival into this magnificent summer's day and their meeting with old friends, with little bright patches of earlier life. Again Sam Martin knew nobody. The pleasure, the rising voices, the laughter and kisses in no way included him. He gave it ten minutes, and quietly slipped past the front door into the road and down to his bungalow. Nobody, he hoped, had remarked his surreptitious exit.

Back home he made tea, opened a packet of chocolate biscuits and pushed out into the studio. There taped to his board was an attempt at the stone bridge on the road down to the sea. Round the unfinished picture lay two photographs and three sketches. He ate and drank, and with difficulty tried to whistle as he cast his eye over the paper where he had painted shapes lightly in before starting the interesting task of deepening and contrasting the shades and colours he had imagined together. This he'd enjoy. He'd paint one layer over another; tricky with water-paints, but possible. He knew from experience that after, let's say, three days' solid painting and looking, he'd decide whether he'd failed, that however carefully he tried to improve his work after that he'd realize that he'd made a hash of it, and that no amount of tinkering would do more than make bad worse.

Sam painted carefully away. Time flew when he was at work with his brushes. Now that his mouth was clear of biscuit crumbs, he could whistle more freely, if just as tunelessly. He had paint on his finger ends and he noticed with dismay a smudge on his white shirt. He shot out of the room to change his funeral shirt and trousers for a pair of cords and a ragged, paint-daubed T-shirt. He concentrated with enjoyment, noticing delicate touches here and there, as well as amateur splodges that needed drastic alteration. His whistling grew to gale force.

The front door bell rang. Sam swore. He glanced at his watch. Ten minutes past five. Not a busy time in the village. He made a slow way to the door, hoping the visitor had lost patience and gone.

Meriel Walker.

'I hope you don't mind my coming round, but they told me

you must have slipped off home so I thought, as I was here, I'd just call round to see you.'

'Come in.' She followed him into the large kitchen.

'What a lovely place. It was such a surprise seeing you this morning. It quite knocked the words out of me. I just didn't know what to say.'

'No.'

He offered her a drink, but this she refused with an unnecessary flurry of words. She sat quietly enough, looking soberly about her.

'I hope I'm not interrupting anything important,' she said.

'No. Not at all.'

'Are you sure?'

'No. I was painting.' He smiled, for the first time. 'Water-colours. Not decorating the house.'

'You didn't do that in my time, did you? I do forget things these days.'

'In your time, no.' He repeated her phrase with ironic emphasis. 'I took it up a year or two after my complete retirement, so that I'd have plenty to do.'

'You went to a teacher? Or a class?'

'No. I read a book or two, and I tried to find my own way.'

'And was that successful?'

'That's not for me to say. I still continue to paint. And it's sixteen, fifteen years perhaps, now.'

'And are you good at it? Do you sell, or exhibit?'

'No.'

'John and Frances have never mentioned it. I hear from them regularly, if not all that often. And they pass on snippets of information about you. They'd said nothing.'

'Each of them owns three of my pictures. That is, unless they've thrown them into the dustbin.'

'I'm sure they haven't.' Her voice rang brightly sociable. She smiled, and moved her handbag from one side of her lap to the other. 'I heard from them both last Christmas but neither said anything about your moving down here to Norfolk.'

'Why should they?' he asked.

'I've always,' she answered in a strong voice, 'insisted that they keep me up to date with your news. I realize that you don't see them very regularly. And one of them, I forget whom, said you were getting to be something of a hermit. Are you?'

'At my age, I don't gad about, certainly. But I speak to people when I go out. I touch my cap to the ladies. I don't run away from them.'

'The same man,' she said. 'On the defensive.'

He decided not to answer that, but sat, fingers locked, looking at her.

'You told the Jeffreys that we'd once been married?' she asked.

'No.'

'I didn't mention it, either, to anyone.'

'That's all right, then,' he said.

'Are you sure I'm not interrupting anything?'

'No. You're not.'

'You're not altogether pleased to see me, are you?' Meriel asked.

'I'm surprised. I didn't expect it. This place is a bit out of the way, and yet you turn up.'

'Yes.' She smiled, calmly. 'But wherever, and in whatever circumstances I'd appeared I don't suppose I'd have been very welcome.' He returned no answer, continued to watch her. 'I was the cause of the trouble. I left you.'

'It's a long time ago,' he said, pacifically.

'Sixteen years. Have you forgiven me?'

'It hadn't crossed my mind. After all I've seen nothing of you. All I heard were the bits and pieces that the children offered me from time to time. I never expected to meet you again, so what good would my forgiveness be? To either of us?'

'That's right,' she said.

There followed a pause. In the silence a bumble-bee dashed itself against the window. Both watched it recover to fly away. He nodded.

'I've never forgotten you,' she began. 'I often think about you, though you're not to know.'

'Thank you.'

'Are you lonely?'

'Sometimes,' he answered. 'Yes, I suppose I am. But it's to be expected. Until just recently I have gone away for a holiday at least once a year. After I first retired, full time that is, I did some part time for a couple of years, I had a couple of cruises.'

'And did you enjoy them?'

'They weren't exactly what I wanted.'

'And? What else?'

'I've been lucky with my health. I can walk and cycle and drive my car, so I'm not cooped up in one place.'

'Still? You're over eighty now.'

'I am, but yes.'

'And have you many friends? Here? Or back in Beechnall?'

'No, not really.'

'The Jeffreys seemed fond of you.'

'I've only got to know them in the last few weeks. Since the Admiral died.'

'Is that so? And the business? Is that going well? I still see lorries with the firm's name on them all over the country.'

'We sold it off thirteen years ago. An American concern bought us out, and they've expanded since then.'

'Were you sorry?'

'No. Morris, Morris Isaacs, arranged it. And we both retained a small interest in the company. That keeps my bank balance healthy.'

'Sam, I think I could drink that cup of tea now if it's still on offer. And if you're sure I'm not interrupting anything.'

He told her to take a turn round the garden for five minutes, and on her return he had set out the tea-tray with his best china and a plate of chocolate biscuits.

'This is cosy,' Meriel said, thanking him. 'To tell you the truth I didn't expect much of a welcome. You're very kind.' She nibbled her biscuit above a protective hand and sipped her tea with relish. 'You're a very kind man, Sam.'

'Oh, sure,' he said.

'And it's nice to look at you. You do seem a little older, but you have a beautiful face still.'

'Not the way I'd describe it.' He'd been both surprised and flattered at her last sentence. Smart, well-dressed women did not usually single out beauty as one of his advantages. He wondered if she was mocking him. She'd never even hinted that she considered him beautiful or handsome when they were married.

Now she began to ask about his garden, and for twenty minutes they enjoyed themselves with technical talk. She had admired his Californian tree-poppy, his Romneya; there was a huge specimen in the Hall gardens, and she'd twice tried to transplant pieces into the grounds of her cottage, but had failed both times. He had no idea of the provenance of the one he owned. The previous occupants had been keen gardeners, and had left the place in good nick. All he'd had to do was keep it tidy this summer.

'You'll make alterations, will you, next year?'

'Things die, or don't prosper. I suppose I'll have to.'

She offered to wash the tea things before she went, but he would not allow it.

'I've really enjoyed visiting you, Sam,' she said. 'It's been nice. You're more hospitable than your children suggest. I thought you might pitch me straight out through the door.'

'I'm an old man,' he answered.

She kissed him warmly on both cheeks.

'I'd like to ask you something,' she said.

'Go on.'

'May I come to visit you again?'

'Well, yes, if you wish to. I'm not very good company, I'm afraid.'

'I could look at your paintings. I don't see any in this room.'

'No. Bedrooms and drawing room.'

'How suitable,' she said.

They laughed together. She made a note of his postal address and his phone number, and said she'd be in touch. She left the house without hurry, and he, finally on his own (he had watched from the gate as her Rover drove off) stood in the brightness of his studio, washing his hands, lonely and chillingly uncertain of his feelings. He was an old man, he comforted himself, who did not like change. The advent of Meriel, Lady Walker, friendly, attractive, expansive, had shaken him. He did not admit it to himself, but took out his stick and made for the beach.

VII

September proved almost as summery as August.

The village was quiet all week, but an influx of visitors on Saturdays and Sundays added a metallic counterpoint to the country sounds.

'I used to love Sunday morning,' Alice Jeffreys had confided to Sam in the street. 'It was quiet and fresh. Now it reeks of petrol.'

'Isn't that an exaggeration?' he asked.

'Oh, you. You know quite well what I mean.'

Sam Martin saw little of either of the Jeffreys. They went to stay with friends on the River Lot in France; Alice sent him a postcard of vineyards, but claimed that she and her husband were living soberly. Mrs St John had spent a week or so after the funeral at home with her children, clearing the Admiral's possessions, and making preparation for widowhood. After that she went off to Massachusetts with her American daughter.

'That all seems sensible,' Sam had commented to Alice who kept him up to date.

'I don't know. Hilda said to me that she wasn't sure she'd want to come back here.'

'You women,' he answered.

'Oh, I think I understand her. The place is,' Alice paused, as if looking for an exact word, 'impregnated with Clement.'

'Good word,' he said. She swiped him, if gently.

He missed Alice now she was in France. She had been lively and sensible as well as beautiful, and never over-serious with him. Life, she suggested, was tricky enough without making a mountain out of every molehill. She bloomed, she claimed now, in perfect health.

His own family did not write, after a burst of holiday post-cards. On one of these John had suggested that he consider spending the Christmas holiday with them. Sam did not fancy the idea, ignored it, hoping John would pursue it no further. In some ways he looked forward, he told himself, to Christmas on his own. One or two, the Jeffreys probably, would invite him in for mince pies or a glass of wine, and he would return the compliment. If they offered him a meal, he would refuse, be in no one's debt. 'You're a miserable sod,' he said, out loud, and laughed mirthlessly at his conclusion.

Emma Craig wrote him a well-spelt letter enclosing a picture, allegedly, of 'Mr Martin' standing on the veranda of his bungalow, garden spade in hand. His most prominent feature, it appeared, was a pair of boots, mud-coloured, and enormous. The Craigs had not yet moved into their new house; Ben quite liked his nursery school; Mummy had joined a yoga class, and Daddy attended meetings in the evening. Emma had written an essay on her holidays and this had won a prize, a medal and a rather dull book, unnamed. They were all well, and she hoped he was. She sent their love. He replied, almost at once, taking care to use print, not joined-up writing, but had so far had no reply. He had pinned her drawing high in the studio.

As for Meriel, he received not a word. He admitted to himself his disappointment over this. Quite what he expected from his ex-wife he did not know, but he thought at least that he'd receive a post-card or phone-call within the first three days. That she had not got in touch meant that she did not mean to do so. She had enjoyed her hour with him, but subsequently had decided against further meetings. Each morning, he waited for the postman.

One Thursday he received a short letter from his former business partner, Morris Isaacs. He was in Norfolk, would like to call round Friday, but had given such short notice because he did not want to put Sam to the trouble of preparing a meal. He'd arrive at 11.30 a.m., they'd eat at the village pub or elsewhere if Sam preferred it. He'd leave early in the afternoon, say at three o'clock. If Sam would like this, would he please ring Morris's hotel in Norwich? If Morris heard nothing he would not come. He did not want to waste anyone's time, least of all his own. Sam telephoned.

Morris arrived ten minutes early.

'I dawdled, but I couldn't go any slower. There hardly seemed any traffic. I always make allowances for hold-ups these days.'

Morris looked well, rather greyer, more heavily jowled but energetic still. He played golf twice a week, badly, with three other twenty-four handicap men. 'The air's good. I'm out of bed at seven and out of Eileen's way before nine. We've not been warned yet for slow play. The time will come . . .' He spread his hands.

They walked round the bungalow and the garden, but Morris insisted that they drive to the pub for lunch.

'All very neat, your place,' he commented. 'You like it here?'

'Yes.'

Clearly Morris Isaacs did not understand this. He kept himself busy with the work he did best. He was called in for consultations by the old firm and two American subsidiaries.

'They pay me to go to the U.S. of A. Twice on Concorde. They must think it's worth their while.'

'And you don't?'

'Oh, I wouldn't say that. Now, tell me what you do.'

'Paint.'

Sam led Morris round his pictures. The friend made deep, appreciative humming noises.

'I never knew you had it in you, Sam. Were you good at Art at school?'

'Not bad. What bit we did.'

'But you didn't do any when I knew you.'

'No. I used to like to walk round galleries when I found time.'

'And you thought to yourself, "I could do as well as that."'

'It never crossed my mind.'

'Well, go on, man. How did you get started?'

'I was finishing work. Meriel had left me. I went to an artists' shop and bought a few things and a little manual and some paper and got going.'

'And you found you could do it?'

'After a fashion. Well enough to keep at it. But I didn't go round shouting the odds.'

'You were always a pretty determined man, Sam. Once you'd sunk your teeth into anything there was no prising you off.'

Morris, strong hands behind his back, padded round from picture to picture, humming and sighing. In the end he confessed,

'Any one of these seems as good as any other.' He walked on. 'Eileen would know. She's interested. All I can do is hit a golf-ball about, very badly. And soon my aches and pains will put a stop to that.'

80

They drove to the Royal Oak, where they ate plaice and chips and drank a pint of old ale outside in the field. Morris continued his interrogation of his former colleague, and ate ravenously, though complaining, 'Beer and fish and chips. I shall be crippled with indigestion all day.'

After the meal they drove down to the car park by the beach, and walked across the links to the sea.

'We have a golf course,' Sam pointed out. 'So if you came to stay with me, you could whack a ball about if you saw fit.'

'It's not the game, Sam; it's the others. My partner's a Unitarian retired headmaster. The other two were a supermarket owner and a high-class furniture repairer.'

'Do you argue, then?'

'Sometimes. Not all that much, and not all that seriously. But we're all competitive, even at this game we're no good at.'

Morris then, switching subjects, pronounced the sea dull, and the sky moderately interesting.

'This sea's dangerous,' Sam warned. 'Nasty currents.'

'It doesn't look deep enough.'

'Don't try it.'

'I wasn't thinking of it.'

They walked back to the car, drove to the bungalow, sat to a mug of Indian tea. Morris had been questioning his host hard the whole time. Sam answered readily, enjoying the inquisition, surprised at his own pleasure. Just before he left Morris Isaacs slapped his arm and smiling with brown teeth said,

'I'm pleased with you, Sam Martin. I had two things on my mind that have kept me away longer than they should. The first was the impression from your children via one or two people at our head office that you'd become a bit odd, something of a recluse, obsessed with small things like watercolours and garden design. That was the primary fear, and it led to the second. I didn't want to come and find it was true, that my old friend had slipped badly. I remember you when we first started together. If there was something wrong with a lorry that the mechanics couldn't handle, you'd be off with your jacket, on with overalls and underneath the bloody thing. The men respected you for it. And I didn't want to find that Sam Martin changed into a crooked, artistic old loony. And you've not. You're into your painting, but I reckon you treat that properly, you've learnt it as you learned the i/c engine.'

81

'Suppose, Morris,' Sam asked, 'you'd found me as these pessimists described me, what would you have done?'

'Damned if I know. That was one of the reasons I stayed away.'

'That's feeble,' Sam said. 'Morris Isaacs without an idea in his head, I don't believe it.'

'There you are. I suppose I'd have rung John and Fran up and reported to them, and asked them what could be done about you. I'd have invited you down to my place for a week or two and asked my doctor to have a squint at you.'

'And play a round of golf? If I wasn't cracked to start with I should have been pretty quick after-that.'

They laughed, slapped each other's shoulders, and marched for the gate.

'Carry on, bloody Rembrandt,' Morris shouted. 'One of these days I'll bring Eileen to have a look at your pictures.'

'You do.'

Sam felt cheerful, though he reached for his indigestion tablets after the fried lunch. Morris was good-hearted. He remembered them in their early times together; Morris thought nothing of a twelve-hour day, and seemed as full of ideas at the end as at the beginning. Without him the firm would never have expanded as it did. They were lucky in that they had begun to chance their arm when circumstances were almost uniquely favourable to road transport, but Morris had not missed an opportunity. Now he was older, and stouter, and slower, and could afford this little, kind visit. It had done Sam good. Morris had something of the younger fire in him still. Sam remembered how his partner would sit him down and say, 'Suppose I was asked to run a regular daily service to carry small pieces of engineering machinery between here and Glasgow and Edinburgh, could we manage it, and how much would it cost? Have we the vehicles, or do we buy or hire? Have we the willing drivers? What would the total cost be, roughly? Here's a list, and pictures, of the stuff they want us to carry. Now, I want the answer in an hour, Sam, and then I've got to go and argue with Stevenson and Goode, and so I want steady, rock-solid figures. They're fed up with the poor and slow service on the railways. Can we manage it? You tell me what sort of lorries we'll need, and how long it'll take, and I'll work out the total cost, and then I'm able to talk straight to them.'

'They're a good firm, Morris.'

'They aren't a charity. As I know only too well. But if I can screw 'em for a bob or two profit, I'll do so. But I want the technical details, boy, so I can blind 'em with science.'

Stevenson and Goode had been closed down for years now, but they'd been excellent clients in their heyday. The world changes even for large firms. Morris Isaacs, the ferocious chaser after work, had rarely showed his social streak, his human kindness; he'd been far too busy. But now, with only occasional consultancies to fan his competitive fire, he went round, if rarely, to inquire into the welfare of dodgy, tetchy, old codgers. It could be that Eileen, Morris's wife, was responsible. Morris's first wife, Verna, had tired of his continual absence from home, his powerful, stressful, energetic, successful search for more business and had left him. At the time Sam had wondered what the effect on Morris had been. He himself had been grieving still after Meriel's desertion, but Morris had shown little sign of undue distress. It had been one further hurdle in a life strewn with obstacles, and one had to clear them. That was that. Sam imagined Morris today at this minute, behind the wheel of his flash Jaguar, face determined master of the road, driving home, curiosity satisfied. Sam all those years ago had been doing well in business, expanding in favourable circumstances, but once Morris had joined full-time that expansion had become an explosion. Morris took big if calculated risks which Sam would not have dared consider, and his boldness had made both old men very well-to-do.

Eileen had come later, at about the time the firm had been sold off. Sam had never met her. The wedding had taken place while Sam was on one of his lustreless cruises, this time to the Caribbean. He had arranged for a suitable present, a Ruskin watercolour, and both sides had made, by telephone, expansive promises to meet. Nothing had come of these. The two men had since run across each other twice, in London, but without consequences. Morris had both times been full of schemes. Possibly, he thought again, Eileen had been influential in fostering this last visit. Morris might just have mentioned the rumours about the loneliness and eccentricity of his old partner to his wife, and she had ordered him, if that was the word, to go and find out their truth for himself. Sam laughed, hollowly, not making much sense of any of this.

He went out to his studio, but decided to take a half-day holiday from painting. He carefully examined the work in progress, determining how he would begin again in the morning. Then he tidied the bench round his drawing board, replacing caps, cleaning up his palette, washing his brushes, clearing the dirty water from his jam-jars and refilling them. Now he could start tomorrow morning without the foolery with his kit that often held him back. He hung his rags on a radiator to dry, and even dusted his bench down including legs and the inside of drawers. He squared up the two chairs, straightened the pictures on the wall, considered cleaning the windows indoors, but thinking better of that returned to scrutinize his picture. Pleased to discover that he had not changed his mind about tomorrow's tactics he stood hand on chin, thinking and doing nothing, when the front-door bell interrupted his charade.

Alice Jeffreys, all smiles, stood there. Her tan suited her.

'Come in,' he invited. 'Delighted to see you.'

'You have visitors,' she said.

'No, he's gone.' She entered.

'I saw you eating in the garden of The Oak as I went past this lunch time.'

'I didn't see you.'

'I was in the car.'

'And I was too intent on my plaice and chips.'

She accepted his offer of tea, and gracefully reclined when he went out to the kitchen into an armchair with *The Times*, much at home.

'Who was he, then?' she asked immediately he had returned.

'Morris Isaacs, my old business partner.'

'Has he retired?'

'Oh, yes. Years ago. Well, as far as he can. He gets pulled in from time to time according to him.'

'By your firm or other people?'

'Both. He loves sorting things out. He's very energetic still.'

'What sort of age is he?'

'Seventy-three.'

'Does he come over to see you very often?'

Alice put her questions with gusto. If she wanted information, she would press for it, not hint but make her inquiries with a friendly bluntness. She had dressed for the call, perhaps to impress his visitor, and looked impulsively, robustly pretty.

'No. It must be six or seven years since I last saw him, and that was in London.'

'But he just happened to be over here by chance . . .?' Her question mocked.

'Not him. He came over, to my surprise, with a specific purpose in mind. And what do you think that was?'

She played with her cup, returned it to the tray.

'He wanted some advice from you about a business venture?'

'No. I'm far too out of date for that. If Morris needed expert opinion he'd get it, or buy it, from somebody actually on the job.'

'To sort out some snag in his private life?' She advanced this less seriously.

'No. He never looked on me in that way.'

'Go on, then. You'll have to tell me.'

Alice trilled with schoolgirl laughter.

'He had heard,' he began slowly, 'at second or third hand that I was beginning to lose my bearings,' Alice frowned at his expression, 'to become eccentric, a loner, tucked away in the back-of-beyond, seeing nobody, hearing nothing. In plain words, I was mad, or near it. That was the story.'

'And where,' Alice asked, 'had these accounts started?'

'With my children.'

'Is that likely?'

'It's likely in the sense that both John and Frances will have reported my move to this place. Why? Because it will have surprised them. At my age. They will also have said that I spend a lot of time drawing and painting, activities they don't usually associate with me.'

'How old are they now?'

'John's fifty-three, Fran's fifty. Both are nicely settled, married, have children, don't need me. We're friendly. Don't get me wrong. Both have been up here. We make occasional phone calls. They are slightly surprised that I have left Beechnall to retire here. I never did any painting when they were young. I was too busy making money.'

'And their mother?'

'Is dead.'

'So you brought them up yourself?'

'No, not so. I did for two years, or nearly. Then I married again. A much younger woman. Only eleven years older than John. She kept the home going.'

'The children went away to school?'

'No. There were excellent day-schools in Beechnall. Both went away to university. John is a barrister; Frances worked for the Beeb, but is married now to a stockbroker.'

Alice sat up, really straight-backed, at the front of her chair, feet together. She frowned slightly.

'Mr Martin,' she said.

'Sam,' he corrected.

'Sam. You don't mind my asking you all these questions about your family, your private life, do you?' There followed a pause. Sam sipped his coffee, apparently deep in thought. 'I mean, I've no right to. We're friends, I hope. Real friends. But, of course, we haven't known each other for very long. I can see that . . . No. If you think I'm too inquisitive, speaking too far out of turn, tell me to shut up.'

Uncertainty twisted her face; she sat awkwardly now, in a fidget. Her eyes stretched wide stared up at him, on his higher chair.

'I've always thought,' he said, measuring his words out carefully, 'that if one wanted to know something, one asked questions plainly about it. Not indirectly, or dodging round corners.' He thought this did nothing to reassure her. 'If you ask me something I don't want to answer, I shall say so.' Again the pause, the awkwardness. 'That's clear enough. You've not asked me anything yet I don't care to talk about.'

Sam sat back.

Suddenly a rush surprised him. She had leapt to her feet, come across, kissed him, burying her mouth onto his. He seemed enveloped by her body, her perfume, her dress. A hand stroked his face, straightening it for the next kiss. Her breasts pressed on to him. Suddenly she doubled her weight, dropped and lay like lead on him. Later he concluded that her ankles had given way, turned over so that she had fallen in heavy intimacy onto him. His wooden chair creaked, then shook, then slowly, or so it seemed to him, turned over depositing the couple, apart, on the floor. Sam's head hit a chair-leg; lights flashed. The chair had fallen free. He could hear Alice's breathing. He sat up, eyes shut. He seemed undamaged. When he opened his eyes, Alice was struggling to sit upright. Her skirts were high, and her legs wide apart.

'Are you still alive?' she asked.

'I think so.'

She straightened her clothes, turned over onto her knees, and then stood, straddling his legs.

'Are you all right, Sam?' she asked, voice anxious.

'More or less.'

He found his way to his feet, much more slowly than she had, and standing righted the chair to lean on it. His breath came short.

' "How are the mighty fallen",' she said.

'Ye'.'

'That spreadeagled us.'

'It did.'

He touched his head where it had caught the chair. His finger ends showed no blood. His breathing proved difficult; slight dizziness affected his vision. He sat heavily down.

'I'm sorry,' she said. 'I must have been too violent.'

'Or I wasn't ready.'

The answer comforted her so that she smiled. She showed no sign of the recent tumble, her hair and dress as neat as ever. Her wedding and engagement rings flashed in afternoon light.

'I was so pleased with you. You'd been so nice to me, so reasonable. I know I'm damnably curious, but you didn't seem to mind. But I kissed you too violently. I'm sorry.'

'Don't think I'm complaining,' Sam said. 'It's not very often at my age that ladies kiss me with any sort of enthusiasm. Any time you like we'll have a repeat performance.'

'Next time,' Alice answered, 'I'll give you due warning.'

His head ached now in earnest; he touched the bruised spot again, cautiously.

'Can I get you another drink?' she asked, suddenly practical. On his reply, she snatched up his cup and hers and bustled from the room. He closed his eyes. This day had proved too much for him. One knee pained him. Breathing came shallow and difficult. His fingers gingerly explored the sore spot on his head.

Alice reappeared with coffee.

'Are you asleep?' she asked.

'Half-unconscious,' he answered.

'Are you all right?'

As they toyed with their coffee, he pulled himself together and invited her to continue with her cross-examination. His voice sounded tremulous, but she showed no sign of noticing.

'Ah, yes,' she said, immediately. 'But where were we?'

'You were inquiring about my family.' He felt proud of his sang-froid.

'So I was. Your second wife, who brought your children up. Is she still alive?'

'Yes,' he said. 'You know her.'

'Know her? Who is she then?'

'Meriel Walker. She was at the Admiral's funeral. We were married for twenty-six years.'

'And?'

'She left me for another man. The children were grown up and married. This was sixteen years ago. She had no children by me and none by Tom Walker, the man she married. Both times there were step-children.'

This information seemed to have sobered Alice, who swilled her coffee quickly down, and sat agog for the next revelation. Her serious expression both soothed and accused him.

'Do you meet her occasionally still?'

'No. The funeral was the first time since the divorce. Sixteen years ago.'

'But you were quite friendly. I mean, you seemed to be chatting amicably enough.'

'Politely, yes. What's more, she came down here later to talk to me.'

'She wanted to renew acquaintance?' Alice asked.

'I don't know what she wanted. Just to check up, probably, how I was faring. She may have wanted to see in what sort of squalor I was living. There but for the grace of God, she thought . . .'

'Her husband was rich?'

'Yes. Not without. He came from a landed family. He inherited the estate. An elder brother was killed in an accident. A bachelor, the brother. Or so I think. The father was still alive when Meriel left me. Died in his eighties. Her husband died moderately recently, three years ago, I think she said. He was a lawyer, a solicitor, quite successful, in Stamford. I'm not sure about details.'

'And he gave up his law when he inherited, did he?'

'Don't know. I don't know a thing about him.'

He closed his eyes again. He felt tired, helpless.

'That's very interesting,' she said. 'It's marvellous how little we know about one another. It's not surprising, though. You lived here for a few months before I even spoke to you. And I had to be taken ill to do that.'

'You've had no recurrence of that?'

'No. It was either the weather or something I ate.'

'You went to see the doctor about it?'

'I did. But he wasn't much help. I was to go easy, and come back to him on the first sign of anything similar.' She looked across at his handling of his cup. 'You're over eighty, aren't you?'

'Eighty-one. Or almost.'

'You don't look it. I'd put you in your sixties.'

He screwed his mouth in sour pleasure, and sounded a note of jovial agreement.

'Would you say . . .' Alice began. She sounded exactly like a television interviewer. People nowadays based their domestic style on television programmes. 'Would you say that you were typical of men of your age?'

'No.'

'Why not? Or is that one of the questions I mustn't ask?'

'I'm a widower. With most married couples it's the other way about. The husband goes first.'

'I never thought of that, but I meant your way of life, the hobbies and habits. Would you say you were typical?'

'I've not the slightest idea. I'm lucky to be able to get about without too much pain, and not to be kept alive with tablets and potions.'

'You don't feel old, then?'

'Yes, I bloody do. Sometimes. Though I'm well, I seem to be hanging on to life with a fine thread that'll give any minute.'

'You think you might die?'

'No. On the whole I feel quite healthy. But I seem to live on the margins of life.'

'That sounds bad. What do you mean?'

'When you're younger and you do something,' he said, 'something quite ordinary, you aren't bothered by the thought that it's hardly worth it because this will be the very last time you ever do it. Such thoughts don't occur.'

'And this makes you . . .?'

'The connection between me and life is tenuous; it can't be long, all things considered, before I drop off.'

'What makes you feel this? Aches and pains? Inability to carry out some job you did easily before?'

'I hear of so many contemporaries dying. Only this week somebody sent me a Beechnall newspaper with a picture and article about a charity I support. And I looked through the rest of the paper, and specially the obituary columns. And there was a name I knew. That of a lad who went to the same elementary school that I did. And I remember walking to school with him one lunch-time, with him and his brother. And he was spinning me a yarn about one of our teachers who used to enliven his lessons with his reminiscences of the First World War. The chap, Johnny Burton, had said he'd jumped out of his trench in Flanders and caught a German artillery shell, and thrown it safely away before he jumped back in the trench, and announced, "There, lads. I've saved you."'

Alice's expression of puzzled delight and disbelief dispersed itself in a wild squawk of laughter.

'You thought it was true?' she asked.

'I did not. Neither did the other two boys. We knew it was impossible. I wondered at the time whether Albert Coates, the boy, had made it up to test my credulity. Yet . . .'

'Yet what?' she asked.

'It stuck in my head. I could take you to the exact spot on the pavement where he told me this, though it's quite different now, all built up. The point is . . .'

'You love the roundabout way,' Alice mocked. 'Talk about circuitous.'

'The point is that I picked up this paper and there was Albert Coates dead, husband, father, grandfather. I'd not thought about him for sixty-nine years. I'd certainly never seen him, but there was the announcement while I was still alive to read it. What's more, when I rang up to thank my friends for the newspaper, they told me about a woman-friend, a neighbour, who'd been to the university hospital for a check-up, had been given a clean bill of health, came home and was found dead in her bed next morning.'

'But she must have been fairly ill to be sent to a hospital.'

'Possibly. But they found nothing amiss. And she was nowhere near my age.'

'You don't know,' Alice objected, 'the detailed history of either of these cases. They both might have been ill for years, for

90

all you know. You're perfectly well.'

'They were my generation, roughly. And though I'm right enough now, I might start getting ill. Statistically it's likely. I can't live for ever.'

'Do you want to?'

'No. I wonder a bit about the manner of my going.'

She considered this, then consulted her wrist-watch.

'Just look at the time,' she said, loudly. 'It's past six.'

'John will want his tea.'

'He's out. And if he's back he can get it for himself.'

'You don't have a cooked meal in the evening?'

'No. Not unless we have visitors.'

'Eat like a king at breakfast,' he said, 'a prince at lunch, and a pauper at night.'

Alice stood. He did likewise. She put her arms round him and kissed straight onto his mouth, but briefly. This time he was ready, but the embrace appeared mannered, stilted compared with the first, rhapsodical, flying kiss. He grinned to himself. She quickly bussed both his cheeks and made for the door.

On his own he turned on the half-completed television news.

VIII

Within the next few days Sam Martin received a letter from Karen Craig announcing that she was pregnant. Her tone was excitable; usually, she scribbled, it was after the move into a new house that one conceived, but here she was, ahead of herself. They were all delighted, Emma especially. He wrote a congratulatory note and asked if they were thinking of visiting Norfolk during a weekend or in the half-term holiday, because he would like to give them a meal.

There followed a few hurried letters and the Craigs arranged to call in on their way back from Yarmouth at the end of October, their half-term holiday. They would be with him sometime on Saturday morning, and they would leave soon after lunch so that they could get home before it was too dark. On that night the clocks would go back.

He told Alice of the visit and she said she would come in and help him. John was away on a golfing weekend so that she'd be glad to have a small purpose in life. She asked innumerable questions about the Craig family, and then set out planning a much more elaborate menu than he had envisaged. She acted, he told her, like a whirlwind.

In some pleasurable way her energy galvanised him. She insisted that he framed one of his watercolours for Karen and then looked through his folders to choose something suitable, a detailed picture of flat sea dwarfed under an oblique sweep of cloud across blue sky.

'Beautiful,' she said. 'Karen will be pleased.'

'Now, choose one for yourself.'

She worked with speed through the folder again, whipped out a second skyscape, placed it alongside the one already chosen.

'Be generous,' she said. 'They make a gorgeous pair. Give her the two.'

'Yes. I'll do that,' he said. 'Now do as you're told. Pick one for yourself, or two.'

Alice did so. Sun on a cottage with a wood behind. Yellow predominated, in a crude brightness.

'That's not very good,' he objected.

'That's for me to say. I've chosen it.'

She kissed him. She seemed to kiss him often, or seize his hand. He did not know what to make of it. A young woman, to him, she could have done better, not wasted her love, if love it was, on his ancient ugliness.

His man in Hunstanton framed the pictures quickly, pressed him to bring down more so that he could put them on display, sell them.

'Could you?' Sam wondered.

'Not so many at this time of year, but in the summer, yes.'

They agreed a price. George Cook would frame a small watercolour and sell it for sixty pounds. He'd take twenty, and Sam forty.

'That's about fair,' he said. 'If there's a run on them, and there might be, I'll up with the price. But get me a few down here soon for the Christmas trade.'

He told Alice of this, and she expressed serious satisfaction.

'A new career,' she said. 'At your age.'

'I don't need the money.'

'No, but it's spreading your name and fame.'

'I don't even know whether I want to sell them.'

'Trust you,' she answered, 'to want to keep 'em in a folder in a cupboard in the dark.'

'I could take out those I like, and frame them myself. As I do now and then.'

'But would you? And how many? You're full of good intentions.'

She spoke to him as a wife to a husband, and he enjoyed it. Alice accompanied him to Hunstanton to choose presents for the others, a big humming top for Ben, reading books and a belled skipping rope for Emma, and for Dad a chaste fountain pen, suitable, Alice said, for a headmaster of modest pretension.

'We'll send them home happy,' she claimed. 'They won't forget you.'

'Or you.'

The visit proved successful, the more so in that Sam had time, with Alice taking responsibility, to enjoy every minute. The children after a quarter of an hour's shyness whooped about the

93

place. The whole party, Alice included, went round the garden though a nip in the air kept them moving. The week at Yarmouth, chosen because Edward had spent a summer holiday or two there as a boy, had not been altogether satisfactory. A sharp east wind had tempered the sunshine and made dallying at the edge of the sea too chilly for absolute comfort. 'And it gets dark so soon,' Karen said. 'Heaven knows what it will be like next week when we've put the clocks back.'

They ate their lunch slowly with talk abounding. Edward was full of his new job as headmaster of the Alderman James Greensmith Infant and Junior School. Yes, he knew who James Greensmith was, had in fact met him; he was an old Labour councillor, now honorary alderman, a decent, diffident, shrewd red-faced man, in poor health at present, but retaining a distant interest in education. He had two sons, both doctors, who had been through the state system, and Greensmith had wanted every child in every school to have their opportunities.

'Isn't that a near-impossibility?' Sam asked.

'The impossibility is for everyone to take advantage of those opportunities. Our job is to see that they're there for those who can.'

'And they are not always?' Alice asked.

'By no means.'

Edward Craig outlined his plans. Of course he was to some extent limited by the national curriculum and by demands of the examinations, but his school drew from a mainly middle-class area, and so they hadn't the mountains to climb that those in inner-city schools struggled up.

'I often think I could deal with the prescribed subjects in a better, more lively manner than our syllabus demands, and that we are forced to ignore matters that would be of more interest and use to the particular children we have from our part of the world, from our social level, but on the whole teachers like to know what's wanted of them exactly.'

'Why is that?' Alice again.

'One, they know what to prepare for; they're not blundering entirely in the dark. And secondly, trivially, they have something to complain about.'

The school was shortly to be inspected, and this had caused problems. But no school existed without difficulties, and it was the duty of head and staff to move these, to clamber over them or slide round them. Craig seemed electrical with confidence, sure of himself, his ideas, his rightness. He spoke modestly, often humorously, had an illustrative anecdote for every point he made, listened carefully to questions or objections. He gave, without doubt, an impressive performance.

Karen, on the other hand, seemed subdued.

She had been suffering from morning sickness, as with her other children. She made no great show about this, mocked herself, but did not look altogether well. 'I thought this time I might have been immune, but it would appear not.' She tried to take things steadily, but would be glad to move into the new house, at the beginning of the Christmas holiday. The old residents were still there. No, she and Edward didn't need to do anything radical when they moved in, but she liked none of the decoration, and that meant repainting pretty well the whole house, or so she feared. They wouldn't start on the work until Edward had got his inspection out of the way, probably next summer.

'Will you do it yourself?' Sam asked.

'That's the idea. Edward likes decorating. The baby will be born at the end of February, or early March, and we shall know how we stand. We shall be in this house a long time, unless Ed chases and gets a job elsewhere, and there's no hurry. I'm not a headlong rusher into things, like some I could mention.'

Craig smirked at this.

The meal and the conversation had been excellent, and it was past two when they rose from the table. What had impressed Sam most of all was the behaviour of the children; they had not only sat at the table without complaint, but had joined in the conversation tactfully and interestingly. He expected as much from Emma, but Ben seemed equally unfazed by the occasion, the constant verbal exchanges. He ate slowly, fairly cleanly, grown-up and at ease. Alice's *tour de force* the pudding, a huge trifle, highly decorated with a kind of cathedral tower the centre-piece, had temporarily struck the children dumb, and though they ate sparingly – they had done too well on the main course – they discussed the beauties of Alice's art.

'It's a shame to spoil it,' Sam said on its appearance. Alice had hidden it from him.

'It's the most beautiful pudding I've ever seen,' Emma gushed.

'You don't have trifles like this at home, then?' Sam asked Ben.

The child stared hard at him for a moment.

'Better,' he said.

'There's a candidate for the diplomatic service,' Sam said.

'Good boy,' Alice said. 'You praise your Mummy when you get the chance.'

Alice and Sam cleared away, produced coffee and then, to the excitement of the visitors, the presents. Each one had been carefully wrapped in suitable, decorative paper. Ben hugged the coloured box in which his top lay wrapped, and seemed in no hurry to have it tried out. Emma looked at the bright covers of each of her books, reading the titles out loud and without error. Finally she removed the tissue paper which disguised the skipping rope. She caressed the shining handles and asked permission to go outside to try it. When Karen methodically unwrapped the paper from her two watercolours, her eyes opened wide with delight and she wept suddenly, helplessly, the tears tumbling down her cheeks. Emma and Ben watched amazed. Edward opened his package, weighed the fountain pen in his left hand and made the brief, perfect speech of thanks for them all. He was used to public performances.

'It's like Christmas,' Emma said.

'Exactly,' Sam agreed.

They walked out for a last trip round the garden. Karen had replaced and fastened the coverings of her pictures. Edward had hidden his pen away; he was not the sort who carried a pocket full of writing implements. Emma lined up her books, reverently with her mother's present, and went first to the garden to whirl her shining rope. Sam noted that she showed no great skill, as if she had never tried to skip before this.

The one awkwardness came from Ben. He would not relinquish his hold on the highly coloured cardboard box in which his top lay, nor lift the lid. His parents offered to open the box for him, and tempted him with descriptions of the gorgeous colours of the spinning top and the musical note if emitted, but the child clung the more tenaciously to his box. The parents were both unflurried, spoke persuasively, were joined by Emma, but to no avail. The child trotted round the garden hugging his covered present, a dogged expression on his face.

'He's like his father,' Karen whispered to Sam. 'Once he's

96

determined to do something, nothing will change his mind.'

'I can hear you,' Edward called back, cheerfully.

The parents did not make an issue of the boy's obstinacy, and all were cheerfully smiling as they took to their car. The farewells were kept short, kisses and handshakes. Ben kissed both Alice and Sam, still clutching his box. Emma carried her present, the white rope now neatly binding the red and blue handles together. Sam and Alice stood by the front gate, feeling abandoned in a place which just minutes before had been crowded with human delights.

'There's a nip in the air,' he said miserably.

'Will they be home before dark?' she asked.

'Might just,' he said. 'Depends on the traffic.'

They trailed indoors where he insisted that she rested while he provided a cup of tea to fill the hiatus. The visitors had not disturbed the room, had left no sign of their stay.

'That,' Alice said, 'was one of the happiest days I've ever had.'

Sam, in surprise, did not question her announcement. In a sense he understood it. Perhaps she exaggerated.

'I love children,' she continued. 'They make things worth while.'

'Yes. You know exactly how to suit them. They seemed pleased, all four of them.'

'Not difficult. Remember I've grandchildren, myself. They visit us occasionally.'

'This lot ate well,' he said. 'Your cooking was great.'

'Yes. They were properly brought up. Their table manners were really good and they had been taught that food was to be eaten, not played with.'

'What about Ben and his box?'

'Yes. I was watching the parents. They didn't make a big deal of it. They pointed out advantages, but when he wouldn't hear of them, they just left him.'

'Is that good?' he asked.

'It is. It wasn't a matter of life and death, so they weren't drawing a moral or exaggerating its importance. He'd open his box when he was ready.'

'But he was missing something. He couldn't see and hear the top spinning.'

'No. But he was his own master. Once that box was open

97

there'd be Dad or Mum or even Emma spinning the top for him. He'd have to stand there, and be expected to admire. And,' she signalled for silence, 'anticipation is often preferable to the real thing.'

'He would know what to expect?'

'Perhaps not. Though they explained it really well. Dad's humming was magnificent.'

Alice herself made a sound, musical, deep-throated, and kept it up as if demonstrating the power of her lungs. He stared in amazement. She finally snatched breath and said,

'Forgive me; I'm excited. I feel that this morning I've done something really worth doing, and that's unusual.'

'But you do all sorts of good things for people. Look at all the trouble you've taken over Hilda St John.'

'She sees it as her due.'

'So that makes a difference?' Sam asked. 'I think what's so satisfactory about this morning's effort was that you got it right. You suggested presents. I'd never have thought of that.'

'You paid for them.'

'And, moreover, you chose gifts they wanted. That takes real knowledge. I'd no idea.'

'I was just lucky,' she said, eyes modestly down.

'Just as you chose the right things for them to eat. If I'd been in charge they'd have had one of the three or four things I can cook. You provide a banquet that suits them all. Ben's eyes stuck out of his head when you wheeled that trifle in. And Edward, he'd be the headmaster in this as everywhere else, a despot and puritan. "Food is necessary (are you listening?), but in moderation." But he took two helpings of trifle.'

Alice laughed at his comment.

'What about Karen and Emma?' she asked.

'If I were a young man Karen's the sort I'd choose for a wife.'

'Is she like your first wife, or Meriel Walker, then?'

'In no way at all.'

'Not even in looks? That's what men bother about in the first place.'

'No. Not either. Joan was taller, and Meriel darker.'

'Would she have had you, d'you think? Karen?'

'Who's to know?'

Alice looked him up and down, not without mischief.

'I would guess you were attractive.' She stroked her chin.

'You had a good head of hair, then?'

'And no double chin and beer gut.'

'Have you a photograph of yourself in your twenties?'

'Somewhere.'

'Handy?'

'You want to see it?'

'If you please.'

He, she noticed, shuffled out of the room like a very old man or an invalid. He seemed in no hurry to return. She wondered if he wasn't sure where the photographs were, or was picking out one or two that flattered him. She settled back in comfort, satisfied with herself, waiting to be pleased.

Sam returned. He carefully shut the door behind him as if he were about to disclose a secret. He carried in his left hand three or four photographs. With something of a flourish he presented her with the first, a black and white picture of himself in vest, shorts and running-shoes.

'Um,' she said, letting her voice rise. 'When was this taken?'

'I'd be seventeen or thereabouts. It's the school's annual sports day.'

'Nice legs.'

She looked hard. In no way could she connect this young man, school colours pinned on his shirt, looking upwards, relaxed for the moment but ready for the loudspeaker announcement which would summon him to the line, the anxious wait for the starter's pistol, with the old man in front of her. The hair bushed luxuriantly, the features were thin, firm-fleshed. The eyes seemed a different shape; the fingers long, the hands unmarked.

'Pretty boy,' she said. Without a word he handed her the second. A tall girl stood, smiling stiffly, in her old-fashioned frock, hands folded in front of her. She seemed attractive, but not beautiful, puzzled at her rôle. Behind her left shoulder stood a young man, awkwardly wearing a suit and waistcoat. With his left hand he held a pipe to his mouth.

'I was on leave from the army. We hadn't been married long. Less than a year.'

'That's Joan?'

'Yes. In her mother's back garden. She'd just be pregnant then with John.'

'It doesn't show.'

His hair was shorter than the schoolboy's, and shone with

99

Brylcreem. The expression on his face lacked animation. The budding athlete had been caught up in the excitement of the day; the young soldier-husband blandly faced camera, world war, absence overseas. Again Alice did not recognize her companion in this slim, old-fashioned type, demonstrating manhood by biting on a pipe-stem. His cheeks were clear still, his lips moist. Little Dorrit bushed at the feet of the couple while tall phlox bloomed to their left. The black and white yet adequately demonstrated the summer sunshine.

'How old would you be there?'

'Twenty-six, seven. I'm not quite sure. I forget. I was in REME. That's where I learnt all about motor vehicles. On loan to the RASC and the RAC.'

He passed over the third card. Again in a garden, but this time Sam and Joan sat on chairs, each with a child. John, seven or thereabouts, stood slightly in front of his father, to a kind of attention, right hand down on his father's knee. Frances sat on her mother's lap, smilingly conscious of her fair curls and her mother's protective arm. This time Alice thought she recognized something of the modern Sam in the expression on the face. It could not be exactly described as a scowl, but determination showed there. 'I've got on, and I'll hold on to what I've earned.' That perhaps overestimated it, but this man was no longer schoolboy or tame soldier, he was a man of business, not quite of substance yet, but on the way.

Alice said as much to him. He turned the photograph in her hand and looked at it again.

'Yes,' he agreed. 'Yes.'

'Were you pleased with yourself? You don't look it.' She scrutinized it.

He shrugged, held out his hand for the photograph, which he lifted from her.

'Joan had,' he said slowly, 'only two years to live.'

'Was she ill when this was taken?'

'No. Quite fit.' His face assumed a wooden misery. 'She died of cancer, tumour of the brain. It was all over inside a month. My mother and her younger sister came in and looked after the children. It was rough for them as they were young. They didn't seem to be able to understand it. Nor could I for that matter. Just when I was beginning to be really successful. I did mechanical engineering at college and joined Westby's when I'd finished.

100

And then just when my dad was beginning to do well, to expand, the war came. I was called up. My father worked himself silly to keep the firm up and running through the war. He had a struggle, but he did some government contracts. Anyway he was there at the end and gradually made progress again. When I came out of the army I went back to Westby's for a year, but the old chap pressed me to join him. Things were getting too large to handle on his own. I was a bit loth, because by now I had two children, but I decided to try it. Westby's would have had me back. In fact, they began to put work in our way, and that helped. By the time this was taken,' he flipped the photograph on the last one which she had not seen, 'we were doing well. We'd expanded the carrying side, and set up quite a large repair business. And then Joan died.'

'Did your mother and her sister continue to look after the children?'

'I could afford home help, and paid my aunt. I think she was glad to get out of my mother's house and work elsewhere.'

'Did they quarrel?'

'Not really. They got on pretty well together, but she had lived with my mother all through the war, and felt she'd never be independent.'

'Didn't she have to work in the war?'

'Oh, yes. She was in the offices at the ordnance factory, but as the men came back she was eased out. Or at least that was my impression. She had lost a job, had a disappointment with a man, a breakdown and that made her even more dependent on her sister. When the chance came to look after the children she chanced her arm, and it worked.'

'Were the children at school?'

'Yes. John was nine and Frances six. I'm telling you all this, but it doesn't seem half the story. Neither with family nor business. It was all much more complicated.'

'In what way?' she asked.

'Every way. How Aunt Alice got on. She had the same name as you. Years younger than my mother. Four or five years older than I was. Yes, complicated. So.' He sighed.

'Go on. It's just getting interesting.'

'No. Leave me one or two of my tatty secrets.'

'Is she still alive?'

'No, she died not long ago. She married a widower, a

schoolmaster when she was forty. They lived in Cheltenham, happy as larks.'

'Had no children?'

'No. Well, not at home. He'd one son, but grown up, who died young soon after his father's second marriage. A mathematician of some sort.'

'And the husband?'

'He hung on into his seventies. They'd been married for twenty years or thereabouts.'

'Was she happy, do you think?'

'When I think back to it (and I don't very often), I'd say that her married life was the best she had. For one thing she lived in a house where the income was regular, and she was allowed to handle part of it. She had lived with her sister, and in my place, and we all messed her about. She had a job during and after the war, and you'd think she would have been independent then, but she didn't seem to be. I saw to it she had money when she looked after the children. I gave her a room at the house. But she'd go back to my mother's in her spare time. That's what she wanted, it seems.'

'Did she seem a colourless personality? A maiden lady?'

'No. A little bit old fashioned in her choice of clothes. But a good-looking woman, really.'

'Have you a picture of her?'

'Must have somewhere. Don't know where.'

Sam looked down at the two photographs, one in each hand, as if he had not noticed them before.

'This is the last. You haven't seen this.'

This time the image of Sam Martin had changed again so that she barely recognized him. In a light grey suit he wore a white carnation in his button-hole but he seemed secondary to the figure on his arm. A bride with veil and wide-skirted white gown down to her ankles, she carried a small bouquet, roses and maiden-hair. The girl modestly looked towards her hidden feet, only half-smiling; she seemed no more than sixteen or seventeen, a schoolgirl. Shown this without instruction or knowledge Alice would have guessed that this solid man was a father giving away his daughter.

'She looks young,' Alice said.

'I was thirty-nine; she was twenty-two,' Sam said, dotting every 'i', leaving his questioner clear in her mind. 'Meriel Rhys-

Davies a.k.a.,' (he thumped the initials in scorn), 'Lady Walker.'

'She's changed.'

'We all change,' he said, 'and mainly for the worse. We were married a long time. And then, at forty-eight, she decided she preferred Tom Walker.'

'Did you know him?'

'Barely. I'd met him.'

'And how did you find out?' Sam sucked air noisily in through his teeth. 'Oh, I'm sorry. I shouldn't have asked that.'

'That's all right. She told me. Plain John Bull. Straight out. I was sixty-five, and preparing for retirement. She was away from home from time to time, some of it with Walker, presumably. But she sat me down one afternoon. We'd just had an excellent lunch, and over coffee she said, "Sam, I've something to tell you. This will come as a shock to you, and I'm sorry about that." She spoke more slowly than usual, as if I wasn't very quick on the uptake. She was nervous, I guess, and not altogether sure what the effect on me would be. After all, I was sixty-five and had had a bit of trouble with hypertension, so perhaps she thought I'd have a heart attack or a stroke. "I'm going to leave you," she said. I just sat there. I wasn't going to make it easy for her.'

'Had you no idea?' Alice asked.

'No. We'd been getting on in much the same way as we had for years. Since the children had left home, at least. I was gradually letting go of the ropes at work, and I'd been planning a cruise or two for us. It was about this time of the year, and I thought I'd book in January and start retirement proper with the cruises in the summer.'

'Did she know about these holiday plans?' Alice inquired.

'Yes. We'd talked about them often enough. Anyway, she waited for me to say something, but I just sat there, dumb.'

'Were you shocked? Or angry?'

'Something of the sort. In the end she announced that she was going to live with Tom Walker, and that she wanted a divorce.'

'And this was news to you?'

'A complete surprise. I can honestly say that I had not the slightest suspicion that there was anything between them. He occasionally visited some friends of ours, the Wilsons, and joined a geological group Meriel belonged to on outings. That was all I knew. He'd been to our house once perhaps when I was there. He was nearer Meriel's age than I was, but hadn't made any great impression on me. I'd rather liked him than otherwise. Quiet lawyer. Clever. Knowledgeable.'

'When did she leave you?'

'Just over a week later.'

'Did you speak to each other during that time?'

'Not much. She prepared sketchy meals at the weekend. Walker was away somewhere. I moved out of our bedroom. I was still at work. She spent her time getting her things together, and seeing her lawyer and her friends. The house was big enough to keep apart in, if that's what we wanted. She told me a day or two before she went when she'd actually be going. That was it. She cleared off as she said she would. I was out; I'd gone to work as usual, and hadn't seen her that morning at all before I left. I knew she'd be out of the house when I returned. She kept her word. When I got back her wardrobes were bare, and bits and pieces of furniture, bric-à-brac, a picture or two had disappeared. She'd left no note. We met twice or three times at a court hearing and a solicitor's office, to sort a settlement out, but that was all.'

'And that was that.'

'Yes. She kept in touch with John and Frances, and they passed on snippets of news. Intermittently. I didn't know, for instance, that Walker had acquired a title.'

'Did you think about her?'

'Occasionally. I was reminded. We'd had a decent, civilized marriage. Or so I thought. It was the end of it that was so rapid. I can't understand it to this day.'

'But you can talk about it calmly enough,' she said.

'Only to you. I never discuss it with my children even, and if I did I have a suspicion that they'd say I was as blameworthy as she was. But it was the suddenness. I no more suspected. . . . It dropped out of the blue.'

'And you were upset?'

He looked at her as if he hated her words.

'Yes. I was. I was angry and shaken. I was on the verge of retirement, and a bit agitated about that. I wanted to do less, to have time to myself, but I'd been going off to work at seven-thirty every morning, Saturdays included, for thirty-odd years. And the firm was expanding now beyond all expectations. And there was a possibility that we'd sell out and make a lot of money. Morris Isaacs had been considering that for some time.

So I was by no means stable, and I hadn't got my old stand-by, work, to fall back on. Or I wouldn't have for long. I was furious. Driven mad. I suppose my pride was bruised. My wife preferred somebody else. But, if I remember properly, it was my ignorance that riled me. Meriel, and I'd lived with her for twenty-six years, found life with me so dull that she decided to clear off, go running to some other man.'

'Did you love her?' Alice asked.

'I wouldn't have used that word. Or not exactly. I'd got used to her. She was there every day. Do you love your husband? Do you now?' His voice rasped harsh.

'Not as I did when we were first married.'

'Do you have sex with him?' He surprised himself with the prurient question.

'Very rarely. John's more active in that line than I am. But elsewhere. With other women.'

'Meriel and I still made love. And she never objected.' He coughed. 'To my advances. Only the week before her announcement, we'd had it. And with no demur on her part. That's what made this so unexpected. I fumed. And kicked the furniture. And swore.'

'When she was about?'

'No. I didn't argue with her. Or ask for explanations. I knew she'd be afraid if she didn't know what I was thinking. And I wasn't going to help her out. She could squirm. It was her own fault. The strength and the intensity of my feeling grew enormously. I didn't think I had it in me. But there it was. Rage. Bitterness.'

'You got over it?' she asked.

'Yes and no. I wasn't myself for months. My temper was shorter. More than once in my room I burst out in helpless crying and flung myself on the bed with my fists beating the duvet. I wasn't altogether sane.' Sam drew in a noisy lungful of air. 'But I gradually hardened myself. Another odd thing at this time was that my partner Morris Isaacs' first wife, Verna, had recently left him. I used to watch him after this had happened to me to see if he showed any signs of distress or anguish or whatever.'

'And did he?'

'Not that I could see. He'd swear about her to me. Accuse her a bit, but it seemed not overwhelmingly important. He'd swear in the same way over a secretary mislaying a letter.'

'Did that help you?'

'Not really. It gave me one extra thing to do, to occupy myself with. But no. For a few months I walked about like a man half-insane. I tried to hide it, kept out of people's way. If I was short-fused or nasty at work people put it down to the proximity or fear of my retirement. No. It was a bastard, and though it's over and done with now, I still don't feel exactly kindly towards Meriel. She wasn't a young, flighty girl. She was a middle-aged woman, had been married twenty-six years. That made it worse.'

'Was the menopause . . .?'

'Menopause? I don't know. Using daft words about it doesn't alter my feelings. She threw me over, and I did not like it.'

'You never thought of re-marriage?'

'No.'

'You didn't expect her to come back?'

'I didn't even hope it. Meriel knew her mind. She'd had enough of me, and if Walker had proved worse she wouldn't have allowed herself to come creeping back. No.'

Alice glanced at him. His anger spurted into these sentences. The rift, ancient as it was, sixteen years, had not healed. She stroked her face, leaned back to look at the ceiling as if at her ease, giving him leisure to recover.

'Well, I've wasted enough of your time,' she announced.

He made no answer. She stood.

'You'll be hungry,' she said.

'That won't worry me,' he growled.

'I'll be going, then.'

'Will John be home?'

'No. He's staying the night with friends. Or that's the story he told me.'

'And you don't believe him?'

'I don't see why not.'

He laughed harshly, almost choking.

'Stay and eat with me,' he said. 'Then there's no need to rush anything. You've done me good today. More good than you know.'

A tear forced itself out of the corner of his left eye, hung in the wrinkles. The hand with which he wiped it off was heavily veined, deeply lined, not altogether clean. He stood like an old man, a prisoner of his ailments, dreading the next blow.

'I shall need very little after that lunch,' she said.

106

'All the easier.'

'You sit down for a bit longer. I have to go back home, close the greenhouse, feed the animals, do the blinds but I'll be back inside the hour.'

He obeyed her, and she crossed the room. She bent and kissed him on his cheek, a sisterly smack, but then leaned forward again to find his lips. The kiss lasted some seconds. Her perfume and her presence dizzied him.

'Sit there like a good boy,' she ordered, straightening up.

He put his arms about her waist, awkwardly, it was difficult from their positions, and pulled her into him over the chair-arm.

'Careful,' she warned. 'You'll have me over again.'

'Would you mind?'

'It doesn't do for old ladies like me to be falling over too often.'

His head rested on her belly. Very gently she pressed it into her, before she shook herself free and said, 'That'll do for the moment, young man.'

'I'm old.'

'I don't think so. But just sit there until I come back. It won't take me long.'

She found her own way out. He heard the front door bang and imagined her brisk footsteps on the brick path. He could barely come to terms with what had happened. He had made his confession to her, something he considered dangerous. She had cared for him, kissed and caressed, pulled him towards her softness. It seemed impossible. He remembered Alice Jeffreys out with her friend the Admiral's wife, two well-dressed, strong-voiced women, making their presence felt not only to tradesmen but to passing half-strangers like himself to whom they'd hardly offer a glance or a greeting. Now Alice, the perfumed Alice, had held him to her, spoken in the low voice of affection, of love even. He could not believe it, dare not. Self-pitying he looked down at his wrinkled hands, and heaved himself from his chair to stand in front of the mirror over the mantelpiece.

He examined his face, found it much as expected, blotched, marred, mole-ugly, lacking grace and symmetry. True, he could read character, experience into the features, but that he did not want; he required beauty to attract Alice, to dazzle her. He knew that to be impossible. He was old, uncomely, impotent, unpre-possessing. Alice was kind, and filling in a boring day helping him with hospitality. He took out a handkerchief, blew his nose loudly, and walked about the bungalow setting things straight.

IX

The end of that day proved disappointing.

Alice returned. At about seven thirty they made Welsh rarebit and drank large cups of tea. They chatted about the village, the visitors, the sea, the Roman road, but made no intimate connections either with words or flesh. In a way that was perhaps better. He wanted no earth-shattering revelations. Earlier events had tired him. By nine o'clock, while she was still strongly talking, he was ready for bed. That was the sort of man he was these days.

'You look fagged out,' she said.

'It's been a long day. And exciting.'

'I'll be away.'

'Come and see me tomorrow, will you?' he asked.

'Not if it tires you out.'

She teased him, a younger woman with an old man. It did not matter now; his eyelids were drooping. He walked down the garden path with her, and stood at the gate long enough after she'd gone, before he shuffled back indoors to lock up. As he was about to leave the sitting room he picked up the photographs which had been laid tidily on the table, Meriel on top. Sam glanced sourly down; that beauty was in no hurry to pay him a second visit. He compared the picture of the bride with the reality of the titled woman he had chatted to after the funeral. He tried to recall who had spoken first as they came together under the sycamore tree. He could not remember, but he thought it was she. What had she said? She'd wished him good morning, afternoon, and probably expressed surprise at finding him so far from the places she expected him to frequent. He tried to recreate the shape of her unusual black hat but could not. When she had visited 'Avalon' she still wore the seemly black coat and tights, but had discarded the fancy head-gear.

Meriel had been pleasant, had suggested another visit but had had second thoughts. He wondered why. She thought it unwise to invite him back to her home where her husband's children would look on his presence with suspicion or disfavour. Meriel had always been a woman of orthodoxy, preferring the accepted idea, the correct appearance. In a way that is what he had liked about her. She dressed, looked, spoke well, saw to it that John and Fran did the right things, said the expected words, attended acceptable events, wore suitable clothes without seeming too conservative. She chose the right furniture, fabrics, carpets, sang the conventional tunes. One was never outraged. That is, until her final announcement that she was to leave him.

He blew out his lips.

After a tour of the place, he went up to bed. In spite of his fatigue he could not sleep. After trying and failing to read, he rose, remade his bed and stood by the window. The Rolls-Royce man passed by with his dogs. For the rest little else but the last of the leaves fluttering in the lights. He could hear nothing of the sea, only the slight restlessness of night breezes. A man in black hurried past, head down. Rolls returned with his dogs; he had not gone far. Sam was just about to return to bed, was winding his French mantelpiece-clock, when he heard his front gate click. He drew his dressing-gown tighter, untied and refastened the cord as he stood behind nearly closed curtains looking out.

A couple, he did not recognize them, had stepped delicately inside onto the path. The taller figure closed the gate, this time in silence. The two stood for a moment, touching, a double-headed darkness. Sam did not in any way recognize the two, but decided that they were male and female as they momentarily parted to stand, listening. After a time, the taller bent to kiss the other and they swayed together. They separated with speed and tiptoed, or so it seemed, into the shadow of his front hedge. There they stood again, making sure of their privacy and safety, and then squatted down. It was difficult to make out their exact movements or stillnesses against the black mass of the hedge and its shadow, but the two were now sitting or lying close. They made no noise, or none he could hear from his vantage point a yard or two above them and twenty-five away.

He watched for development, opening his curtains another inch. He felt an instant of excitement, though he condemned himself as a Peeping Tom. But. These lovers, if that is what they were, trespassed on his land. Why had they chosen this spot for their love-making? There must be dozens, if not hundreds, of

110

more private, sheltered, out of the way arbours further down towards the sea where they could roll, and thrust, be penetrated, scream without attracting any attention at this time of the night.

Were they a decoy? Had they clicked the gate to attract attention so that an accomplice could break in at the back? That seemed very unlikely. He could have rung the police and inside twenty minutes he'd have a patrol car with vulgar head-lights and two heavy-booted bobbies trampling round his house. That would suit neither fornication nor larceny. Sam moved away to make a quick survey of the back garden from studio, kitchen, bathroom. He found no evidence of invasion.

Back at his front window he could imagine the same vague black shape in the velvet dark of the hedge's shadow, but this time he noticed a slight change. From the edge of the darkness onto the grass a woman's leg protruded. There was little of the erotic about this; he could see nothing above the knee. In the half-light he found it difficult to judge the age or shapeliness of the leg, though he was sure he could see her shoe. The leg moved, rather slowly, without passion, and in the end was withdrawn, in one or two hesitating jerks back into the darkness. He listened but the lovers were silent. Had they made any sound he would have picked it up, for his window stood open. An owl hooted as the wind toyed with the last leaves. He stared at the darker darkness that represented the couple.

He drew up a chair. He would do his spying in comfort. He had not occupied his seat above a few minutes when a fierce thirst troubled him. On his bedside table he kept a carafe of water and a glass, but he did not want to leave his position. He resisted the urge for a time, but in the end yielded, as he knew he would, rose, poured out his drink, and returning sipped it sitting. The thirst had disappeared. He put the glass down on the carpet between his feet. The pair in the garden could not be seen or heard, only imagined. He snatched his glass up again from the floor and gulped the contents down. He coughed, choked, swore at his impetuousness, relaxed again to lethargy, the front of his dressing-gown damp.

Guiltily he kept his place.

What was an old man like him doing here? The couple, as long as they did no damage, should be left to love. In any case he could not see them. For all he knew they might be lying on their backs side by side innocently studying the stars. If he were

111

young again, he wouldn't want some dirty old man observing his sexual antics. He remembered Joan, that mistress of the proper, in a field, on holiday, frock-ends up, legs wide. They could have gone indoors, they were married, but she had tempted him somehow, for even then he'd preferred comfort, to this outdoor wildness, this natural snatch of pleasure. There had been no spare light then; these were the black-out years of the War. She had intended this, had walked him from the cottage they had rented by the week, out into the garden, and then to the field beyond. It had been deliberate; Miss Prim had decided to shock her husband in the fresh air, to please him beyond his cautious ways, his kindly loving, his loving kindness. She wore no underclothes, and moaning, uninhibitedly ripped at his hair. At the moment of his climax, a sheep in the next field had bleated; it sounded exactly like the cough of some bronchitic old man, and he had for a moment lain still inside her, terrified that they were being observed.

Sam Martin smiled, and took his eyes away from the hedge-bottom. Spying on this couple had perhaps revived this memory from the first home-leave of his marriage. He had not remembered it for years, and now as an old man he recalled it not with lust or prurience but with tenderness. She had prepared herself for him, dressing only in a summer frock, (what was its colour?), and a light mackintosh. She had presented herself to him, a willing wife, near-naked on the edge of a field under a copse; body and soul they had come together. Now she had been dead, returned to earth for forty-odd years. Again he found himself weeping, not largely, not ostentatiously. With the back of his hand he wiped the small wetness from the corner of his eyes.

Alice's kindness earlier in the day had perhaps pre-destined his mood. She had given something of herself to him, in a less overt way, but offering herself in her acts of efficiency, her unusual gentleness, her soft kissing. That was all his old age called for, was capable of receiving.

How long he stood with these thoughts he could not say, but he felt locked inside himself, seeing nothing, hearing no sound. He peered back into the crack of his curtains and was surprised that his lovers were now standing. He was quite sure of this because they had moved slightly nearer the house so that the head and shoulders of both appeared above the darkness of the hedge. The two were much of a height. He and Joan would have

112

appeared so to an onlooker; she was a tall girl. He could make out little of the present two; the woman's hair was longer than the man's. They stood apart and moved, as if stamping their feet. He concluded that they were adjusting their clothes. This done, they closed together in a kiss, long-held, static, statuesque. So he and Joan had embraced under the summer night sky fifty-five years ago, in undying love, one flesh, one spirit united against the dangerous contingencies of a world at war. Sam sighed.

The couple made their way towards the gate. He saw them pause at, then step over, a narrow flower-bed. They let themselves out of the garden in silence, without hurry. They stood for a brief time in the road; he could see them top to toe but without recognizing them. To him they were nobodies, leaving him bereft of their company. They had enjoyed each other, and he, who could barely see them, who had to imagine their ecstasy, felt alone, deserted by these his, the word echoed, friends. That was ridiculous; they had not even known he was there. They would pass him in the street tomorrow; he would walk by them, stand in the queue, maybe even speak, but with neither side acknowledging or suspecting the joint participation in that nocturnal act of spending and waiting.

Wide awake he went to the kitchen where he made himself a mug of hot chocolate which he took back to bed. Sitting up, on his elbow, he drank it, drew sheet and duvet about him, and was asleep within minutes.

Next morning Alice called round to see him straight after breakfast. He had washed his few pots, and had determined to walk out at the front to examine his lawn for damage. That meant normality had returned. The postman rattled bills through his letter box, and two minutes later Alice arrived. It was not yet a quarter to nine.

He unlocked, unchained his front door.

'Hello,' she said. 'You've got your anorak on. Were you going out?'

Sam described last night's experience, said he was going to examine the lawn for damage.

'How interesting,' she said. 'What a den of vice. All unbeknown to me. Come on, Sherlock Holmes.'

They walked down the path, she first. She had made her way onto the lawn as he examined the gate.

'You'll find my fingerprints there,' she said, over-loud.

'And the postman's.'

'I hope you don't draw any conclusions.'

He could do without her whimsicalities at this time in the morning. He wished that he had been on his own, with no demands made on him.

'I can't see any damage,' she called.

He trampled across the lawn to where she was standing. The grass, cut for the last time this year, had grown little. He thought he could see the slightly flattened place where the lovers had lain together. He was not sure, asked her opinion. She took a long step towards the spot which he indicated, and stooped.

'No,' she said. 'I don't know. I can't see anything.'

Suddenly, she seemed volcanic with sharp movement this morning, she jerked upright and pointed. A yard from the hedge bottom lay a condom.

'Evidence,' she said.

'A french letter.'

'Don't pick it up,' she warned.

He looked about him, found a twig which he poked under the sheath, and at the second try lifted it, neatly balanced and comical, to eye-level.

'I'll put it in the dustbin.'

He walked away, rounded the house, dropped both contraceptive and twig into the bin. He stood for a moment at a loss, then made a limping way back.

'Done,' he said to her. 'Disposed of.'

'I wonder if it will make this part of the lawn especially fruitful,' she laughed. 'The pagans used to have fertility ceremonies like this.' She pointed to the ground. 'You'll have to see if the grass is particularly green just here.'

'And if it is invite them back?' he grumbled. 'I wonder why they came in here. There must be better places.'

'There are some people who like to make an exhibition of themselves. There was a possibility of being seen, and they took it.'

'Why didn't they use the middle of the lawn, then?'

'They maintain a balance,' she answered. 'A slight possibility of being seen. An element of risk. It adds spice.'

'Does it?'

'Oh, we're grumpy this morning, aren't we? Are you envious? Just because you're not likely to want to do it, you mustn't

114

begrudge other people their little pleasures.'

'I wonder who they were.'

'You didn't recognize them at all?'

'No.'

'What time was it?'

'Just before midnight.'

'Did you notice if they had a car? If they hadn't it's likely they'd be village people.'

Both shook their heads, he without relish, she in mischief. They trailed along the path, unspeaking, up the steps to where they stood on the veranda, staring back to the far end of the garden.

'It's not very warm out here,' Sam said. 'Let's go indoors.'

'You wouldn't think of dropping your trousers out here, then?'

'I would not.'

'And it must have been even colder at midnight.'

The kitchen warmed them as they stared down the length of the back garden. Alice expressed surprise at the varied deep reds and yellows of the raspberry rows.

'Ay, autumn's here,' he answered.

As they stood quietly, making little of the vista before them, a heavy hammering on the front door interrupted the vigil.

'Who's that?' Sam asked.

'Lover-boy come back to claim the valuable gold ring he dropped last night in the throes of passion. Go on, answer the door. Find out.'

'Why the hell don't they use the bell?'

'No one here can really tell. Keats,' she giggled. High spirits ruled this morning.

Sam made for and opened the front door. A big young man, in blue jacket open over a sweat shirt, confronted him.

'Ah,' he said. 'Is Mrs Jeffreys here?'

'She is.' Sam waited for further information.

'Mrs-The-Admiral's back,' the young man said. 'Mrs St John. She told me to knock her up next door, and when we got no answer, she asked me to call in here to see if I could locate her.' He seemed pleased with the word.

'Come in.'

The young man darkened the passage. Alice came through the open kitchen door.

'Hello, Jim,' she said. 'Hilda's back, is she? This is very early.'

'Picked her up at Heathrow. Got a fax yesterday. Her and her daughter.'

'Nothing wrong, is there?'

'Not that I know. She got fed up with America, so the pair of 'em came back. To be here and back for Christmas. They had some early snow, she said.'

'What about Carolyn's husband and family?'

The young man pulled a sour face, and shook his head.

'You'll have to ask her.'

'How did she know I was here?'

'She didn't. She thought you might be away when we couldn't get any answer at your house, but she said Mr Martin might know where you were.'

'Did she want me urgently?'

'I don't think so. She just wanted you to know they were back. They were going to get a bite to eat, first of all, and then an hour or two's nap. They'd been hanging about.'

'Thanks, Jim,' she said. 'I'll give her a ring. What are you doing?'

'Home. Breakfast.'

'Kip?' Sam asked.

'No such luck. I've got to run the old man to Norwich. Then up to Wells.'

'No rest for the wicked,' Alice said. 'Thanks, Jim. I'll give her a bell.'

The hallway felt empty after the young man had removed his bulk.

'Does the local taxi,' Alice said. 'Very reliable. You must have seen him about.'

'Why did Mrs St John send him round here?' Sam asked.

Alice laughed, pulled a comical face.

'Here? She wanted you to know she was back. Or perhaps in some way to catch me out. But it's typical. Hilda was a very pretty young woman. The men flocked about her. You might not think so now. But that's as may be. She knew that she was attractive, and acted on the assumption that she was so. And the habit dies hard.' Alice looked to determine whether or not she was convincing her hearer. 'She likes ordering men about, and so, instead of telephoning you to find out if you could tell her where I was, she

116

orders Jim Tate to call in on his way back home. It's her style.'

'Is this true?' Sam asked.

'It's my interpretation, and is as likely to be right as anything else you hear.' She cleared her throat. 'I'll call in.'

'I can't make out whether you like her or not.'

'I don't know either.'

'That means "no", doesn't it?'

'She's a bit older than I am. She was two years or so ahead of me at school. I remember her, but I doubt if she remembers me. I was a junior nobody. She says she does, but I don't think so. We can recall so many people and happenings, she imagines she ought to and so she'll say "Oh, we were at school together" and people think we were bosom friends.'

'And what do you think?'

'Nothing. In my usual cynical way. I've been useful to her, and company when there was nobody else, and John does all sorts of bits and pieces for her. Saves all the hassle and hanging about for plumbers and handymen.'

'Your husband finds her attractive.'

'He can see that she was. And he likes her manner. And he and Clement got on well, that is, when Clement was all right in his head.'

Alice suddenly thrust her arm through the crook of his elbow.

'It's getting late,' she said. 'Have you been to collect your newspaper yet? Neither have I. We'll go along together.'

She whirled him round and kissed his cheek. He kissed her mouth. She returned this in strength, and her tongue explored his as she pushed him back against the table.

When she released him he felt only relief; he could breathe easily again.

'This is getting serious,' she said.

'Do you think so?'

'Don't you?'

She straightened his collar, then took her small, lace-edged handkerchief, wet it with the end of her tongue and scrubbed lipstick from his cheek and lips. It reminded him of his mother.

'There you are,' she said. 'Fit to appear in public.'

They walked together to the newsagent's, talking like staid old people. A young couple passed them, looking away. He imagined what they'd think: a married pair of ancients, tottering out, past all pleasure.

117

'I wonder if they were the pair on your lawn?' Alice asked, a few yards on.

'No.'

'Why are you so certain?'

'The woman was taller.'

'You said you couldn't see them properly.'

They laughed, parted to conduct their transactions in the shop. He had to wait while she and Mrs Newman, wife of the proprietor, exchanged views on the post-Christmas pantomime at the Church Hall. This was now under rehearsal and giving rise to the annual quarrels, spats, arguments. Alice was acting as pianist in these early stages, teaching the cast the ridiculous songs the church organist would not touch. She enjoyed this for a week or two, but was too bored to continue or to perform on the three nights though she was, in fact, a far better pianist than the music teacher who was dragooned into the job.

The early stages were seen as a catalogue of misfortune. The vicar's wife fell off the stage, and no one knew why. One night the piano was locked and those who knew the hiding-place of the single key were all mysteriously absent. Alice had gone home, leaving an instruction that they could recall her when they had a piano ready for her to use. No message ever came. A young woman, new to the village, had threatened the producer with her husband. Nobody knew the nature or extent of his wrong-doing. Many suggestions, some fantastic, flew about.

Alice delighted him with these stories on the way to the butcher's which was at the far end of the village. He expressed his surprise at the eccentricity, even the vice, of the inhabitants and wondered how much Alice exaggerated.

'Does your husband perform?' Sam asked.

'No. He's not had the time. Or the inclination. He likes to organize his own pleasures.'

'Is he at home now?'

'No. He's away. On business. And you may well ask on what business. I often do, and get no answers.'

'Is that upsetting?' Sam delighted in the tact, the understatement in his query.

'I'm used to it.'

They reached the Admiral's house, and Alice stormed up the path to ring the bell. The lengthy peal could be heard yards along the road by the retreating Sam. He remembered how he had looked at Mrs St John and Alice only weeks before as they had walked round the village, letting the plebeian world know their business as they talked, shouted rather, in their upper-crust style. When Alice spoke to him it was all much quieter; she whispered conspiratorially, giggled, loosened her shoulders. The grand lady of the village disappeared, replaced by the gossip, the joker, the interpreter.

Alice, without argument, bloomed feverishly in his imagination. He could not understand why such a woman could take an interest in an old man as he was. She'd have no idea how much he was worth. Neither his appearance nor his bungalow was in any way prepossessing. He could easily have appeared as a schoolmaster, a petty official or a small shopkeeper. Perhaps he was the only man available, but at least he had not disqualified himself by his appearance or behaviour. When, about four thirty, Alice phoned and asked him to call in, 'if you're taking a turn through the village later this evening', it seemed no more than he expected. No, that was not right. His head had not been turned to that extent. This brief, brand-new connection had proved exciting; he felt as he had as a seventeen-year-old when anything could happen, but he'd another sixty-odd millstone years hanging round his neck to warn him that miracles by their very nature are rare.

Now at eight o'clock he sat upright but at ease in a small room he had not known before in her house. Curtains were drawn; the walls beat heavy with warmth. He occupied the single armchair in the place. Alice leaned back on his legs. She had thrown down a huge cushion at his feet and then neatly dropped onto it, asking if he was comfortable. He felt much at home. A glass of whisky and water had been put on the small table to his right. He had hardly drunk spirits since he came to the village, but he'd already taken an appreciative sip.

He closed his eyes, remembering his final move from Beechnall at the end of the previous year. The old house he had let, but on that misty late November morning the removal-men were carrying out such furniture as he had decided to take with him. Already several valuable pieces had been packed away and despatched to John and Frances. He had ordered new beds for 'Avalon', and they were already in place. The Beechnall house had been over-furnished for modern tastes, so it still seemed comfortably habitable, but he could see the empty spaces; they stood proud as recent scars. He walked into the cold street to watch the removal-men pile his belongings into their pantechnicon. He wore a jacket, a pullover, a collar and tie, but the cold drilled into him; the mist dripped thick as drizzle, but chilled him to the bone.

He exchanged a few words with the workmen, as they passed. They sounded cheerful, but later that evening they'd be at home, with wives and families, looking over the same old possessions, cursing them perhaps or at least wishing they could uproot themselves and start again in a new place. And he, at eighty, who had no need to move, no need to leave the town and settle amongst strangers at the seaside, stood shivering on the pavement under brown, low dampness of skies. He wondered what his neighbours thought; one or two would be watching behind their curtains. Three sisters opposite had been there since he had moved in a year or two after his marriage to Meriel. Then they had been young, lively well-dressed women, flaunting their busts as they set off for work. Their parents had since died; one of the girls was now a widow; one had divorced; the third, the most handsome, had never married but had received a substantial bequest, so rumour had it, in the will of a city alderman and factory owner who lived in the corner house at the end of the street. They had all retired from work, and had returned, in two cases, from their own homes to join their sister in the large house which the parents had left equally to the three.

This morning, he guessed, one would be on watch for his departure. The other two would come running upstairs at moments of crisis or excitement. He could well imagine their comments over lunch, for this was not one of the days when they went into town to eat, and a new topic of conversation would prove welcome.

'Poor Mr Martin,' one, Betty the divorcée, would say, 'he looked lost. Just like a little old man.'

'That's what he is.'

After Meriel had flown he'd looked on Helga Drew with some favour. She was the youngest, most uninhibited of the girls, barely fifty and without encumbrances. They spoke together in the street; she made no secret of her pleasure in the conversation, but it had gone no further. Meriel had crippled him emotionally, he had decided, made him unfit to try matrimony, even consider its early stages. Nothing had come of it; she had smiled brightly enough at him, but that had been all. They were neighbours and no more.

Now in the brilliant light, the almost palpable heat of Alice Jeffreys' room he touched her hair, stroked her cheek. She looked up at him in some surprise, but showed neither resentment nor shock. She had been telling him about her playing for rehearsals of the Christmas show.

'Every year I swear it's the last,' she'd said.

'And what changes your mind?'

'I like the Rivingtons who produce it. And we make considerable money for cancer research. I don't play the real performances, or at least not more than one.'

'Who does?'

'A man called Gross. From Hunstanton. A schoolteacher.'

'Is he any good?'

'Oh, he'll pass muster.'

Alice, it appeared, had considered making music her career. Her teacher had been very good, and she had passed diploma examinations in her late teens, and had played successfully in concerts and accompanied singers in north London where she had lived. After she had married John Jeffreys at the age of twenty-three she had hardly touched the piano for four years; they had not, in fact, had an instrument in the house, but as soon as she was pregnant with Janice, John had presented her with a new upright, and she began to spend time almost febrilely, she claimed, making up for lost opportunities.

Sam stroked her face and she took his hand to kiss his palm. This was life.

'Do you ever give concerts hereabouts?' he asked.

'Jeremy Rutherford in Hunstanton persuaded me to play last year.'

'And was it good?'

'I enjoyed it. He worked very hard filling the seats, and drumming up performers. I don't suppose his charities made a great deal of profit, but Jeremy's the sort of man who glories in rushing round and organizing people.'

'What did you play?'

'The Bach Italian Concerto, some Brahms, the *Intermezzi* Op 117, and some Chopin and Liszt.'

'Did it go down well?'

'Yes, I think it did.' Sam interrupted his caresses to pick up his glass and drink. 'The trouble is that though I had done all these things before it took me a great lot of practice and effort to get anywhere near the standard I once had.'

'But you made it?'

'Within reason, yes.'

The normality of the conversation contrasted strangely in his mind with the smooth feel of her cheek, her ear, the soft lips, the hair. Whisky had affected him; he leaned forward to touch her breast as she continued to describe some fearsome technical difficulty in the Liszt which had almost defeated her.

'If I hadn't told myself that at one time I could rattle this page off without any difficulty, I don't think I'd ever have managed it.'

'Did they have a good piano?'

'Yes. They moved Jeremy's own piano out. It's quite a big Steinway. You'd be amazed how much that cost just to move it, oh, less than a mile.' She stroked his leg. 'And just a week before the concert I had to take over the job of accompanist to Eleanor Jacobi.'

'Who's she?'

'The opera singer. She's pretty well retired now.'

'I'm not up in these things.'

His hand explored, without haste, inside the low-cut neck of her dress, the lace edge of her petticoat. He seemed not to be on or of this present earth. His eyes he kept closed. His life existed and blossomed in the tips of his fingers.

'She did some Schubert. Very well. Her usual accompanist had been taken ill. Again I had my work cut out. She was a nice woman.'

'Nice?'

His fingers learnt the warmth of smooth flesh.

'Yes. Though she knew exactly what she wanted, (she'd done these songs with Moore, and Geoffrey Parsons, and Graham Johnson amongst others), she wasn't ever unreasonable. She'd suggest a crescendo or rubato, that sort of thing, and when we got it right, she'd congratulate me, but without any hint of patronage. I had the impression that we'd managed it, together, the pair of us, thought it out between us. We have, in fact, decided to do another concert in the New Year in Norwich. A whole lieder recital, this time.'

'How long will you practise together?'

'A month. Perhaps less. I'll have her marked copies before that.'

'Are you pleased?'

'Yes, I am. And especially as Jeremy Rutherford told me that Eleanor wasn't keen on female accompanists.'

'That was before she tried you?' Sam asked, facetiously.

'Of course.'

She lifted his hand from her breast and stood up.

'I get stiff down here,' she said. 'More whisky?'

'I shall be drunk.'

She poured a moderate tot into his glass and kissed his mouth, but did not resume her position at his feet. She smiled down at him from one of the two upright chairs.

'Are you comfortable?' she asked.

'Very. I think heaven must be something like this.' He amazed himself. 'You'll have to play for me sometime. Is John interested?'

'He knows very little about music, but I think he likes to see me out at the front performing, and then being praised by all and sundry. He was a very good golfer at one time, still is to some extent, and he knows what it's like to be at the top of the tree.'

'He's not jealous?'

'No. Why should he be? I'm not trespassing on his ground. It's a kind of feather in his cap. Your health.' She cheerfully raised her gin. They drank. 'I shall have to kick you out shortly into the cold world, because I've my duty to do, to go in next door to see that Hilda's all right.'

'Isn't her daughter there?'

'Yes, but she's flying back to the States at the weekend.'

'How will she shape once she's on her own?'

'That's what we don't know. She's apprehensive. But she has her bits and pieces, meetings and so forth. And John will call in on her. She'll like that. She might even want to see you. I'll ask her. Whenever she's mentioned you, she's said something complimentary. I think she was impressed by the picture you gave me.'

'It wasn't marvellous.'

'Marvellous or not, she thought highly of it.'

They talked on for another half-hour, friendly, sometimes with animation, but not touching. He wanted to put his glass down, ease himself up from his chair, cross the tiny room and

123

take her in his arms. But he was shy as a boy. He'd cut a ridiculous figure struggling up from the low arm-chair, and then standing there uncertain exactly what response he'd get from his ancient hips when he took his first step. And how would she accept the advance? A not very tidy, impotent old man struggling with his arthritis to paw her could not be her idea of the climax of an evening's pleasure.

Alice kissed him by the front door and gently slapped his buttocks.

'I wish I was that size,' she said.

It struck cold on her garden path so that he made haste along the road, whistling. Even at this early hour of evening, not yet nine o'clock, nobody walked about. He thought of turning back and calling in The Royal Oak, but he'd no idea who'd be there. Standing at the bar, topping Alice's whisky with a cold half-pint or two had little attraction. He'd get home and to bed.

Swinging his arms he reached his front gate. He paused at the latch, and his eye caught a glint. He bent and picked up a ring, which he slipped into the pocket of his coat for closer examination indoors. He closed the gate with silent care. Half way up the path he tripped on an uneven paving stone. He felt the sharp jolt on his foot, then an instant of dizziness as if his brain could not compensate for the suddenness of his stoppage and he fell forward. One hand and one knee hit the ground hard, jarring his whole body. He lay on the path, in the darkness. He was too far from the porch for the automatic outside light to come on. He did not move, satisfied with still safety after the violence of his impact with the flagstone.

He felt no great discomfort as he lay and concluded he had broken nothing. He moved arms, legs, fingers carefully one at a time, but still did not rise. Had he been out in the street he would have scrambled immediately to his feet, but here in the private darkness of his own garden he could sprawl unobserved, gather his wits. Now he pushed himself up and stood, listening for what? He heard not a sound in the dark. Confidently now he made his way to the steps, the veranda, and opened his door. He undid and hung his anorak in the entrance hall. The place was warm, thank God. He looked at his hand. It was black with mud, and injured in two places. It bled little but a flap of skin peeled back from the wound. He made at once for the bathroom, then carted his first-aid box into the kitchen where he washed his hand, sore now, under the tap. There was water already in the kettle which he boiled. Dettol in the basin of water, he cleaned his hand with cotton wool, then dried it. The wound looked wet but no longer oozed or bled. He dried it, and awkwardly, left-handedly covered it with a plaster.

His right knee hurt so that he hauled up his trouser-leg. In the middle of the kneecap he'd ripped off a circle of skin, large as an old-style half-crown. He bathed it, congratulating himself that he had not thrown away the disinfected water. He dried and covered the sore place. He pulled up the other leg of his trousers and found no damage. His legs looked thin and white, disfigured with varicose veins. Now he straightened his trousers, and found no mark, no stain, no tear on them. The crease ran as straight as before. His thigh ached, but that could wait. He returned the repacked first-aid box to the bathroom, before disposing of water and cotton wool.

He sat by his central-heating boiler to examine the ring he'd found. It looked strong, expensive, with a cluster of small diamonds round an opal, an engagement ring, he guessed, really quite valuable. He'd put a notice on the board in the newsagent's window, and ring the police. His knee and hip were sore as he hobbled over for kettle and instant coffee. He dismissed himself and his thoughts as trivial; the day had ended with a sharp lesson. He had sat, imagination ablaze, like a young lover in Alice's house, but as soon as he was freed he'd fallen. That constituted a warning. He was lucky; he might well have broken a wrist, an arm, a leg; he'd escaped with a scratch or two. Dismissed with a caution.

Limping he locked up, and lay shivering in his bed. Nobody depended on him these days; he was free. He ought to invest in an animal for company or cupboard love, but that would not be fair. At his age, even an unlucky, short-lived dog or cat would outlast him. He shuddered.

That night he slept fitfully thumping at his pillow. In the morning muscles ached and his eyelids drooped leadenly. Every job proved a burden. He rang Alice, but no one answered.

X

Three days later Sam mooned at his breakfast table.

Outside the sky loured, low and almost brown. He had not wanted to get up that dark morning, had to force himself unusually. Now he ate his toast awkwardly, leaving buttery finger-marks on his post, two advertisements and an early Christmas card from the widow of an old friend. She'd written a cheerful message, poor woman. Sam remembered her husband with gratitude, a thoughtful man, eagerly on the look-out for ideas. Whenever Sam thought of him, it seemed to be spring, the sun just beginning to be warm. George Barker had been an energetic man who'd filled his time in properly, but cancer had finally reduced him to a speechless, helpless shell. Sam begrudged that death. If anybody had deserved to live to a hundred it was G.H.B. He would not have wasted those extra years. Now his wife wrote, beautifully neat, saying she was busy, healthy and not grumbling. Sam wished he had been born saintly. The front door bell rang. He swore, jumped up quickly for it might be Alice, whom he had not seen for three days, and knocked his injured knee on the underside of the table. He limped out.

He clumsily withdrew the two bolts, loosed the chain and unfastened both locks. A smart young woman, perhaps late twenties, stood there, heavily gloved and scarfed.

'Mr Martin?' she inquired.

'The same.'

'I believe you have found a ring. I reported it to the police and they gave me your name.'

'And your name, please.'

'Heather Oliver.'

'Just step inside, will you? It's too cold to be standing about here.'

He led her to the sitting room, but to his chagrin found he had not yet drawn the curtains. That was one of his first tasks in the morning. He apologized.

'I'm not myself today. The winter's getting at me.'

Sam motioned her to a chair, where she sat and removed scarf and gloves. The room smelt stuffy to him and not quite warm enough.

'Would you like a drink?' he asked. She refused. 'When did you lose the ring?'

'I'm not exactly sure. You see, I don't always wear my engagement ring, not often in fact, and the main reason is that it's rather loose.' She held out her left hand; he saw the thin gold of her wedding-ring. 'I ought to get it fixed. But I came down here oh, four days ago, Friday. Did you find it on the road somewhere near here?'

'Yes.'

He wished he had straightened, dusted the room, squared up the pictures. He was not usually so fussy. The windows, thank God, were recently cleaned. Mrs Oliver sat bright as a new penny, straight-backed, interested, black-haired, almond eyes dark, a fine bloom on her cheeks, and indicating no hauteur, no disdain for the untidy room.

'You'll want me to describe the ring?' she asked.

'Yes.' He had been wondering how he could put the question politely.

'It's quite valuable. I ought to be more careful with it. It's ridiculous. And when I lost it, I'd no idea where. My husband reported it to the police station. He knows them there quite well; he's a solicitor. And they rang back to say you had left a message you had found a ring.'

He wondered why she'd offered this introduction, why she didn't precisely describe the missing object. Perhaps she was waiting for a clue from him. His curiosity aroused he posed an irrelevant question.

'Was your husband with you when you walked along here?'

'No. I was with a friend. We had been to visit a mutual friend.'

She did not say whether her companion was male or female. He bit his lip, not hurrying the conversation. Perhaps she was one of the couple who had copulated at the bottom of his lawn. It did not appear likely. She was too well-dressed, too well-spoken. Involuntarily he blew out his lips, baffled by his own speculations.

He fiddled in his pocket, and luckily found what he wanted. He took his spectacles from the case and put them on. He could see no better, they were meant to assist his reading, but they would denote keenness of intellect to her, he hoped, and he could peer at her over the top.

'Well,' he said after another pause, 'perhaps you could describe the ring as accurately as you can to me.'

She answered immediately, giving a good idea of the thickness and shape. She added, 'It's said to be 24-carat gold.'

'That's the finest, isn't it? Pure gold?' he asked.

'Yes. Though I don't know how we'd know.'

Again Heather waited for him. He said nothing, so that after a few seconds' awkwardness she described the opal set with six diamonds. He had no idea whether that was right; he had not counted the diamonds. He should have done so. He tried to visualize the jewels, but failed. He snatched his glasses free from his face, and waved them at her.

'Are there any other distinguishing marks?' he asked.

'Inside the ring there are my husband's initials and mine. TO and HC. Timothy Oliver and Heather Carter.'

'Are they your full names?' he asked, stupidly.

'No.'

'Nor any date?'

'No.'

'What colour is an opal?' he asked. She must think him dim, if not mad. He was now convinced by the initials that it was her ring. He had no idea why he had asked this unnecessary question.

'Milky,' she answered.

'Ah, yes.' He said this as if it settled the matter. 'If you'd be kind enough to wait a minute.'

He went out to the kitchen, retrieved the ring from the back of a knife drawer, rechecked the initials, and held his left hand out to carry the treasure back in some style in his palm. He closed his hand on the ring to open and close the door, then shuffled across to stand in front of her. He straightened his hand.

'Is that it?' he asked.

She scrutinized the ring from about a foot above his hand, then picked the ring up.

'Yes,' she said. 'That's it.'

To his surprise she had placed the ring back in his hand which he had left outstretched.

'Take it,' he ordered.

She lifted it up, examined it again, then slipped it on her finger, where she turned it, rather quickly, nervously.

'Thank you,' she said. 'Look, it's too big.'

She smiled as if the demonstration proved something.

'Thank you so much.' She set off again. 'I'm very grateful. Very grateful indeed.' He did not reply. 'Is there something I could do for you? In return?'

'No, thanks,' he said gruffly. 'I'm glad it's found its rightful owner.'

'I was absolutely certain it had gone for good. And I'd no idea where I'd dropped it. Where was it exactly?'

'Just outside the front gate. A few inches further and it would have been in the ditch where there's almost always an inch or two of water at this time of year. I saw the light flashing on it.'

'It's very kind of you.'

'I put a notice in the newsagent's about it.' He had no idea why he extended the interview with these trivial questions or remarks. 'Were you shaking your hands about just here? Gesticulating, you know?'

'I've no idea. I'd have said, I can't really remember, that I'd had my gloves on, if it was a cold night. Perhaps I pulled one off. To get at a handkerchief. I've no recollection.'

She spoke ordinarily and convincingly, in no way embarrassed.

'I'm glad you spotted it,' she continued.

'Yes. An engagement ring. It must have sentimental value for you.'

'Yes,' she answered. 'We don't know, do we, until we've lost the thing? I must get it altered.'

'Or eat more.'

She looked puzzled, saw the point, tried to laugh.

'Your husband will be pleased.'

'Yes. Though he's more careless than I am. In some ways. In his work, he's a solicitor, he's meticulous, finicky even. Everything must be exactly right. But with his possessions he's hopeless. He can't remember where he's put his car keys down. I tell him to get into the habit of putting them in the same place all the time, but he can't be bothered. Too much regimentation in the office. He's not interested. He's thinking about more important things. Or so he says.'

'Have you been married long?'

'Eight years.'

'That's not a great while.'

She sat, mildly at his service. In the end she rose.

'I must be going now,' she said.

'Could I not get you a cup of coffee?'

'No, thank you.' She had half hesitated. 'It's my morning to do the weekly shopping in the supermarket. And I'll call in at the jeweller's and get this ring done, so there are no more mishaps. And again thank you so very much. You've been most kind. I ought to do something for you. Is there nothing I can do in return?'

'No,' he said again, then suddenly adding. 'I'll give you something.'

He darted, speedily for him, from the room to return with a plastic pot in which the tips of hyacinths were just beginning to emerge from the bulb-fibre.

'There,' he said, presenting it to her. 'Hyacinths. White. For weddings. Keep them in the dark, and cool, for a bit longer, and then put them out. They'll probably be a bit too early for Christmas. But you'll know all that.'

She thanked him, and dashed a kiss onto his cheek. Her perfume spread delicately.

'Call in again,' he invited, 'any time you're down here.'

'I will. And thank you so very much. You really are most kind.'

She rattled off her thanks all the way to the front door and beyond. He watched her negotiate steps and path, and heard her car drive away. He rubbed his hands together, bemused. He could, he concluded, do with a visit like that once every two days. That was his trouble, loneliness. He wanted people to drop in from time to time to entertain him. The paint-brush and television screen didn't occupy him sufficiently. He slipped on his overcoat and marched off to the shop.

He had not seen Alice for days, but as he passed her house he saw her husband out on the garden path. John Jeffreys called out to him. Sam approached the gate.

'I've a little favour to ask of you,' John said, in a loud voice. 'I have to go away for a couple of days. And Mrs St John's gone somewhere or other. Now she's asked Alice to pull the blinds at night. One or two lights come on automatically. But Ally doesn't like going round a dark house at this time of the year. I don't know what she thinks will happen to her in a village like this. Though you hear of some very strange goings-on these days. Even in out-of-the-way places. So I suggested she asked you to walk round with her. Will you?'

'I don't think I shall be much good fighting off burglars.'

'It's the appearance that counts. Two of you to deal with. Now, will you?'

'Right. I'll do my best. When does my escort-duty begin?'

'Tonight. I leave straight after lunch. I'm supposed to have retired, but they keep calling on me to suss this snag out or meet that man.'

'Aren't you pleased?'

'I complain a lot, but I suppose I am. There's not much happening in this village in winter. We can't even get a regular four for bridge. You don't play, do you?'

'Sorry, no. I don't. Can't you join this pantomime group your wife plays the piano for?'

'You must be joking. Alice will ring you to give you instructions.'

She did so; he was to be outside Mrs St John's house at six thirty.

'It'll be really dark, then.'

'What difference does that make?' she sounded snappy.

'I thought the burglars came in at twilight if they haven't the nerve to break in in broad daylight.'

'I'll warn the neighbours to listen for the alarm. But I have to go out. In fact, I'm late now.'

Alice put the phone down with vigour.

At half-six exactly he stood outside the St John front gate. Alice arrived at thirty-six minutes past.

'Am I late?'

'You are.'

She did not apologize, but rattled a bunch of keys. Once they had entered the hall, she switched on a small table-light, and scrabbled in her pocket for a sheet of paper.

'This is the list of blinds to be drawn and lights to be left on. You stay here a moment until I've dealt with the alarm.' Then she led him round the rooms on the ground floor and three bedrooms, where they drew the curtains. 'That's it. I'll do the alarm and lock the front door.'

'What about the lights that we've left on?'

131

'They should go out automatically at eleven thirty. What time do you get up?' He told her. 'Right, we'll pull back the curtains and walk over the whole house at nine.'

Outside she thanked him, linked her arm through his.

'You're a good man, Sam Martin,' she said.

At her front gate he faced her with a question.

'Do you know a Mrs Oliver?'

'I don't think so. Who is she?'

'She came to visit me this morning. About a ring she'd lost. I'd reported it to the police, and they gave her my address.'

'Lucky woman. What do you say her name was?'

'Oliver. Heather Oliver.'

'Where does she live?'

'Hunstanton, I think. Or thereabouts. Her husband's a solicitor. Timothy Oliver.'

'Oh, Oliver and Rempstone. They're King's Lynn and very well known. We don't use them, but Clement and Hilda St John do, I think. Is this Timothy an elderly man?'

'I don't know. But that's not my impression. He'd be young, like his wife. Early thirties.'

'Is that her age?'

'Yes. If that. A very attractive young woman.'

'Aren't you lucky? Where did you find her ring?'

'On the verge right outside my gate. I was coming back from your house. It must have been lying there some time, but I saw nothing of it on my way out. She'd been to see a friend.'

'Who was that?'

'She didn't say, and I didn't ask. She was with a friend at the time, she said.'

'Man or woman?'

'Again she didn't say.'

Alice grimaced, wagged a finger at his inefficiency. For a moment she turned her back on him as if to come to terms in private with her thoughts, and then wheeled round on him. She paused before she spoke, long enough.

'Did it cross your mind,' Alice said, emphasizing each word, 'that this woman might have been one of the pair of lovers who performed in your front garden?'

'It did. I didn't recognize her. She was tallish as was the other woman. But there was nothing else to connect her.'

'Didn't you try to find out?'

Sam laughed aloud at her curiosity.

'I put one or two well-directed but tactful questions to her. But either she didn't cotton on to what I was asking about or . . .'

'She brazened it out?'

'Yes. She seemed in no way embarrassed. Her behaviour was exactly what I'd expect from a woman who'd lost a ring. She was grateful. And pleasant. She in no wise aroused my suspicions. The thought had occurred to me, as it obviously did to you. But then again I'd have thought I would have found the ring inside the garden, where we checked, if you remember. I had another fairly close look there, but found nothing. Not a sign anybody had been there.'

'I see.'

'I gave her a pot of hyacinths.'

'You did what?'

'I gave her a pot of hyacinths.'

'Why ever did you do that?'

He paused now, stared Alice straight in the eye. 'She made a very favourable impression.'

'You're quite a ladies' man, aren't you?'

'I do my best for you.'

'You never presented me with pots of hyacinth.'

'True. But I have a couple ready for you. But I'm holding them back so that they'll be out at Christmas.'

'You mustn't take what I say too seriously, Sam, you know.'

'I treasure up every word.'

Alice came across and kissed him in on the side of his face. He twisted his head to kiss her on the mouth. Her tongue briefly explored him, before she laughed curtly and broke away.

'We don't want any heart attacks,' she said. She smacked then caressed his left buttock. 'Canoodling in the street won't do our reputation any good.'

'Nobody can see us just here.'

'Thank God for that. I'll see you at nine tomorrow. I'll ask John about your Mrs O. He's usually well up on local tittle-tattle.'

'Won't he be here to help you draw the curtains in the St Johns' tomorrow?'

'I doubt it. He's out this evening and won't be back. That's why I must get on. He'll be home for lunch tomorrow, and that will be our main meal.'

'Lucky man.'

'He doesn't think so. Nine o'clock sharp tomorrow.'

She slapped a hand across his left arm, and made off through the gate and up the garden path. He watched her all the way in the darkness then finally in the coarse brightness of the automatic lights. She did not look back. Here outside it seemed cold. He made off quickly, remembering that he had not mentioned his fall to Alice. The wind from the sea, the east chilled him. He had noticed nothing of it while he had been with Alice. He had no sooner made himself a cup of hot chocolate than the phone rang. Alice Jeffreys announced that she had looked up Oliver and Rempstone; she did not say where. There were two T. Olivers: T.J. Oliver, LL.B., and T.R.S. Oliver, LL.M.

'They must be father and son,' she said.

'And how many Rempstones?' he asked.

'One. H.R. Rempstone, M.A. (Cantab) And four other men. And two women's names. The firm was founded in 1906. They have four offices.'

'Anything else?'

'Commissioners for Oaths.'

'Sounds very respectable.'

'Indeed, but we'll wait and see what dirt my husband will dig up.'

Alice giggled, reminding him of tomorrow's chore, and rang off.

Next on the telephone Karen Craig gave him a bulletin. They were well, the children especially and all looking forward to Christmas. Edward grew busier than ever; after one parents' committee he wasn't back until midnight. He complained all the time, but she was confident he did what he wanted to. Was there any chance that he could drive over in the holidays? They'd look forward to it. The children often talked about him. The humming-top had proved a tremendous favourite. She chattered on about members of her husband's staff, the education committee, the government. Though it sounded sane, even interesting, she seemed to talk too much, as if she was lonely, needed adult companionship. He played along with her, piling question on question. Her final anecdote, almost epic in length, concerned the grand-parents of one of Emma's friends who were conducting a furious feud with their neighbours in the courts over the height of a hedge. It must be costing them a bomb, but had become an obsession.

'What sort of people are they?' he asked.

'Quiet. Pleasant. Unaggressive. He's a retired sanitary engineer. But this quarrel seems to have sparked something off.'

'Have the courts decided anything yet?'

'No. It hangs on and on. I don't think the Talbots mind. Their daughter, a very sensible woman, says it's doing them more good than a holiday ever would. It's keeping them alive. And they're both as bad, wrapped up in it to the exclusion of everything else.'

'And what about the neighbours?'

'Awkward and old and idle. They'll lose in the end, but they don't want the Talbots to put anything over on them. Their son's a lawyer and he keeps telling them to come to some acceptable compromise, but they won't hear of it. It's been in all the national as well as the local papers. Perhaps you've read about it.'

He could not recall the case, he said.

'And how are you keeping?' he asked. 'Never mind the rest.'

Karen confessed herself run off her feet, but the worst thing was the shortness of the daylight. She was at home with the children, and once they were in bed she was left to her own devices.

'Isn't that good?'

'No. I'm a social type. I do go out once a week, to a literature class. To study modern novels. But do you know, Edward wanted me to play truant this week so he could have an extraordinary meeting of his parent-teacher association? I just told him it wasn't on. "I go out one night a week, and I don't see why I should give that up because your parents won't change their bridge night or miss their darts matches or pub quiz." He was quite angry, I could tell, but he tried to sound reasonable. "There's nothing I'd like better," he said, "than a quiet night in at home with my feet up." "Then you organize it," I said. "It won't take a miracle."'

'And what happened?'

'He got one of the young women on his staff to babysit for us. But he wasn't best pleased.'

She must have talked to him for more than half an hour, filling in the lonely evening. He felt surprised, defeated, remembering, regretting the nights he had left Joan, and then Meriel, at home with the children. It had not seemed unfair at the time. He was making good money then, and his wives could spend it (he encouraged them) on themselves as they liked. It seemed long enough ago, and like everything else these days of little importance to him.

He was early at the St Johns' house next morning and found Alice, late again, taciturn if not surly. They drew the curtains in silence, and did not stop for conversation when she locked the doors or let herself into her own front gate.

'I shall have to be getting on,' she said. 'Johnny'll be back any time now.'

'Anything I can do for you?'

'No, thanks.'

She tried to smile. Her face was powdered unevenly and her lips roughly daubed with unsuitable lipstick. She seemed untidy, as if her dressing had been interrupted by bad news or the onset of illness.

'Are you sure you're all right?'

'Yes.'

She marched away from him, a determined woman.

Back at home he tidied the place, then rushed by car into Hunstanton. That seemed crowded, though the schools had not yet broken up. Back by eleven, he had barely opened the morning paper when the front doorbell rang.

John Jeffreys, dressed to the nines.

'The boss has sent me round for two things. One to say thanks for helping her out opening and closing the St Johns' house, and, two, to let you know that you won't be needed tonight or tomorrow morning as I shall be at home.'

'Are you coming in for a cup of coffee?'

'Yes, thanks. If I'm not wasting your time.'

He entered, asked for tea rather than coffee, spread himself comfortably in a kitchen chair.

'No golf today?' Sam asked.

'No, I've been away most of the last week or two and so I'm at the boss's command, to run errands, such as this, or lug something about the house. She's a great changer of furniture is our Alice.'

'Do you mind going away?'

'Not in the slightest. It's connected with my work, and it makes me feel needed.'

'You're not retired then?'

136

'Officially, yes. Two years last summer. But from time to time they call on me to do them some job. They think I know the ropes. And I suppose I'm efficient. But it's charity, really. My old second-in-command is managing director now, and he likes to flash his patronage about. And it makes me feel wanted. I imagined I looked forward to retirement, but I didn't really. I was busy; I was on top of my work; I didn't want to stop. Don't you feel the same? Sometimes?'

'I'm over eighty.'

'You're not, are you?'

Something boyish about Jeffreys suddenly touched Sam. This large man, energetic, beautifully suited, had come out with the confession that he hadn't enough to fill his life. Married to Alice, presumably comfortably off, fit enough to play golf, even tennis and squash whenever he liked, he still felt at a loss. The man held his teacup in two hands in front of his face, as if he were lifting a trophy to the plaudits of fellow competitors. He appeared both puzzled and pleased, like a bright child with a still-wrapped Christmas gift, trying to make out the nature of the present from the shape of his parcel.

John Jeffreys enquired about Sam's firm. He nodded seriously through the account.

'You'll still see some of the lorries about with my name on them, but we were taken over years ago. Apart from a Christmas card or fancy publicity handouts and an annual balance-sheet they don't bother me much. Just pay money into my bank.'

'You don't miss your office?' John Jeffreys asked.

'I did at first, I suppose. But it's a long time ago.'

'But you moved here?'

'Yes. Years after I retired. They say that's just about as stressful a thing as one can do at my age. Mark you, I covered my retreat. I've still kept my house in Beechnall. I could get back to it fairly quickly if I wanted to.'

'Why did you move?'

'To tell you the honest truth, I don't know. I thought this was a good place to paint in. There are professionals about. Not in this village, I find. But I don't think that was it. Not exactly. It has its drawbacks. It's a bit out of the way if my children want to visit me. Not that they do very often. But. I can live privately here.'

'Out of the firing line? You mean you don't want people bothering you.'

'Something like that.'

The two looked steadily at each other.

'But don't you ever want people bothering you, dropping in? Now you've tried it?' Jeffreys asked.

'Occasionally.'

'We'd bought our house some years before I retired. It exactly suited Alice. I kept a small London flat, so that at busy times I'd be home only on Saturday nights and Sundays. It suited us both. Alice had met Hilda St John again. She was interested in finding decorators, doing the house up exactly as she wanted it. Every time I came home she was bursting with new notions. I've never known her so happy, and I gave her her head. She was an organizer, would have done well in business, and now with a biggish house and garden she could let rip.'

'And had she got it straightened out by the time you retired?'

'Oh, sure. Except she always hankered after change. She's creative. Artistic. She was a first-rate pianist. I sometimes thought that by marrying me she put a stop to an interesting career.'

'And she was beautiful?'

'She was. And sexually attractive, ready for it.'

The vulgarity silenced Sam who turned again to his cup.

'You paint pictures, don't you?' Jeffreys asked, unaware of his gaffe.

'Yes.'

'And that fills in your spare time?'

'It helps.'

'What else do you do?'

'Walk about the world.' Sam could not think why he used the phrase.

'You mean you travel?'

'Not now. I go down to the sea, or tramp about the lanes. And I have to cook and clean the house and dig the garden.'

Jeffreys nodded, scratching his chin. He was the same well-dressed, bustling, muscled sportsman who'd rung the doorbell, but now he seemed less certain of himself, on the edge of difficult questions, and for that reason a more interesting man.

'When you look back at your eighty years,' he said, having cleared his throat, 'would you say your life has been a success?'

'That's not easy.' Sam coughed. 'I sometimes give it a thought. It's not driving me mad. I'm not boiling over with

138

regret or resentment. No. A funny thing. The last time I was down at John's I got talking at a party there, in Hampstead, with a professor of English literature, about that.'

'He was an old man?' Jeffreys asked.

'No. Fifty perhaps. And just about to go back to Cambridge to some notable post. Very smart man, full of life. And humour, and go. Could talk about all sorts of matters. Pop music, for instance, without seeming silly, if you know what I mean. I don't. And when I asked him this same question he said this. Thomas Hardy, one of our greatest nineteenth-century novelists, and possibly the greatest of all English twentieth-century poets said of himself, "I have achieved all I meant to do, and I wonder if it was worth doing".'

'Was that at the end of his life?'

'Just a month or so before he died. He was older than I am. High eighties. This professor said Hardy always took a fairly gloomy view. And he was ill at the time, and may have been having a bad day.'

'And that's how you feel, is it?' Jeffreys asked.

'I don't know. I worked hard to build the firm up. And I was lucky enough to throw my lot in with Morris Isaacs who really changed us, and fairly quickly, from a large local firm to a national and international concern. That counts as success, I imagine. It means I don't have to worry about money. Not that I need much. I eat pretty frugally. I don't throw money about. I give a bit to charity; I could do more in that direction, I suppose. But I never look back and think I ought to have tried something else. Or made even more money. Or ended up in the House of Lords. The past doesn't worry me all that much. I often hear people say that old folks live more in the past than in the present, but it's not so with me. That's because I'm healthy. I can walk or drive out any time I wish. I don't like this time of year, but I can see well enough still to draw, on the long nights – I don't fancy painting by electric light, good as it is – and I can read and watch the television. But if I get toppled with illness, and I become incapable of looking after myself, and that happens to be dozens of people who are nothing like my age, I'm pretty sure it'll change my mind for me.'

'Oh.'

'As it is, even with my health and strength, I still seem to be living on the margins of life. Nothing much depends on me. I don't see children or grandchildren too often. They don't bring trouble but neither do they ask for help.'

Jeffreys breathed deeply.

'I'm sixty-four,' he said, 'and I think about dying. That's morbid, isn't it?'

'No, as long as it doesn't obsess you. I've wondered for years how I shall go. Heart attack, stroke, cancer. In my case it can't be too far off, but while I'm fit I don't worry myself unduly.'

'But when you feel ill, then it's different?'

'It is. But I'm basically optimistic. I've recovered before, I'll recover again. But one of these days I shan't.'

Again Jeffreys held a long silence, out of which he seemed to struggle slowly, like a man heaving himself out of a freezing pond.

'It's funny,' he said, 'to be talking to you like this. Seriously. I hardly know you. We don't talk like this at the golf club, not even at funerals. Well, perhaps now and then when we've drunk one or two more than usual.'

'You don't talk to Alice about it?'

'Certainly not. Wouldn't think of it. If anything happened to Alice, I don't know how I'd manage. She'd be all right if I snuffed it. Money-wise, and in herself. She'll always find something interesting to do. That's what she admires about you. You paint. Beautifully, she says. And that's better than whacking a ball round a golf course when there's nothing to show at the end but your marked card. Not that she objects to that. If I enjoy it. She thinks you're young for your age.'

'Good.' Sam smiled his contentment.

'She has her bad days.'

'Why is that?'

'If something's gone wrong or she feels a bit off; bad cold, touch of rheumatism, you know. Or when I've done something she doesn't like.'

'That can't be often,' Sam said, pulling a clown's face.

Jeffreys raised a warning finger.

'We'll say no more.' He narrowed his eyes, and comically lowered the finger. Sam took it that his companion was obliquely drawing his attention to sexual peccadilloes. Jeffreys now stood. 'Well, friend, we've sorted the world out between us,' he said. 'And I've thanked you. You won't mind continuing with the good work, I hope.'

140

'No. A pleasure.'

'And Alice enjoys your company. You're unusual, she says.' He laughed. 'And I'm not so sure she doesn't think to herself that you might need looking after. She'd nurse you.'

'I hope that won't be necessary.'

Jeffreys rose, buttoned his coat. He loomed large, tweedy, strong as a horse.

'She'll give you a ring, or call in, when you're next required for the St John Watch.'

He waved a high hand.

XI

The time up to Christmas proved disappointing.

Sam helped Alice with the house-watch, since Hilda St John had phoned from America to say she would not be back until the spring. Alice assisted him with presents for the Craig children; he chose and wrote his own Christmas cards grim-faced, puritanical in duty. For the Jeffreys he made an exception, painting a card of the summer pathway to their front door. It did not seem altogether suitable, but it was a well-executed little sketch which he hoped she'd keep. She threw her arms round his neck the morning after its arrival and kissed him with almost painful energy.

The weather gloomed. Dun skies matched muddy earth. Sam continued to walk out both morning and afternoon in spite of rain and head-colds. Life had slowed down; he had barely enough tasks to fill the short days, and he spent the evenings warmly nodding off in front of television programmes which rarely interested him. Having painted Alice's card by electric light, he started on two larger pictures, but he lacked enthusiasm. Nothing happened. The news on wireless and TV seemed factitious, dredged up in default of anything more important. The Radio 3 music did not stir or hold him. It was his own fault, he knew, but try as he might he could manage no improvement. His age was to blame. He did not expect more, he told himself. He should shuffle from one domestic triviality to another, thankful that he could carry out his chores at least efficiently. John's eldest son, his grandson Charles, was injured in a car accident, and was prosecuted by the police for dangerous driving. A short, stiff note presented the facts. Sam had not seen the boy for some years now; he'd be twenty-eight. Sam began to ring regularly for information, but once it became clear that Charles would recover and was unlikely to go to prison the parents lost interest or appeared to resent the grandfather's intrusive calls. He invited the young man over, but Marti, his mother, thought the visit unlikely. He didn't drive for the present. He lived on the other side of London, in any case, and they saw little of him. 'He ignores us,' Marti wrote, 'follows his own life and has done so since he left university. He only appealed to us over this accident because he needed our advice and money for solicitors. He was temporarily short. Now that's over, or nearly so, he's dropped us like a hot cake.'

Sam, slightly annoyed by her simile, said it was sad. She said it was exactly what they would have expected. These phone calls to his daughter-in-law tested him. He did not know Marti well, was not even sure about her name; he suspected Martina or Martine. A small, dark, darting woman, she seemed the last wife he'd expected respectable, legalistic John to have chosen. She was polite to Sam, treated him as an equal on the telephone; she would have been unwise not to have done so. She and her husband looked forward to a substantial inheritance from Sam's estate when he died. When he thought of the quick-eyed Marti, Sam considered this 'filthy lucre'. He wondered what they'd do with it. Nothing much, he feared. More up-market, splash out on a house in the Dordogne or Malaga; something static, solid. No yachts, flying lessons, wild expeditions. John would see to that; he was a hard-working barrister, good at his job, careful with his own property as with other people's. He had no need of money from his father; he could live comfortably on his own earnings. Marti always looked, to Sam's untutored eye, extremely well-dressed, even gaudily so.

And now their son, Charles, had transgressed. He might well have killed himself or some other motorist. From the way the parents talked this had not been unexpected. Charles led a rackety life. He had a job, was no remittance man: John would have seen to that. Sam had no idea what he did. He had been married, once at least, for Sam had sent him a wedding present, but beyond that his domestic arrangements were beyond his grandfather. Was there some little great-grandchild somewhere in the background? He feared not. If there had been some respectably born child John would have informed him.

'Is there anything I can do?' he asked Marti over the phone.

'I don't think so.'

'Money, I meant. Fines, legal fees. You know.'

'No, I don't think so, thank you. I'll ask John, but I guess he'll have all that covered. In any case, Charles isn't short of money. Well, just occasionally.'

'What does he do?'

'He works in a finance-house. You'd think, or I would, that a job of that sort would mean steady living, sobriety and all the rest of it.'

'And it's not so?'

'Not in Charles's case, for sure.'

'But he can hold the job down?'

'He's clever, did well at university and in his professional exams. He's no fool. But his private life is highly spiced.'

'Not criminal?'

'No. He might take drugs. That's criminal, I suppose.'

'Is he married?'

'To one woman, though he lives with another. We're never sure of his domestic arrangements. We never see him. He doesn't visit us, and we certainly aren't invited to his place. It was his partner who rang us about this accident.'

'Did she seem sensible?'

'As far as we could tell. He was in hospital, out of it for the moment. But she rang for legal advice. John invited her to lunch near his office and talked to her, gave her the information she needed. A very good-looking girl, he said. Charles was by no means pleased when he heard that she'd consulted his father. But she could stand up for herself. And he took the money we offered.'

'And what about his wife?'

'We hear nothing about her these days. They're not divorced, as far as we know.'

'Does he support her?'

'I shouldn't think so. She does much the same sort of thing that he does, and earns as much.'

'That wouldn't stop her squeezing a bit more out of him, now, would it?'

'You're probably right.'

'Is he back at work?'

'Yes. The case hasn't come up yet. He'll be disqualified, John thinks, but won't go to prison. John hopes it will sort him out.'

'Will it?'

'Can the leopard change its spots, or the Ethiopian his skin?' She laughed, nervously high.

144

Sam enjoyed the conversation, forming a new, favourable impression of Marti. He said as much, and invited her over.

'John's hardly any spare time. And when he has he just wants to lounge about at home. Old age is setting in.'

'He's only fifty-three.'

'I know that. But he works hard, and is very set in his ways. I make him have a good holiday away from it all at least once a year. We shall have three weeks in the Seychelles.'

'And will he enjoy that?'

'He'll idle about, and swim. He won't make or take phone-calls. I hope it shows him that he's not indispensable, but I doubt it.'

'He enjoys his work.'

'In his dry way, yes. Or he's good at it. People look up to him, depend on him. We all like that.'

'Well, persuade him to come up here, to the seaside.'

'I'll do my best, but I'm not very optimistic.'

'Come yourself, then. And let the old stick-in-the-mud prepare his own meals.'

'Perhaps I will.'

Sam went whistling about the house, thinking of interesting places he could show to Marti. Slightly surprised at himself, for he'd not found his daughter-in-law very attractive at their former meetings, he concluded that her adversity or his boredom had worked the oracle. He whistled louder, certain that his euphoria would not last and fairly confident before the day was out that she would not pay him a visit.

Alice Jeffreys called in on him while his mood was still gracious. He gave her an account of the phone-call and Charles's difficulties. She listened, eyes alight.

'So they'll come up to see you?'

'For a half-day at most. John makes out he's up to the ears in work.'

'Will they invite you down there?'

'Doubtful. And I don't want to go.'

'But you say you've invited your daughter-in-law up here?'

'I have. I must have been out of my mind. I've never seen much in her. Perhaps she's at her best on the phone. Or perhaps she's improved over the years. Anyway, she won't come.'

'What's she like?' Alice asked.

'Small. Dark. Colourfully dressed in a tasteful way. A bird of paradise.'

'My, my. She doesn't sound like a dry barrister's wife.'

'Now, don't get me wrong. Just because she prefers bright colours it doesn't mean she lives a wild life. I guess she's very respectable, keeps a tidy house, entertains perfectly. She might even have lost her penchant for bright clothes.'

'Penchant?' Alice laughed. 'She's impressed you.'

'You,' he warned, 'are letting your imagination run away with you.'

'Exactly. It pleases me to think of this brilliant little woman dressed in bright oranges and blinding blues chasing you about the house.'

She kissed him. It happened often these days. When she judged she'd gone beyond accepted limits of criticism or teasing, she would walk across and kiss him on his cheek. At the same time she pulled him towards her, submerging him for a second in spicy perfume, before releasing him almost immediately. He enjoyed the momentary contact, but could not elucidate it to himself.

This morning she seemed especially attentive, because she had told him that she and John would be away from Christmas Eve until the day after Boxing Day. They had changed plans suddenly, and she attributed the alteration to her husband.

'We shall take the dog with us, but it means that both our house and the St Johns' will be empty. I'll inform the police, but do you think you can manage to look round both twice a day? It's a bind, I know. Especially on holiday, when you might want to . . .' she paused in search of plausibility, 'do something else.'

'It'll fill my time in,' he said, grimly.

'Are you sure?'

'Yes. A short walk morning and night will keep me lively.'

'But the weather might be awful.'

'I'll risk that.'

'I don't think that there's much need to draw all the curtains. Tonight I'll show you what I think might be a minimum.'

'Don't you think I'm capable, then, of making a judgement?'

'Efficient and intelligent,' she said.

He thought she'd dart across, and kiss him again. She did not.

'John,' she said as she left, 'is very pleased about our acquaintance. He tells me so about twice a day.'

'Why?'

'Perhaps because he thinks it in its small way makes up for his

146

fancy friendships with various ladies.' Her voice rose and dipped with sarcasm. 'He doesn't think there's any sexual hanky-panky going on between us; he wouldn't like that at all. He'd be jealous.'

'But he's not averse . . .?'

'Yes. He'll commit adultery from time to time. If that's what you mean.'

'And you don't mind?'

'I wouldn't quite say that. John and I hardly have sex together. Not now. Some people keep up, I understand, excellent sexual relations in their sixties. But we don't.'

'You don't love him, then?'

'I didn't say that. I guess one can love somebody very, oh, deeply without any sexual contact. I'm not claiming that, either. We don't show much overt affection, as we did when we first knew one another. We've changed. We're both too conservative to have split up. He's too comfortable. He likes to come back home, after an excursion, to a warm house, a good meal, a soft bed just as he did when he had to go away on some business trip.'

'And you're prepared to put up with this?'

'Shouldn't I be?'

'I thought that most people looked on their spouse as somehow their property. And like your house or your job or your position in society it gave you, however differently, your sense of status, of worth. And when one of these is taken away from you you feel degraded; your self-esteem is damaged. And whether or not marriage is losing its importance in our society, because people just choose to cohabit, as they call it, or because of the high number of divorces, I have the opinion that people who do take their marriage vows feel disgraced, deceived, degraded, if their partners desert them.'

'You felt like that?' she asked.

'I did.'

'When Meriel left you?'

'Yes.' They paused, both wondering if they had gone too far. 'I doubt if it was on religious grounds, that solemn oaths before God had been broken. It was that my life, my everyday domestic existence was radically changed. I was just approaching retirement. That would take some time, a few months, I thought, and I was looking forward to a change of life. Holidays every day.

147

Cruises. Trips abroad. But I got the sort of alteration I didn't expect. It made me hang on longer at work than I had intended. Just to keep myself steady, and my mind off my troubles.'

'And you managed it?'

'I don't know about that. My partner's wife, Verna Isaacs, left him at much the same time, and I'd no idea whether he was bothered or not. He showed not a sign, a glimmer. And I was racked. In despair.'

'Perhaps your partner and his wife had had enough of each other. And you didn't want to lose Meriel.'

'Maybe you're right. Certainly I didn't want to give her up.'

'But you got over it?' The question, recalling their earlier conversation, sounded triumphant.

'I wouldn't say that. Not exactly. Some days, some weeks I never give it a thought. But then I suddenly feel this black gap she's left. It doesn't happen often, but it surprises me that it happens at all after this length of time, sixteen years since the divorce. The worst thing is that though it's not often, for a moment it's powerful. I feel torn apart. I get over it, but it's nasty while it lasts.'

'I see.'

'I ought to have recovered, to feel at worst, let's say, a mild regret.'

'And when you actually saw her again? At Clement St John's funeral?'

'I was surprised. That was the main emotion. I recognized her at once. She looked older, of course. But she was a woman. Flesh and blood.'

'I don't quite follow you,' she said.

'I was able to cope with the living woman in a way that I could not with the image in my mind.'

'Why was that?'

He considered her poser, and at length.

'Ah, you have me there.'

Sam stumped across the floor.

'I'm sorry I raised all this,' Alice apologized.

'You do me good. When you're here I'm in touch with life. Otherwise I'm just a nothing. A leaf or twig on the stream. Buffeted by the wind, twisted by currents and likely any minute to be caught up and stopped for good in some island of debris.'

'That's quite poetic,' she said.

148

'That's what I mean. When you're here I can try to say what I mean, to describe what I feel.'

'Have you been looking at twigs on a stream?'

'Every day.'

They stood there, bewildered, enmeshed in their own uncertainties. This time Alice kissed him, and they clung together. When she released him he swayed.

'I feel dizzy,' he said.

'Sit down, then.' She spoke like a nurse, friendly but to be obeyed. Alice stayed with him a few minutes longer until he claimed to be steady. After he had shut the door, he leaned on it. He had opened a box of troubles for himself. He hammered the wall with the flat of his hand.

Next morning he had a letter, with the last two or three late Christmas cards, from Karen Craig. She wrote, he decided, with guilt. The letter began ordinarily enough thanking him for their as yet unopened presents, saying how excited the children were becoming, and describing her own preparation for the festivities, and her ever-increasing workload and her pregnancy. Then the tone altered.

'I am glad that I have so much to do, and I'll tell you why. I oughtn't to write this to you. Would you please destroy it when you've read it. You can do nothing about it, but I must get it off my chest to somebody before it drives me frantic. In the last two weeks I have had two separate letters delivered on different days. Neither had either address or date. Both made the same accusation against Edward, that he was having an affair with a member of his staff. One named her; one did not. The woman was Victoria Cox, aged twenty-five, who had joined the staff, as Edward had, last September. The first letter made the accusation, said that it was the talk of the school, and she should know. The second, more detailed, had claimed that the writer had herself (Karen took it both were women) seen the two in a passionate embrace, and on another occasion walking hand in hand brazenly in the centre of town. The second ended with a paragraph saying that a man of his age, position, the head of a school, father of a young family ought to be ashamed of such behaviour.'

Karen said that the letters had upset her. She had harboured no suspicions against her husband until they had arrived. True, he had been out more often in the evenings than before, spent

149

longer hours in the school, but she had expected all this. They had discussed such drawbacks when he first thought of applying for his new job. At home he was kindness itself both to her and the children. She detected no change in the man himself. She had met Miss Cox once or twice on her visits to the school; she was a pretty young woman, well-dressed and, according to Edward, good at her job.

She had not shown these letters to her husband. Perhaps that had not been sensible. He had, in any case, plenty to occupy him what with one thing or the other. Perhaps she was herself being silly. Edward had enemies in the school. One man had been expected, at least by his cronies, to succeed in the headship and made no pretence of hiding his disappointment.

Karen felt awful about this, because since the arrival of these letters she had harboured suspicions about her husband. She was beginning to wonder if Edward would take a sudden day away from home in the holidays ostensibly to attend a conference but in reality to spend time with Miss Cox. 'I shall see her tomorrow at the nativity play, and shan't know where to look or what to say. This is terrible. If you don't mind I'll give you a ring before term ends to talk about this. There's barely a minute when it's out of my head. I know I ought to have shown the letters straight away, or at least when the second arrived, to Edward.' She was his, with love, Karen.

He thought about it, came to no conclusion, did not destroy the communication until the next day.

Suppose she had showed the letters to her husband that would only have set her mind at rest if he had been innocent. Edward had made a good impression on Sam; a smart, well-organized, athletic young man who'd be admirably suited as a headmaster, because he had ideas, wasn't afraid of decisions, could stand up for himself, loved children. Yet such a man could be caught out by some pretty young woman who was as efficient at her job as he was, supported him against the foot-draggers, and who compared favourably with the domestic, flushed, child- and kitchen-bound, pregnant woman at home in her apron. It wouldn't be the first time. Temptation dogged every successful man.

Stumbling about his house, Sam Martin shuffled these ideas.

He could tell Karen nothing for her comfort. Yes, she'd do well, however late, to face her husband with the letters, and if it turned out that they told the truth that would be enough; she'd have to learn how to put up with it. Sam bit his lip. He felt depressed that such trials were visited on attractive families like the Craigs, but at the same time slightly elated that he was involved, however obliquely. His own life had now become so colourless, and partly by his own choice, in this seaside village that he welcomed the misfortunes of others to alleviate the boredom. He should get enough from the newspapers. The sexual antics of politicians and pop stars, the murderers, the perverts, all personally unknown to him, should provide him with gaudy entertainment to add garish splashes of colour to his grey days. Karen would be at her wits' end: Emma and Benjamin troubled by their mother's behaviour towards them; Edward, guilty or not, marking the changes in his wife, the little woman becoming the little devil at the slightest provocation. Sam clenched his teeth, set about vacuuming the bungalow in preparation for the Christmas visitors who would not come. He felt better when he occupied himself with housework. No cold blocked or tickled his nostrils, neither rippled his spine nor beat inside his head; his scalp did not prickle with incipient influenza. He pushed the cleaner, a fit man, looked over his handiwork and felt satisfaction with himself, ten or fifteen years younger than his age by the calendar. He spent the afternoon until near darkness cleaning windows. He spread his Christmas cards round; more than he sent out, he reflected with a grimace. His rooms looked bright, smelt of polish, glowed warm, welcoming. He found that evening after he'd listened to the Six O'Clock News and eaten a spartan tea that he could not sit. He had already ventured into the cold at five o'clock to deal with the curtains in the Jeffreys and St John houses, but now once he had washed and put away his crockery and cutlery he drew on his topcoat and a tweed hat, locked up and made for the outdoors.

Sam delighted in walking down to the sea in summer at evening-light. The trees, the sky, the rustle in the hedge bottoms, the greetings of pedestrians (and he was always surprised at the number of people and cars about at that time of night) made the walk comfortable, accompanied, social. Now in December the breeze disturbed twigs, with the sky starless and overcast, while darkness hung almost palpably between the hedges. He could hear his steel-tipped heels clang on the road, and he whistled as he swung his arms. He stepped onto the wet verge as a single car drove past. He wondered who was out driving, and why. He increased his pace. Near the end of the road, past the car park, by the public lavatories he stopped and listened. He went gingerly into the urinal which was lighted by two bulbs hung with black, surrealistic cobwebs. Surprised that the place was open, for he expected the council to close the place against vandals at the end of the season, he looked round again. The convenience was not exactly neglected, but lacked the disinfected cleanliness of summer. He pushed out into the road, uncertain whether to turn left for the sea, or right for home and warmth.

'Evening,' a man's voice called. 'Open, is it?'

'It is.'

The man crossed the road but remained an unrecognized shape in the faint light from the toilet bulbs.

'Amazing.' The voice sounded elderly, bronchitic.

'Open for Christmas,' Sam answered.

They laughed half-heartedly together.

'Going down to the sea?' the man inquired.

'I had thought about it.'

'Mind if I walk with you? I shan't be so apprehensive, then. After I've paid a call in here.'

They set off together. Sam felt uncomfortable. He did not know the voice, nor anyone in the village who wore a jaunty Dutch miller's cap. He could make that out now his eyes were accustomed to the darkness. His companion was shorter than he, and wore an abbreviated top-coat.

'We ought to be locked up going out on a cold night like this,' the man began.

'Do you think so?'

'Are you a widower?' the man asked. 'I am.'

'Yes,' Sam answered, half in truth.

'My wife died in September. After a holiday in Wales. We got back home, and she seemed to be doing really nicely. But she had to go into hospital again. She died there. Well in a hospice.'

'You didn't expect it?'

'Well. I knew it was cancer, and terminal. But she'd seemed so nicely in Porthcawl. I thought we might have a year or two. She couldn't do much, but I took her wheelchair and we sat about and watched the sea, and the other people. And she seemed to perk up. She ate a bit more. And the weather favoured us. It's a long way, but we stopped on the way there and back at my younger daughter's. Porthcawl's a quiet place. Down at the bottom end there's a fun-fair and a lovely stretch of beach below it, but we never went near that. Up our end, north-west, there was no sand only rocks. They'd built a kind of swimming-pool on the edge of the sea, and we could watch the kids larking about in the water. And there were shelters, so if the wind got up, we could sit there in the sunshine out of the draught. "I never thought, Jack," she said, "that I'd enjoy another seaside holiday." And, do you know, she'd eat an ice-cream. I've not known her do that for years. "Lilian," I'd say, when she'd finished and folded her silver paper and given it to me to drop in the litter basket, "I hope that hasn't put you off your lunch," and she'd laugh. She even got a bit of colour. And seemed so lively when we arrived back. I was amazed. But it didn't last. They tried some new chemotherapy, but that made her so ill, they took her in, and then put her into a hospice that was part of the hospital. She didn't last long.'

'No?'

'I used to go in every day. It wasn't far.'

'Where was that?'

'Norwich.'

'You're a fair way from home, aren't you?'

'No. I'm staying at the pub. The landlord's my nephew. He knew I'd nowhere to go.'

'Not your daughter's?'

'No. They're going to his parents' place in Worthing.'

They tramped on in silence until they reached the gap in the dunes. Both men were breathing heavily.

'Not as fit as we were,' the stranger offered. 'How's the time, please?'

Sam squinted at his watch in the darkness.

'Seven thirty or thereabouts. I think it's time to turn back.'

'Right.'

The two men did not immediately move on, but stood staring out to the sea. In the darkness they could barely distinguish sand-banks from sea pools. The main murmured in the distance, an indeterminate noise, so that the listeners were uncertain whether reality or their imaginations determined the vague sounds.

'I like to stand by the sea,' the man said. Sam made no answer. 'It all adds up, in the end.'

'I don't follow you,' Sam answered.

'Every little bit fills your day up, and gives you something to think about.'

'You're lonely, then?'

'Yes. Aren't you?'

'Sometimes. I try to give myself things to do. I paint. Watercolours. I walk about the place. Even on dark winter nights. I manage a bit of DIY. At present I'm looking after two houses while the owners are away.'

'But it's not enough, is it?' the man asked.

'Not always, no.'

'When I was younger I was invariably looking forward to something. I was a schoolteacher, a master in a grammar-school. I taught maths, and a few periods of French or English if they wanted it. Maths teachers were in short supply in my day. But in my various schools, I moved about a bit in my first years, there was always something happening. They kept us busy. I taught at one place five and a half days a week, and then was expected more often than not to turn out on Saturday afternoon to umpire a cricket match or referee rugby. We got longer holidays than other schools, but, by God, they got their money's worth out of us.'

'Did you mind working on Saturdays?'

'I didn't think too much about it. I was used to it. It was a good school. We were paid above the odds, and the place was pleasant enough to work in. You don't miss what you never had. Did you have to work at the weekend?'

'I worked for the family firm. It sometimes meant Sunday as well.'

'A big concern, were you?'

'It grew. Road haulage. Martin and Isaacs.'

'You've retired?'

'I have.'

Now, with a last look at the sea, they turned.

'On a good day in summer I've seen Boston Stump from here through field-glasses,' Sam said. 'But it's not an exciting place.'

'Nowhere is exciting for old men,' the other said. 'That's good. It's partly that we make it so. If we had a terrorist explosion we'd look away. We can't stand too much. Old men make it easy for themselves. Or try to. I'm sixty-nine. Three score and ten next year.'

'I'm eighty-one.'

'You do well.'

'I don't know about that.'

154

They had now crossed the wildness of the bird sanctuary having walked sedately over the thin strip of golf course.

'Are these marshes dangerous?' Jack asked.

'I don't think so. We're supposed to keep away from them, especially in the nesting season. You could get your feet and trousers really wet if you weren't careful, but I don't think you'd come to much harm. To tell you the truth, I've never tried. I stick to the paths. That's what they're there for.'

They tramped on, in a moody silence.

'We're unusual,' the man said. 'By the way, my name's Jack Brentnall. Unusual in that our wives died first. It's mostly the other way round.'

'My first wife died; my second left me,' Sam said, gruffly.

'Oh.' They stumped on. 'Do you ever think of dying?'

'Yes. Sometimes.'

'Seriously, I mean.'

'I occasionally wonder how I shall go. Will it be after a long illness or a quick heart failure? It can't be too far off now.'

'Are you frightened?'

'I'm not sure. I was once seriously ill, very seriously, and I felt so weak and uncomfortable and full of pains that I don't think I would have minded going. There are things I'd hate to miss, about my grandchildren, about my friends, about science. I'm interested in these space probes. They've got machines outside the sun's orbit now, and they can still pick up the messages that are radio'd back.'

'I've had two small strokes and a heart attack,' Jack said, not to be deflected.

'Recently?'

'One since my wife died. Heart attack. I'm supposed to have angina. It frightened me. That I can tell you. Bad pain. In the middle of the night.'

'What did you do?'

'Rang the ambulance. In the end. When things got no better. But when people tell me they're not afraid of dying, I don't believe them. I was.'

They had reached the edge of the golf course and were walking in single file along the last stretch of path before the tarmacadam road. The wind swirled. The air struck colder.

'Have you got your car up here?' Sam asked.

'No.'

'You shouldn't be out on a cold night like this? With angina?'

'I'm well wrapped up. I have my tablets to hand. That's one thing I don't want to do, make an invalid of myself. I was terrified of the pain that night; I don't mind admitting it. But I don't want to think myself into dragging about, waiting for the next blow.'

They were marching now between hedges in the middle of the road.

'I tell you what mainly bothers me,' Sam said. 'I seem to be miles behind the rest of the world. I went to the dentist in King's Lynn the other day, and while I was waiting I had a look at a magazine called *Hello*. It was full of pictures of actresses receiving awards and all sorts of famous people I'd never heard of.'

'Well, if you stick yourself out of the way in a poky little place like this, what do you expect?'

'But they'd appear on telly, wouldn't they?' Sam asked.

'Yes, but you look at the wrong channels, or listen to Radio 4 like me, or read the wrong newspapers.'

'Or I don't remember what I do see and read.'

'That's possible. You can't be expected to know all about, oh, let's say, pop music. You don't spend a great deal of time with young people who'd direct your ideas that way. When I was teaching I'd try to talk to my pupils about their interests. Now, I either make contact with people nearer my own age or with nobody at all.' They proceeded steadily, and Brentnall seemed able to talk without discomfort. Clearly he missed, after all these years, a captive audience. 'I will tell you what does trouble me. Now I'm interested in music and when I was younger I used to know the names of composers who were at work. The Third Programme kept me abreast. In England Britten and Tippett and William Walton and Vaughan Williams. He'd been going for years, of course. But where are their equivalents today?'

'It's no use asking me,' Sam answered.

'Tippett's still about, but he's very old, and nearly blind, I think. I could offer you a few names. Radio 3 keeps me up to date: Maxwell Davies, Birtwhistle, Goehr, Holloway, Turnage, Osborne, Matthews, Weir, but I don't know much about them. Mostly names to me.'

'Is that their fault, or yours?' Sam had been impressed by the list.

'That's the trouble. I read and listen a fair amount, but I fall further behind.'

'Wasn't that always the case?' Sam asked. 'When you were younger you were so busy, so immersed in what you were up to, that you didn't care what you missed. It didn't matter.'

'I don't want to be both a geriatric and an ignoramus.'

'But that's better than being a cabbage. And you're at least mobile. You can get about and see and hear and try new things.'

'I suppose so.'

They continued in uncertain silence; twigs rustled. The men stopped at the small bridge to stare down at the stream. They heard more than they saw.

'Well,' Jack Brentnall said as they set off again, 'we've managed to make ourselves miserable one way or the other.'

'You speak for yourself.'

They had turned now into the main street, still bucolic near the lane.

'Some very pleasant houses along here,' Jack said. 'Big. Take some upkeep.'

'People are prepared to pay for what they want.'

'Are they? Or is it for what people tell 'em they want.' He went on to describe a colleague who'd bought a six-bedroomed house on retirement. 'I thought he was mad. His children were away. And the place was, to say the least, remote.'

'And?' Sam pressed.

'He seemed happy as the day's long. He'd plenty to do. He was a craft teacher. He did some painting. His wife had her friends out for meetings and so forth. They made a kind of tapestry for the church. Their children and grandchildren could come along. He grew no end of stuff in his garden.'

'And what happened to him?'

'Still there as far as I know. I had a card from him for Christmas.'

'And what's the moral, then?'

'He wanted to live in a large house with plenty of spare rooms. He'd lived in a semi all his teaching career. This house was going at a bargain price, I'll admit, but more than their own place fetched, though. So they had to blue his lump-sum and part of their savings to buy it. But they both wanted it. It's six years ago now. He taught till he was sixty-six. But it's been a success. They've both kept well, so it doesn't matter about the doctor's

157

surgery being three miles away. They are still able to decorate and mend and improve. What'll happen in a few years' time I don't know. But they've had six good years.'

'You would have advised them against taking the place?'

'Wouldn't you?'

'Nobody asks me that sort of question,' Sam said, 'nowadays. People in this village like the Jeffreys and the St Johns live in houses far too large for their needs, but a house confers status. You can't have retired admirals living in poky cottages. They've got to cut a bit of a dash, however inconvenient to themselves. And it would be the same with your friend. For the first time in his life he could afford to live in a large detached house. They might have to economise, cut down on food bills, do without holidays, but if it's what they both wanted, so be'it. As you say, it might not have lasted long.'

'I'm not sure about his wife. She just fell into step with him. But. He'd achieved his dream.'

'Not many of us do that,' Sam said.

'Didn't you?'

'We made our firm large and profitable. Yes. But that wasn't the be-all and end-all of life.'

'It depends,' Jack Brentnall said. 'This chap had been the woodwork teacher, and in some of the schools I knew that damned him. He was clever enough, but he hadn't been to university. Full stop. Woodwork, I know, changed into Design and became an "A" Level subject, and he coped with the lot, but to some of them he was just a carpenter, an artisan.'

'And this retirement into a large house put his detractors into their place.'

'He probably thought so. Not that these "scholars",' irony twisted his word, 'would ever think of visiting him. But if they did, he was ready for them.'

'That's an interesting story,' Sam said. 'Will you come in for half an hour?'

They were within a few yards of his front gate.

'No, I don't think so, thanks all the same. I've been loose long enough. My nephew will be sending a search party out before long. I've enjoyed every minute, and I hope to see you again. My motto is: Never protract a pleasure too long. At our age, especially.'

'What was the woodwork teacher's name?'

'George Champion. Why?'

'You made his story very interesting to me. You ought to write it down, together with other bits from your life. It would make fascinating reading. Damn' sight better than the stuff the library van brings round.'

'Odd you say that, because I am writing something.'

'About schools and so forth?'

'No. It's about myself. But in cloud-cuckoo land. The last sort of thing I thought I'd be putting down. But it must wait. I'll tell you some other time.'

'I'll look forward to that.'

'Good night, Mr Martin.'

'Good night.'

Sam had forgotten the stranger's name, but he stood and watched the small, trim, broad figure progress under the high but inefficient street lamps. The trees almost barked as the wind strengthened. Two old men occupied the road between them, one strutting along, one watching. Sam realized that he wouldn't recognize the man's features if he saw him again, only his short coat and the jaunty Dutch cap. And, above all, the plain school-master's voice, making everything clear. The complications of it all.

XII

Sam's Christmas Day proved quiet.

He heard the clatter of people returning from midnight mass, but opened up the Jeffreys' and St Johns' curtains at the usual hour. He ate his breakfast cereal, took a dish of prunes and indulged himself with two cups of coffee. He had made up his mind about his lunch: a large piece of a bought Christmas pudding with custard. He'd finish it tomorrow cold, with cold custard and cream. He examined the label, mocking himself. During the morning Alice Jeffreys rang to ask for a report on her house; she seemed cheerfully distant, had been out to dinner the night before and had eaten and drunk too much. Yes, it was all good of its kind; people gave her news of old friends and sometimes somebody would say something interesting. 'Do you know we all went out for a walk yesterday afternoon, though the weather was nothing like decent, and I was walking along with an old acquaintance, a banker called Terence Curtis; I'd known him since I was a schoolgirl. And he suddenly half-stopped, and turned (there was a yard or two between us) and said, "There are two women with whom I'd have liked to have a child, and you're one of them." I was flabbergasted. Though we'd known each other for so long we had never met regularly, we were more acquaintances than friends, and yet he came out with this.'

'Is he married?'

'He was. His wife died quite recently. They'd four children.'

'Is he attractive?'

'Not really. A dry, little man. He was desiccated when he was young.'

'And he'd never said anything like this to you before?'

'Never.'

'Nor made any advances?'

'No.'

'So why did he start now?'

'Drink.' Alice giggled.

'Is he a boozer?'

'Not to my knowledge. Nor did he smell of alcohol.' She hummed down the phone, happily. 'I used to think when I was about eighteen that he was a bit sweet on me. He'd be four years or so older than I was. But he never said anything, well, not seriously.'

'Did you know his wife?'

'Yes. Slightly. We met occasionally, you know. Later. When he was married. I think he'd met her at Oxford. She seemed pleasant enough. He's pretty well-to-do these days. I don't know why he was down there in Essex.' Alice and her husband were staying with her recently-widowed sister, who had retired to the village where they had lived as children. 'Down to have a look at the old place. He lives in London now. I asked him why he wasn't staying with one of his family, and he said he'd been determined this year to look round the scenes of his childhood again. It had been rather an obsession this last year, and though Christmas was not a good time, he'd chanced his arm.'

'Who was he staying with?'

'Nobody he knew. He'd taken a room in the local hotel, The Windmill. He'd written to various people, once he'd fixed that up and they'd invited him over for meals. He was no trouble. My sister had him in, with others, and that's when we took this walk. It's odd, isn't it, what people tell you?'

'Do you think it was true?'

'I've no idea. I had no such feelings about him.'

'It's made me jealous.'

'Why?'

'That he could dare to say such a thing. I don't think I'd ever risk it. I envy him.'

'Sam,' Alice said. 'I'd sooner have had a child by you than by him.'

'We didn't know each other then, when it was possible, I mean.'

'No,' Alice answered coolly. 'No.'

He realized he had said the wrong thing, but the conversation continued civilly for a few more minutes. She and John would be back on Saturday, and she'd call in on him some time on Sunday afternoon. She'd heard nothing from Hilda St John.

After his lunch, such as it was, had been eaten and the pots washed and put away he telephoned the Craigs. He first spoke to

161

Emma who said what a marvellous Christmas they were having. She listed her toys, and her brother's, then her parents'. His presents were rated highly. Emma still seemed to believe in Santa Claus. Her grandparents were here, and they were nice, though her grandpa nodded off every time he sat down, because he couldn't sleep at the proper time when he was in bed. Yes, they'd had turkey and Christmas pudding and crackers with paper hats and riddles. Her present from the cracker was a small, silver boot.

'What's it for?' Sam asked. 'This boot of yours?'

'It's an ornament. I shall keep it on top of the chest of drawers in my bedroom. It will bring me good luck.'

Emma, in the end, fetched her mother.

'Are you very busy?' he asked Karen when the seasonal greetings had ended.

'No, not really. The men, Ed and his dad, are washing the dishes.'

'That means I'm breaking into your leisure time. You could be sitting there with your feet up.'

'No. Not at all.'

'Are you all right?' Sam asked.

'Yes, thanks. Busy, you know. At everybody's beck and call.'

'I hadn't heard anything from you.'

'No. I meant to ring, but I never seemed to get round to it.'

'I was a bit concerned. About the letters, those two letters you had.'

'Yes,' Karen answered, and fell silent. 'That sorted itself out in a way. To some extent.'

'How do you mean? Did you show them to him?'

There followed a pause as if she were checking that all doors were closed.

'Well, half and half. I showed him the second letter, and made out it had just come. If you remember there was no date on it. I told him there had been another in a completely different hand-writing, but I said I'd burnt it. I had, just before I let him see the second.'

'And.'

'He read it, and asked me what the first had said. I thought he'd be angry, but he wasn't. "Just park yourself down, Karen," he told me, very quietly. It was evening. The children had gone to bed. He sat there reading the letter, as if he was thinking out how to answer me. In the end he said, in a whisper, "This has upset you, hasn't it?" I didn't say anything, so he said, "It's not true, Karen."

"Who sent it?" I asked him.

"Obviously somebody connected with the school, a member of staff or the governors. Even, it's a possibility, one of the parents," Ed answered.

"And why would they send it?"

"You don't believe these accusations, Karen, do you?"

"I didn't know what to think. It was possible. You hear of much worse things. I mean, you're out of the house much more than you were at the old school, but I expected that."

"Have you noticed any change in me?" he asked.

"No. Except you seem more tired now or preoccupied."

"Yes."

Then he looked at me, and sat with his chin on his chest.

"It's untrue. All these accusations are untrue, Karen."

"Who made them?"

"I've no idea. None at all. This looks like a woman's writing. Was the other?" He did not wait for an answer. "I'll tell you about Victoria Cox. She and I were the new ones on the staff. She, I expect, aimed to make a good impression, and so found it easier to fall in with my ideas. She is, moreover, more gifted as a teacher than the majority in the Bentinck School or any other I've known. There are one or two there who resent me and my new broom."

"Why didn't they say so to your face?"

"One at least did. But they're afraid I'll block their progress."

"But this seems a mean way to get their own back."

"Yes. Perhaps they thought I favoured Victoria more than I should. It's possible. She was new. It was my job to see she settled properly. Perhaps they didn't like it."

"But you don't know who it would be?"

"No. I didn't know the letters had been sent. Or I could have been on the watch. I've samples of the handwriting of all the staff, at least. Do you mind if I keep this?" He had tucked the letter into an inside pocket. "One other thing. Victoria Cox is engaged to be married at Easter."'

Sam admired the sharp way in which Karen had conveyed the conversation to him. He could imagine the pair, sitting opposite, faces serious, with each uneasy movement a mirror to their uneasy minds.

'He convinced you?' Sam asked.

'Yes. I think so. I should have told him before, but I was so . . . Look out, there's somebody coming.' She obviously turned away from the phone. 'Oh, Ed. It's Mr Martin on the phone. Would you like a word?'

Sam talked freely, friendly to Edward Craig for a few minutes. The family were having a wonderful time, but already the headmaster was thinking about the next term. He spoke at some length about his plans.

'What are your staff like?' Sam asked. 'Good?'

'Above average. But we're all being pressed by the government and the inspectorate to reach higher standards. That'll stimulate some and flatten others. My lot on the whole will cope. I'm optimistic.'

'Are there some teachers who are outstanding?' Sam asked.

'One or two. But teaching's a long-drawn-out job. And even the best have their bad days.'

Craig talked on; the subject appealed. He liked to lay down the law about his ideas even on Christmas Day. Sam wondered what he would be like to work with. He'd seemed a practical man when he dealt with his own family, but in charge of some hundreds and under public scrutiny he might show a different face. And what of Miss Victoria Cox? Let's say he had been, put lightly, a little tactless, too effusive, enthusiastic in his dealings with her, those letters to Karen had shown that someone closely connected with the school was not only unfriendly to Craig, but probably disturbed. That could mean danger. Craig showed no signs of apprehension, but instructed Sam in his magisterial manner, and, his listener admitted to himself, sounded intelligent and thoroughly sane, a man to be trusted.

At the end of the conversation Sam sat in front of his electric fire to eat an apple. What did Emma think of her father? Or Edward's own father? Headmasters have parents who remember them as occasionally careless children. Sam bit into his Cox, which he had not peeled, gnawed it to a small sphere of core, and fell asleep. He woke half an hour later, thinking himself back in his Beechnall house, with one trouser-leg almost scorched. He hobbled out to the kitchen to drink a glass of water. The day outside grew greyer by the minute.

The pub did not open on Christmas Day, and for only an hour or two on Boxing Day so that Sam saw nothing of his new acquaintance, Jack Brentnall. On Friday evening he decided he'd call in after a stroll, and the landlord said, Sam not having mentioned the man, that he'd call his uncle down. The old chap had spoken of their walk and conversation several times.

Brentnall trotted in, smiling, to join Sam. He carried half pints. He wore a blazer and some club or college tie. He looked both slimmer and younger; his grey hair was thick, neatly parted and plastered down into a shining helmet. The old men described their eventless Christmases to each other. Sam made much of the fact that his main sustenance had been slices of Christmas pudding. Both laughed beyond reason. Jack had eaten like a horse, for his nephew and his wife were excellent cooks, and had filled the hungry with good things.

'They share the same trouble,' Jack claimed. 'They can't rest. You'd think they'd be worn out with the hours the pub has to keep open these days, and all these meals and the trips into the markets, only too pleased to put their feet up. Not they. They've got muzak thumping on all day, and they're rushing about, one room to the other, discussing the next move or order at the tops of their voices. They're lovely people, but I want to say, "Sit down, slow down, shut up." '

'And if you did?'

'They'd look at me as if I were speaking Greek. They're into habits of rush and shout and nothing's going to change them.'

'They sound a decent pair.'

'They are. They are. They needn't have had me over this holiday. I'm just an added complication. But some people court disturbance. They're on top of the world. If you were an outside observer you'd write them down as an energetic noisy pair, often at odds with each other and who didn't care who knew it. But they're in command of their lives as I'm not; they can bawl, and rush round because they know they're winning. Whereas if your observer watched me he'd see me as calm, unmoved, but it's the quiet of lethargy, of defeat. I'm as I am because I know I'm finished; my best days, poor as they probably were, are over. I sit here and let things happen to me. They don't. They organize.'

'But you travel abroad a bit, don't you? And read? And go to concerts or the theatre?'

'Yes, I do. But more and more reluctantly. Yes, that reminds me. Do you remember I told you that I was writing something?'

'Yes. About cloud-cuckoo land.'

165

'That's not quite right.' Jack Brentnall drew himself together, like a teacher about to begin on the crux of his lesson, making sure the class was ready and receptive and he fully prepared to deliver it. 'It's a bit more realistic than that in one way. I'm away on holiday in a foreign, European city. Zürich, Prague, Budapest, you know.'

'Have you been to these places?'

'All three.'

'Which do you like best?'

Brentnall looked affronted as the course of his story was interrupted.

'Prague,' he said finally. 'Praha. Well, there I am out in the foreign street. Now you expect it to be different in some ways, odd-looking tram-cars, strange names over the shops; though nowadays I'm surprised at the similarity of cities. But in the story I'm writing everything goes exactly opposite to my expectations. I stop a taxi, and call out the address I want to be taken to, and the door suddenly closes in my face before I can get in. I stop to ask for a direction from some very respectable-looking woman out shopping and she bursts into tears. I walk up some steps which begin to crumble away. As I stroll through a park the gravelled path becomes a quicksand. I look at my reflection in a shop window (I'm always doing it; I must be very vain), and I'm tall and thin and stooping. Other people look as they are, but I am nothing like myself. When I order a meal, I'm given not a Barmecide's feast but some crusts of bread and fishbones.'

'All these odd occurrences are all unpleasant? Is that so?'

'Yes, it is.'

'And can you say why you write like this? Your taxi could turn into a Rolls Royce with a very obliging chauffeur. Your respectable woman in the street could change into a young beauty who threw her arms round your neck to kiss you.'

'Not likely.' The gloomy voice denied the twinkling eyes.

'I thought the whole point of your story was that everything was unexpected.'

'It is.'

'But why unpleasantly so?'

Brentnall rubbed his chin, staring into the furthest corner of the ceiling, above an unexpected palm tree.

'Yes. I've never really considered that. I'm so intent when I'm

166

writing to make it all sound real, realistic, possible, that your other consideration has never entered my head. When we go abroad we want it to be different; that's the point. More sunshine, different language, romantic buildings, odd customs, strange meals. We don't want it to be too much like home-life. On the other hand, we don't wish it to be too far removed. I don't want, I can tell you, to be using chopsticks every day or suffering from gippy-tummy all through my holidays.'

'You could be served soup, couldn't you,' Sam asked, 'only to find you've only been given chopsticks.'

'In my sort of story, yes. Thanks for the idea.'

'Are you writing for publication?'

'I've not even considered that. The reason is that I have somehow to prove to myself that I'm in my right mind. I've noticed in the last year or two that I can't immediately call on a word. I know I know it, but it doesn't immediately come to the tongue. These are usually words that I don't commonly use. I was trying to think of the word "alienate" this morning, but could I get it? I feel cross, miffed about this, because I'd always considered myself a fairly literate man. If it happens I just leave it, and sooner or later the word presents itself. That's not much use in conversation, but in a letter I can always leave a blank. In conversation I try to find some other way of saying what I want, and it's not always easy. Do you find this?'

'Yes, I do. Often,' Sam answered. 'Most old people are in the same boat.'

'What I fear most is that one of these days I shan't be able to find the word at all, even after a time, that it will have disappeared for good. That's why I'm doing my bit with the pen in the belief, mistaken for all I know, that regular practice at formal writing will keep my vocabulary intact.'

'You're doing pretty well so far,' Sam said, laughing.

'That's why I do it. But the nature of my writing I can't account for. This story is about abroad. Well, I'm getting near the end of my foreign trips, so I'm perhaps trying to prove to myself that I didn't waste my time when I did gad about or perhaps trying to make up to myself for the fact that I'm not as capable of dashing on and off trains and planes as I was once. And that perhaps accounts for the unpleasant nature of the subject matter.'

'What will be the end of the story?'

'That I don't know. I've not finished it.'

'I see,' Sam said. 'You're not leading to some almighty catastrophe, then?'

'Such as?'

'Switching off your light in your strange bedroom on your first night,' Sam said, enjoying himself, 'only to find it was the button that triggered off a series of nuclear explosions that have destroyed the whole world.'

'By God,' Brentnall said, 'you've got a vivid imagination.'

'I'll try not to use it too much.'

'And I'll tell you the good thing. At least we're well. Or moderately so.' Brentnall nodded sagely as he spoke. 'Until I had these turns of mine I didn't think about my health at all. Now I know that there are plenty of people of my age, never mind yours, who've died or are terminally ill. I'm as good as new now, my doctor says, as long as I'm careful. But you and I, the pair of us, can get about, aren't crippled with pain, haven't been told what we shall die of, and when. So we can walk down to the beach, or drink a pint or two without half killing ourselves.'

'God bless the Prince of Wales,' Sam said.

'We used to say that when I was in the forces.'

'And worse, I expect.' They snorted.

'Yes. I wonder who'll read my story after I'm gone? You've got your pictures that somebody will put up on their walls. It's something. It really is. May I ask you a favour? May I come up and have a look at your work before I go back?'

They arranged a time for a visit the next day, drank another cheerful half-pint. As Sam left, Jack Brentnall accompanied him to the door. They stood outside in the lights of the car park.

'What'll you do once you're home?' Jack asked.

'Straight off to bed.'

'Will you sleep?'

'With luck.'

They stood in the chill, and Sam was surprised when Jack wheeled, held up a hand and began to declaim, if quietly,

'Now cease, my lute this is the last
Labour that thou and I shall waste
And ended is that we begun;
Now is this song both sung and past
My lute be still, for I have done.'

168

He finished and stood like a statue, his white hair comically spiked upward, one hand raised as if in blessing.

'What's that?' Sam asked.

'Sir Thomas Wyatt. Lived at the time of Henry VIII. When I was a student three or four of us used to go down to the pub, The Traveller's Rest, on a Saturday night. We took girls sometimes. We didn't drink much. We hadn't the money. Two small halves. And one of my friends, Tom Carey, used to say that verse in the street at the top of his voice every time we came out. He did it so often I learnt it by heart. We made a ceremony of it in the end, joined in, if you know what I mean.

Now cease, my lute, this is the last . . .

He was studying English. An odd young man, with thick eyebrows.'

'Is he still about?'

'I've no idea. I've not heard of him, or from him, for years.'

The statue moved, held out a hand. The two odd men shook, at a loss, surprised by the strength of their feelings.

'You get inside,' Sam ordered, 'or you'll catch your death.'

They shook hands once more. The headlight of a car entering the park momentarily lit them, casting long shadows, then deserted them to deeper darkness.

XIII

The next morning Alice Jeffreys telephoned to say they'd return on Sunday so that his work of supervision would be over. She did not sound unduly happy, but grumbled that being away from home was no real pleasure at this time of year. One of the Mediterranean islands or North Africa or the Caribbean might warm her old bones, but not Ross-on-Wye. He had thought she was in the Home Counties. She talked exactly like the woman he used to see in the street. A smart, well-dressed, wealthy person of note, sure of herself and her status, more inclined to complain than praise; she hectored him, as she might make her wishes clear to a home-help or shop assistant rather than to a friend. Sam tried not to show his disappointment, and cut short the conversation after five minutes. When he'd reported on the pile of mail, she'd answered that there'd be nothing important, mostly offers to lend them money, or to buy luxuries she did not want or already had. She sounded thoroughly disagreeable by the time they'd finished.

Jack Brentnall had arranged to come for coffee at eleven, and Sam therefore did not want to start painting only to be interrupted as soon as he was thoroughly immersed. He felt as grumpy as Alice, and he'd no sooner fetched out and plugged in his vacuum cleaner than the phone rang again.

This time Karen Craig called. She sounded lively; her period of pregnancy progressed without snags.

She wondered if the family could come over for lunch in the holidays. She realized there were not many free days left, and they were short of light, but the children and Edward had expressed a wish to visit him and the sea. Sam at once fixed a date. They'd start very early.

'You needn't do anything,' she said. 'We'll take you to the pub for lunch. The children'll love that. They're at an age where going out for a meal in public is highly regarded.'

'Even Ben?'

'Even Ben. He's getting to be really grown up. And Ed thinks a blow of sea air, however cold, will do us good.'

'He's all right, is he? Edward?'

'Yes. Very well.'

'No. I meant: Is all well now between the two of you?'

'Yes.' Karen sounded faintly hesitant. 'Yes, we've talked it over again once or twice. I think I was quite right to show him the letter and bring it all out into the open.'

'Good.'

'There might have been a smidgen of truth in it.' Her choice of vocabulary led him to think she was mistress of the situation. 'This girl went out of her way to please him. They were both new. He perhaps showed her more favour than he should.'

'Kissing her? Holding hands together in town?' His rancour against this morning's world dictated the questions.

'That's possible. I don't put it past him. I'm not sure. He's a man craving for affection and admiration and he'll return them.'

'Has it happened before?' Sam asked.

'Not to the best of my knowledge. I shall always be, well, very slightly suspicious. From now on.' Her voice grew richer, as if she enjoyed the revelation. 'But this present battle's over. He's back at home. He's had warning that he's being watched. That can't be bad for him.'

'And you're pleased?'

'I don't want major upsets now while I'm pregnant. Or at any other time. When I think about it two or three awkward things came up at the same moment. Ed had a new job. I didn't perhaps make the fuss of him that he thought he deserved. We were moving house. Our sex life was, let's say, not quite as satisfactory as it might have been. He needed cossetting, and I didn't do much about it. So he looked, or was tempted to search, elsewhere.'

'But it's straightened out now?'

'It seems to be. The next thing we all look forward to is the new baby.'

'Does Edward?'

'I'm sure he does. He adores his children. Of that I *am* sure.'

They hummed pleasure and congruence of ideas together without words. He thought that marvellous. She suggested a time of arrival. If it was fine Edward would drive them all down to the

171

beach car park, and then back up to the pub. He told her about Jack Brentnall.

'He sounds interesting,' she said. 'Will he be there when we come up next week?'

'I expect he'll be back at home.'

'Will you keep in touch with him?'

'I never know that sort of thing. It'll depend on him, I expect.'

'You won't make the effort?'

'I don't know. When you get old, like me, you tend to fill up your life with all sorts of little jobs, time-consuming affairs, and they sap your energy so that you haven't the opportunities to be branching out.'

'Have you a good number of friends in the village?'

'No. Not really. There are the Jeffreys. You met Alice when you were here. There are plenty of people I speak to. The newsagent and odd bods in the pub. They're all very cheerful and affable, but I can't claim that we're close. My life consists of chance meetings, casual happenings.'

'And some days are blank?' she asked.

'Yes. There are days when I don't speak to anyone. Some days, in winter, I don't go out of the house. And that's bad.'

'Oh, dear.'

'We need company, companionship, even of a casual kind. It's depressing to stay indoors, day after day.'

'You wouldn't do very well as a hermit?' Karen asked.

'I would not. They're saintly and think they're in touch with God. The only person I'd be in contact with would be myself, and though I'm vain and self-regarding and all the rest of it I'd soon become bored with my own company. No. When you're younger you have a job that fills your days up, or did in my youth, and you had responsibilities to your wife and family and home. You often feel resentful about it, wish you could have ten minutes you could call your own instead of people harassing you to do this, that and the other for them. But I had some drive then. Now I drag my feet.'

'That's not my impression. You play with the children like a man half your age.'

'No. My life consists of trivial, unconnected incidents. Fragments. I'll admit it could be worse. I could be confined to a wheelchair, or locked in a nursing home, or incapable of dressing myself.'

172

'You might still be alert in your mind.'

'I don't know whether that wouldn't be worse.'

Karen broke off to say she was off shopping in the supermarket with a friend. They went once a week using one car only, and had a light lunch. And talked the leg off an iron pot. This had been made possible by putting Ben into a nursery. He didn't mind. He was a sociable little soul, and would be delighted when he could join a real school. In this he exactly took after his father.

'Right, I'll see you all next week.' Sam smiled at the phone. 'I'm glad things go well for you.'

'Thanks, Mr Martin. Don't worry yourself.'

Jack Brentnall arrived exactly on time, and smartly dressed.

'One thing I learnt from National Service. Be on the parade ground five minutes before time.'

Sam helped him off with his coat, silently admired his silvery bow-tie, and sniffed the tactfully applied aftershave. Brentnall's cheeks shone pink and his hair was brilliantined.

'Are we cheerful today?' Jack asked.

'Moderately. Two ladies have rung me already. And you?'

Jack shook himself with the vigour of a dog emerging from water. It looked odd coming from so neat a man. He let himself carefully down into a chair.

'Ah, I feel off today.'

'Why's that?' Sam asked.

'I think it must be talking to you. About what we're doing or trying to do. I didn't sleep very well, and when I did drop off I dreamed.'

'Nightmares?'

'Not exactly. Very unpleasant dreams, and this is unusual for me. I don't dream a great deal, and when I do I don't seem to remember much.'

'But this time was different.'

'Yes.' He tapped his fingernails on the table top. 'When I first married, forty-odd years ago, our first house was a cottage. It wasn't very picturesque, and we bought it for next to nothing because we knew it was to be pulled down when they built a new by-pass. In fact we lived in it, comfortably enough, for five years, or nearly so. Then we were told to clear out, and bought a more suitable place. That's where we lived until I changed my job again. Now in this dream, and remember I hadn't thought consciously about the place for years, I was a young man again. We'd cleared the cottage and were living in our new house, but I'd decided to go back to have a last look round and make sure we'd really moved everything out. Nothing like that happened in real life. When we left I employed a local professional furniture-remover, and as for the bits and pieces which were left, some house-clearing agent, a friend of the removal-man, shifted the lot. When I examined it for the final time the weekend after we'd quitted the place was bare. They'd made a thorough job of it.'

Sam listened to the flat narrative, and watched Brentnall's nervous movements of arms and legs, his grimaces. The man appeared thoroughly ill at ease, as if he'd jump high from his chair and scream. So far the narrative seemed to the listener to present no cause for such distress.

'And then?' Sam said. An ordinary voice.

'In the dream I'd just arrived at the back door. There was nobody about, because the cottage was rather out of the way, at the end of a lane with hedges. I got hold of the door-handle and pushed, but couldn't get the thing open. I knew for certain I hadn't locked it the day before. I looked more closely and I saw that the door had been nailed shut, presumably against vandals, though I couldn't see much reason for this. The transport authorities were going to knock the place down, anyway, and as I said it was well away from the town. So there I stood outside in the yard.'

'And this upset you?' Sam asked.

'No. Not unduly. I was surprised that the authorities had taken the trouble, that's all.'

'So?' Sam coaxed him on.

'I looked through the back window into the living room. It wasn't very well lit, but I could see clearly enough. The room was stripped, except for one thing. On the far wall, opposite me, where we used to keep the piano there was a horse fastened. I don't mean tethered; I mean fastened by bands round the body, the legs and with nails, huge-headed nails, through the torso actually onto the wall, the hooves two or three feet from the floor.'

'Dead?'

'No. It was not.'

The two old men stared each at the other. Brentnall's face drained white and puckered round the lips.

'How did you know?'

'It moved its ears, and its head.' Brentnall clutched the wrinkled skin of his neck. 'The most outlandish thing about it all was that it wasn't a full horse, not three-dimensional, but more like a skin. I could see that, but it made no difference. I was convinced that it was alive and suffering.'

'And what did you do?'

'By this time I was on my knees by the back doorstep. I knew what I had to do, that is, get in touch with the police who'd contact the RSPCA. But I didn't want to do it. I knelt there, with my hands clasped and my eyes shut, as if I was praying, but I can tell you I wasn't. I was in an agony because I knew my duty, but hadn't the strength of mind to do anything even as simple as that. All I needed was to get home to a telephone and set the rescue in motion. But I couldn't, and didn't want to. "Why me?" I kept groaning aloud. "Why not somebody else? Why is it left to me?" I had no strength, only pain, and self-pity. And there I knelt, rocking, swaying, every bit of manhood and sense drained out of me.'

Sam watched his companion's face with something like terror. It would not have surprised him if Brentnall had not dropped to his knees here, moaning and swaying on the carpet. The man was caught up in the ferocious despair of his dreams, thrashed by its panic.

'What did you do?' Sam asked, voice phlegmy with his own fear.

He had to wait for his answer. Jack kept his eyes shut tight. His body did not move, ugly in its crooked paralysis. After a time, as he lifted his head his mouth dropped slightly open.

'I woke up,' he answered dully. 'I'd made up my mind, or I think I had, to get in touch with the police, and I was struggling to my feet when suddenly I was awake, terrified, but awake. I was shaking still, and groaning, though I was wide awake.'

He drew himself up, essayed a weakly smile, as if to convey his present equanimity as opposed to the hopeless, searing impotence in the dream.

'Yes,' Sam said, 'yes. Not good. These dreams seem so real.'

The two old men sat, as in reverie, occupying chairs to no purpose. Sam was the first to recover.

'Have you any notion,' he asked, 'about the cause, the basis of the dream?'

175

'Well, in some way,' Brentnall spoke slowly, putting words together like pieces in a jigsaw, 'it reflected my present, my, well, state of life. Physically I was useless, and even morally so. My weakness was compounded with cowardice.'

'Yes,' Sam said. 'Why a horse?'

The other jerked as if in anger. He would have looked so, Sam thought, when one of his pupils had asked an impudent question. Skin tightened round the jaw bone. False teeth appeared.

'No idea.' Snapped.

'Have you any connection with horses? Kept them or ridden or driven them?'

'No. Never. I'm fond of animals. But I've not once in my life sat on a horse's back.'

'So it doesn't represent anything? It might just as well have been an elephant or a fox or a cat?'

'Umhh.' A cross-patch grunt accompanied a shake of the head.

'Had your wife any connection with horses? Did your children ride them?'

'No to the first question. My daughter had riding lessons. But I had no thought about them in the dream.' He began to speak more slowly, shaking his hands in front of him as if feeling his way. 'I'd say, if I had no option but to answer, that it reflected, if that's the word, my present state. I'm old; I'm getting weaker; I've no great principles, only a few habits I've acquired over the years, so that when I'm asked to do something I regard it as an intrusion on my life, a threat to my small comforts.'

'But the horse?'

'I don't know. Don't think I haven't tried to offer myself a solution. The nearest I can get, and this may be complete rubbish, is that it is a picture of my present state of mind. The moving house represents death. I'm going somewhere else. In real life, all that time ago, we were only too glad to move. We knew it was inevitable, and the new place was miles better than the old. You and I have spoken about dying, and we know it can't be too far away at our age.'

'Go on.' Sam was interested now.

'The empty room must have represented my life. Nothing there to show for damn' near seventy years with that one awful exception, the tortured horse. All I've done since I have been on earth is worthless. But there's this dying animal to account for. I don't know what it means. You asked me, "Why a horse?", and the only answer I can think of is that a horse is large. It's not small, a rabbit or stoat or even a cat. It's large; it can't be ignored. My life has this big, cruel crime to answer for. I can't explain what it is. I have done nobody any violent wrong. Or at least as far as I can remember, and I would remember that, wouldn't I?'

'Have you any beliefs about an after-life?'

'None at all.' Brentnall answered with brusque firmness.

'So you're not expecting a Last Judgement?'

'No. This was it, perhaps.'

'Do you know,' Sam said, puffing, 'that I've neither given you a cup or coffee nor showed you my pictures?'

'No, you haven't.'

Sam rose at once to repair his failure of hospitality. Jack held up a hand.

'Thanks for listening to my drivel.'

'I can imagine how frightening it was. If that's the word.'

'Do you have these terrifying dreams?'

'No, I don't. Like you I don't seem to remember even.'

He turned and marched with all the speed he could muster from the room. He took his time over the preparation of coffee. When he returned he affected cheerfulness.

'You're honoured,' he told his guest. 'I've fetched the china cups out for us. I'm a mug man, myself.' He poured, then pushed forward a plate with its tastefully arranged pattern of biscuits. Jack Brentnall raised his coffee gratefully.

'Delicious,' he pronounced. 'Delicious.'

Sam sat and reached for a thick finger of shortbread. Brentnall now appeared easy in mind and body, catching crumbs from a chocolate biscuit with his left hand. For the next quarter of an hour they talked of sport and television.

'Do you ever go to the cinema?' Brentnall asked.

'Never. Though there is talk of starting a film-club in the village. Nor do I go to the theatre. The last piece of drama I saw here was a rehearsal for the village pantomime.'

'Was it good?'

'Better than I expected. Alice Jeffreys played the piano for some of the rehearsals. She kept me in touch with the progress of affairs, and she dragooned me into going. But I was pleasantly surprised.'

177

'Is she your lady-friend?' Jack asked.

'She has a husband.'

'That wouldn't stop you now, would it?'

Sam blushed. Jack did not seem to notice, only that his little pleasantry had not exactly suited the mood of the moment. He moved the topic at once. Now he spoke, knowledgeably, Sam thought, about red wine. They each drank two cups of coffee but restrained themselves to one biscuit. They had momentarily lost intimacy and Sam led his visitor to the drawing room where they stood, discomposed, in front of the half-dozen pictures there were.

It was immediately apparent to Sam that his visitor had no real interest in painting. He was capable of cobbling sentences together that conveyed appreciation or understanding, but he would rather have talked of something else. His formerly expressed wish to see Sam Martin's pictures had been an excuse to visit the house, to be received in it, to find out how the host lived. Sam hurried his friend round, saying little, but politely answering questions. Do you begin a picture at the top or the bottom, the left or the right? How long does it take you to complete a painting? Do you ever try to sell the finished works? Do you use a camera at all?

They stopped only once at a picture hanging in the dining room. A horse looked up gently from grazing. Sam thought little of this as a composition, but his grandchildren had admired it on a visit six or seven years ago, and he had framed it with the intention of sending it to them, but had never got round to it, chiefly he thought because he was uncertain of its aesthetic merit. In the end he had hung it on his own wall, in a darkish spot. Jack Brentnall stared morosely at it.

'The colour of the horse in your dream?' Sam asked.

'No. Too brown. Mine was a light beige. Not grey. Faintly brown. I don't know what the technical term is.'

'Neither do I,' Sam said. 'What's a strawberry roan?'

'No idea. Presumably a horse with a reddish brown coat. Or is that a bay?'

'Don't ask me. So it's nothing like your horse?'

'Nothing is like my horse. It could not be.' Jack sounded offended.

They walked out into the garden where the wind bit into their old bones.

'Not much to be seen at this time of the year,' Sam said.

'Ah, but it's neat. You clearly cleaned it up at the end of the growing season. Do you do it all yourself?'

'I do. It's a bit painful at times. I get short of breath, especially when I'm bending, and I've all sorts of aches and pains that I didn't have, or ignored, when I was younger. I get a bit of help.'

'I have a man in since my heart attack. He's worse than useless. Ignorant, but he keeps it tidy. You're lucky again. Able to garden and over eighty.'

'Did you have discomfort when you were younger?' Sam asked. 'I can remember that when I was a boy I used to have shooting pains in my legs. People called them growing pains.'

'I had them,' Jack said. 'It seemed as if everybody had them. You never hear of them nowadays. I wonder what they were. Rheumatism? Muscular strains? Some dietary deficiency?'

The shared thought of the mystery seemed to cheer both men as they stared down at cabbage stumps, sober shrubs, the crinkled bark of ancient apple trees. They trotted on, comically.

'These look well,' Jack called, pointing at camellia leaves. 'Plenty of buds.'

'Won't be too long now before they're out. That's the beauty. Exotic blossoms so early in the year.'

'By God,' Jack said. 'I look forward to the spring.'

'And I. It soon comes round, but, by the same token, it soon goes.'

'Cheer up, man.' Brentnall did a further tripping run, half a dozen grotesque ballet-steps, arms out monoplane-wide.

'Steady, the Buffs.'

A dog barked in the distance. Grey skies grew blacker in the wind to the north, and cleared as quickly after a few icy splashes.

'Does you good,' Jack said. 'This sea air.'

'If I stand around here much longer,' Sam answered, 'it'll be shrinking pains, not growing, that I'll be suffering from.'

They turned, urged themselves laughingly indoors. In the warmth of the kitchen Brentnall, still gaping down the length of garden, recovered his breath to speak as he leaned over the sink.

'By God, Sam,' he said, gasping still, 'this morning's livened me up.'

'Would you like another cup of coffee?'

'No, thanks. I've had stimulants enough for one day.'

179

'Come and see me again. We'll get that horse of yours down off the wall.'

'That's the way to beat nightmares, so the experts say. Rerun it, and then tack on a happy ending. But it reduced me, I can tell you, kneeling outside that nailed back door.' Brentnall pointed at a writhing holly, black against the sky.

'Was your wife glad to move into your new house?'

'Yes. She didn't much like the cottage. It was by no means ideal, and we didn't want to spend money on it because we knew we'd have to leave at any time. I reckon the three or four years in the new house were the happiest in all our married life. We moved south next, to St Albans, and we both got on well there, had teaching jobs, in schools we liked, but we shifted again, to Leeds, and then back to my first school in Norwich where I was head of mathematics.'

'You liked that?'

'I was invited to apply by the headmaster. I was already head of department, but my wife liked this part of the world.' Jack sniffed. 'You've done me well, my friend, I came in this morning so low I could creep under a snake's belly, and here I am now with my chest sticking out a yard.'

They talked for a further ten minutes before Brentnall hurried off saying they didn't have lunch proper at the pub.

'There's plenty of food, but we take it and eat it when we can. I'll give a hand in the bar midday. I can manage that when it's not too busy.'

'You'll be able to reckon the change, at least.'

'I can. Come down this evening, will you? I've not felt so cheerful for months.'

Sam watched his friend, Dutch cap and sailor's roll pre-eminent, strut down the road. Jack looked back once and waved.

Sam, indoors, swilling coffee cups, felt pleased. As he prepared to reheat yesterday's casserole he sang out loud. 'The people that walked in darkness have seen a great light.' He took another stroll down the bleak garden, still singing.

XIV

Alice Jeffreys called in on him the same afternoon. She had brought a small present, a pot of yellow chrysanthemums, a reward for looking after the houses. She questioned him about his Christmas, seemed interested in Jack Brentnall, saying she'd not met him nor heard of him.

'Neither Hilda nor I used the pub,' she said. 'It didn't seem quite the place. I can't say I've never been in, but it must have been a year ago at least.'

'And John?'

'Oh, he'll call in now and then. And they hold committee meetings there. And if we want something out of the ordinary, a very large joint of beef, or some special poultry, he'll get the landlord to order it from his own butcher. He's very obliging.'

'This man's a teacher of mathematics. Or was.'

'And nice?'

'Yes. Like me, though not so old. A bit lonely. Nobody to complain to.'

When Sam mentioned the Saturday visit of the Craig family, she immediately consulted her diary and offered to give him a hand with the arrangements.

'What about John?' he asked.

'He'll be away.' She pointed at her handbag in which lay the diary. 'In London, and then Guernsey. I can give you all my time.'

'Won't it be boring for you?'

'No. I'll enjoy it.'

'There are no meals to prepare. They're suggesting we eat at the pub. I'll be delighted if you can join us. I really will.'

'And before that?'

'If the weather's fine we'll go down to the sea. Car to the car park, then an hour chasing round. They want to be back home in good time.'

'Right, I'll be here. Will your new friend be with us?'

'No. I should think he's had more than enough of children.'

'But he might like to talk to Edward, is it?, and Karen about teaching.'

'It never crossed my mind.'

'What do the pair of you talk about? The good old days? Service in the forces?'

'We do mention the past. That's true. All old people live in the past, they say.'

'Do you?'

'Not really. I remember things often, good or bad. But not all the time.'

'But when the two of you get together, don't you boast about the triumphs of your youth?'

'A bit. We don't know each other well enough yet to want to score over the other. But we'll see. I shall be down at the Royal Oak tonight to talk.'

'Good,' she said. 'Great. I'd like to hear you.'

She left, bustling. The few days at her daughter's had left her plenty to do, she claimed. She had buttoned her coat and made off down the front path before he had chance to detain her. He felt disappointment. He had looked forward to her return, and now found her brusque, efficient, rather distant, like some official from social services, polite, interested, but needing to get your poor bit of business over before rushing on to the next. He faintly caught her perfume in the kitchen where she had talked to him, but her voice had been harsher than he remembered. This was Hilda's friend, a person of importance, not afraid to let people know it.

That evening he made his way down to the Royal Oak and settled down in the lounge, which was comparatively empty.

'They're all at home,' the landlord said, 'finishing off the Christmas bits. Tomorrow, they'll start coming in. Men don't like it too much with the family.'

'Don't you?'

'Home and work are the same place to me. I'll give Jack a shout, tell him you're here.'

Ten minutes later Jack Brentnall appeared, in a dark grey suit, with a white shirt and a plain gold and navy silk tie. He carried his own drink in, and waved it at Sam.

'Your health, sir,' he said. 'I've reason to be grateful to you. This morning, oh, this morning. It's the weather and the long nights. S-A-D they call it. And yet after an hour in your house, I was a different man.'

'Do you miss your teaching?' Sam asked.

'A captive audience? I spent my time in grammar schools with willing pupils. God knows we wrote some of 'em off as stupid and unteachable or badly behaved. But compared with the schools in some of the inner cities these places were havens of peace and scholarship.'

'They've got rid of most of the grammar schools?'

'Yes. And I suppose that's probably right. But I knew two old colleagues who both taught on, part-time, until they were seventy. Nobody nowadays stays on much beyond sixty. I was sixty-one.'

'And you'd had enough?'

'Yes. I handed over my department to a young man with up-to-date ideas. It's ironical that they'd regard me as right now, good old back-to-basics, none of your fancy pupil-oriented curricula.'

'That's a curious word.'

'Latin for a ground where they did their chariot-races. Curriculum.'

Brentnall was now launched, and talked at length about his subject, and how one built on already acquired knowledge.

'Why are so many people poor at maths, or frightened of it?' Sam asked.

'Because they've been badly taught. Though,' he thumped the word and held up his hand to keep his listener silent for the rider, 'at all levels one can set puzzles which will defeat very many who have acquired the necessary knowledge. And people remember this, how they were unable to take the two or three mental twists that would have solved the problem.' He nodded, gravely, to himself, perhaps recalling when he had been found wanting or perhaps proudly able to provide a solution when the rest had failed.

He had now gone on to regret that he had never taught girls.

'People wrote them off too soon.'

He was launched into the story of a girl he had coached first for O and then for A Level. She had been discarded by her, female, teachers as incapable.

'And yet I tell you once she'd shed her original and baseless dread of the subject, and learnt the rules, she became interested

183

and really quite competent. She wasn't a genius, but she managed an A grade at A Level in Maths and Further Maths. Confidence and interest are vital.'

'Have you ever taught any really gifted mathematicians?'

'Two or three. They'd be through some difficult solution before I'd half-understood the question.'

'Was that embarrassing?'

'No. I had to fall back on my experience. But I tell you it was marvellous to explain things to such as these. They'd pick it up and be on to the next three or four steps before you'd got anywhere near them. In one case the boy was so talented he'd be adding bits and pieces of his own. I'd guess these ideas of his would exist somewhere on paper, that someone had thought them up in the past, but he, as it were, improvised with the best, right out of my class.'

'And what's that boy doing now?'

'He holds some prestigious chair in an American university.'

'Did all these really clever boys become professors?'

'Two out of three. One went into economics.'

'Banking?'

'No. I think it was something to do with airlines. These people who make the enormous salaries we read about in the newspapers need different skills altogether. They'll understand the bit of mathematics they need, but they don't have to be outstandingly talented at the subject. They'll use considerable gifts, I'm sure, though I'm not quite certain what they are. Steadiness under fire. Something like that. Or dash. How to gamble convincingly. Boldness. These are part of personality, as I think mathematical gifts aren't altogether. There are gifts, personal traits that a mathematician must have; he must be prepared to work hard, to be competitive and all the rest, but . . .'

Brentnall let his arms hang loosely in front of him as if he were puzzled beyond his capacity. After a time he recovered and talked about 'ceilings' in mathematics: one could do brilliantly at GCSE, or A Level, but fail hopelessly to cope at the next stage. He could not, he said, understand this, but he'd observed it often enough.

Sam asked about the National Lottery. Very clearly, very seriously, Jack set out the odds against winning a supreme prize. He quoted figures with confidence, calculating how often one would win under the present rules, playing twice a week, and discussed whether it was worth buying ten or a hundred tickets instead of one.

'I take it you don't enter?' Sam asked.

'Oh, but I do. I don't smoke so I spend five pounds every weekend.'

'Have you a system?'

'No. I fill in my birthday, my wife's, my son's, and add others at random – day of the week, cost of apples that morning, some intuition I've had.'

'Have you won anything?'

'Small prizes, twice.'

'So you're out of pocket?'

'Oh, yes. I knew I would be. But I'm buying excitement.'

'And your knowledge of statistics doesn't deter you?'

'No.'

'You're not prepared to learn from experience?'

Jack Brentnall set out his views on life. One paid for one's pleasures, and this mild flutter at the weekend was a small island of joy in the ocean of boredom that washed round old age. He began to list his other diversions, a diminishing list, one of which appeared to be eating. He was beginning to describe with enthusiasm his love of Italian cookery when the door of the lounge was flung confidently open and the Jeffreys, John and Alice, smiled lordly at the almost empty room.

'The man himself,' Jeffreys announced flinging an arm in Sam's direction.

'May we join you?' Alice asked.

Sam introduced the newcomers to his friend. Their confident way of stalking across the room impressed; they constituted an occupying force. Jeffreys, having shaken hands, made for the bar with strides that dwarfed the furniture. The landlord had already taken his position polishing the richly gleaming top of a tray.

At the table both Sam and his friend were standing to greet Alice; Jack held a chair for Alice, who thanked them both with an old-fashioned, emphatic courtesy that matched theirs. She immediately turned her full attention on Brentnall, inquiring how he was passing his time in 'our little backwater'. He, obviously attracted, described his daily régime, and told her how much he enjoyed his conversations with Sam Martin.

'And we've interrupted one of them,' she said.

'Oh, no. Not at all. I'm delighted you've come in. Delighted.'

Over at the bar the landlord was head to head in an almost inaudible conversation with John Jeffreys. Their faces were close, conspirationally alight.

'Man to man,' Brentnall said sarcastically.

'It'll be some golf club arrangement, or the dinner at the opening of the bowling season,' Alice said.

'Do you attend these functions?' Jack asked her.

'The functions, the meals and the presentations of medals and prizes, but not the games. I don't play.'

'Not tennis? Badminton? You look the sort of fit lady who'd excel on the match-courts.'

'No.'

Jeffreys had now cornered Sam, and in the same whispering baritone he used for the landlord he said how pleased he was that Alice was coming along to the bungalow to help entertain the Craig family on Saturday.

'I shall be out of the way at six thirty. First stop Hayes, Middlesex. She'll enjoy it with the children.' He seemed to know all about the family, had discussed it with his wife, and remembered the details. Sam was surprised. 'I feel guilty to some extent,' Jeffreys confided. They paused momentarily to register that Brentnall was now claiming to Alice that his game was rugby union, but that it was nothing like the sport he'd played forty years ago. Jeffreys laid a hand on Sam's arm to return him to their topic. 'She'll enjoy it, I know. I'm supposed to have retired, but no sooner are we back than I have to set off on this trip.'

'For how long?'

'Until Tuesday or Wednesday night. Sunday'll be golf and drinking but the rest will be useful. We're meeting some Japanese businessmen. And they think an old white head like mine adds weight, gravitas to our team.'

'And does it?'

'You judge for yourself. The MD and his Two i/c know what they want, and how they're going to get it. I'm a bit player.'

'And does that annoy you?'

'Not really. I'm interested to know how the business is progressing. I've a small financial stake in it still. That was part of my retirement package. So I listen.'

'Do they ask your advice?'

'About technical processes, now and again. I must be of some use to them, or they wouldn't call me in. They'd drop me without a qualm. They're a pretty ruthless bunch.'

'And the golf?'

'I can still beat any of them. I can't match them for distance, but I drive straight. They think they ought to be able to whip me with their superior strength, but they can't. Or not often. Perhaps when I'm old and decrepit they'll forget me. We organize a match, two foursomes against the Japanese group. They speak English, or most of them. They play like demons to win. And this year they've got some very good man here, pretty near professional standard.'

'If they beat you, they're more amenable to your ideas?' Sam wanted to know.

'I've not noticed that. No. Money talks with both sides in this lot. No, we all enjoy the game and the hospitality and work all the harder after the relaxation.'

'Do you talk business on the course?'

'Yes. Put suggestions. We have two long sessions on the Saturday. That's why I have to start out at such an ungodly hour.'

Jeffreys spoke with friendliness; he obviously enjoyed talking about his work to someone who understood its drawbacks and advantages. He was pleased to have retired but not to have been left in desuetude. A decent man, Sam decided, who'd made something of his life and continued to do so.

Not for some time did Sam consciously notice how deeply Alice and Jack Brentnall were engaged in their own talk. Jack was clearly out to create and impress. The two other men had broken off their own conversation, and Jeffreys had laid a hand on his companion's arm as if to prevent him from starting up again. It hardly seemed possible to Sam that two couples could have sat so close and yet have been so oblivious of each other. Brentnall spoke with a quiet eloquence, an intensity about rugby football. He leaned forward towards Alice, his white hair gleaming and his face red with effort and excitement. He tapped with his forefinger on the table top, Alice sat, as it were, away from him, her mouth slightly open.

'All I can do now,' Jack pronounced, 'is watch the game on TV.'

'And is that worth it?' she asked.

'In some ways, yes, in some ways. A few years ago I learnt to hate the Welsh.'

187

'But surely . . .'

'Their crowds sang with such passion. It was terrifying. You'd hear them altogether,

> "Bread of 'eaven, bread of 'eaven,
> Feed me till I want no more",

and then their fly-half would punt the ball seventy yards up the pitch and one bounce into touch right into our 25, 22 they call it now, metres, ridiculous. And our side had to toil sweating back. Bread of Heaven, oh, I hated them.'

'Oh, dear,' Alice said. 'It all sounds very violent.'

'They're not so good now. The game has changed. Money has intervened. Some of their best players have gone off to Rugby League. The English clubs . . .' He broke off, sighed, shaking his head. Inside a brief minute he had changed from a sharp, galvanic energy to shaky despondency. Alice observed the transformation, well back from the table. Brentnall sipped at his half-pint for comfort.

The conversation became general. Jack compared his suburban district with this village. John Jeffreys spoke about the Admiral.

'Was he well liked?' Jack asked.

'Yes. The last year or so he barely went out of the house, but before that he'd always speak to people in the street, and cough up for local charities. He'd always got this quarter-deck manner, but when he smiled at you it smoothed the edge off it. Hilda, his wife, took more getting to know. That's so, Alice, isn't it?'

'In a way.'

'There was something of the old nobility about her.'

'Did she come from aristocratic stock?' Sam asked.

'Oh, yes. Her grandfather was a lord. Not that she ever mentioned it to me. And, d'you know?, for all her frozen exterior, I'd say she was a passionate woman.'

Jeffreys stopped, awkwardly. Perhaps he realized he had overstepped his mark. A faint smiled twisted Alice's lips.

'If she supported or opposed anything,' he said, digging himself out, 'she felt for those causes very powerfully.'

Alice laughed. Tension disappeared. They discussed, not uncritically, the characters of Hilda and the Admiral. Jack listened bright-eyed.

'This is what pubs are for,' he said. 'Good talk dissecting the character of people.'

'Maliciously,' Sam said.

'No.' Jack dismissed the suggestion. 'No. This is judicially done, and charitably.'

'Do they go together?' Alice asked.

'Yes. I don't see why not.'

Next Sam raised the matter of the village pantomime, a run-through of which he had seen just before Christmas and enjoyed. John Jeffreys complained that he barely laid eyes on his wife during the rehearsal period. They exchanged views about the performances of the principals, and the difficulty of training a lively chorus. Alice intervened.

'Some people, and it doesn't matter what they're like in real life, once you put them up on the stage become as wooden as apple trees. And nobody seems able to take them out of it. There they stand, gnarled and expressionless. I can't understand it,' Alice admitted. 'They're hidden amongst others but they act as if every eye in the audience is on them.'

'But they aren't as bad as the show-offs?' Jeffreys laughed.

'I'll say nothing,' his wife answered, 'or I'll be naming names, and then I'm in trouble.'

Brentnall began to talk, fluently and with apparent expertise, about the annual school play at his last grammar school, well-known, he claimed, for its reputation for its high standards in drama, anything from Sophocles and Shakespeare to musicals and music-hall. At least three well-known television and film actors had made their first stage appearance as scholars of the place.

Jack confidently laid down the law as to what constituted a good performance, apportioning relative success or failure between production and histrionic ability. He appeared to know about scenery, and discussed what could or could not be done on a small stage, and spoke almost professionally about modern lighting systems. He flashed technical terms, and though he spoke with a low voice, he delivered his views as in a public lecture, looking round his audience, making a gesture from time to time with a small, well-manicured hand, in the direction of one of his auditors.

'Did you produce plays, then?' Sam interrupted.

'No. But my assistance was often called on.'

189

He immediately continued with his exposition and included a quite long, rather dull disquisition on the art of cutting Shakespeare plays.

Sam found this intriguing: Jack spoke with peremptory assertiveness, as if he'd been delivering this lecture every night of the week for the past six months. Sam, however, noticed that both Jeffreys were bored, their eyes glazed or closed from time to time, and in Alice's case she once half-hid a yawn with a well-stretched hand. Brentnall, intent on his subject, observed nothing of this. Sam wondered how a mathematician and rugby-player could be so well-versed in the theatrical arts. Jack now rhapsodized about Richard Strauss's *Metamorphosen*. If he had any music at his funeral it would be that.

'Hey, not so much of that,' Jeffreys jovially grumbled. 'You're only about our age.'

Alice suddenly stood, silencing them all. She pushed her glass into the centre of the table, and said,

'Come along, John.' She spoke in a voice not to be contradicted. 'We've a great deal to do before you go off on your jaunt.' Her husband drained his pot, and rose. The two stood magisterially by the table, dwarfing the two old men, who were now awkwardly and politely pushing up to their feet. All shook hands. Alice said how much she had enjoyed Brentnall's conversation, and asked when he was leaving. He told her on Saturday morning.

'All the best men disappear that morning.' John guffawed to himself.

'I think I'd better make my way home,' Sam said.

'Don't let us spoil it for you,' Alice said. 'We just have to start organizing ourselves. One doesn't know what tomorrow brings, and in any case John is out most of the day so we'll have to decide on the principles at least tonight.'

'Principles?' Sam asked. He buttoned his coat collar.

'Will you come in tomorrow evening?' Brentnall asked him, and was reassured.

Outside the air nipped their faces, and the road seemed suddenly black after the flare of lights in the car park.

'How old's your friend?' Jeffreys asked Sam.

'Sixty-nine.'

'Same decade that we're in, sweetheart,' Jeffreys said, flinging an arm round his wife's shoulder. 'I'd have thought he was older. Smart and all that, but getting on for eighty.' He'd lied to Jack's face.

'Did you like him?' Sam demanded of Alice. She did not immediately answer as they swung along, the three out of step.

'He's a funny, little man,' Alice murmured. Sam, surprised, said nothing. She, feeling the need for further explanation, continued. 'He's too fond of the sound of his own voice.'

'He says some interesting things.'

'Such as?'

'Teaching mathematics to women.'

Jeffreys brayed laughter.

'No,' Alice said. 'He was too pleased with himself by half.'

'Isn't everybody?' Sam asked.

'You aren't for one.'

'My,' Jeffreys, laughing again. 'Praise indeed from my wife.'

They continued at a good pace. Sam, disappointed at her view of Brentnall, searched his mind. She judged objectively; he enjoyed Jack's company because he mended a hole in a dull, leaking life. They reached the Jeffreys' gate.

'I'll see you on Saturday morning,' Alice said. 'What time will the Craigs arrive?'

'They talked about an early start, so probably they'll be here just before ten.'

'I'll be along soon after nine, then. I'll have cleared our house of all John's mess, and I'll help you get straight.'

'These men,' Jeffreys said.

'There won't be much to do,' Sam argued. 'In any case we're out for lunch. All we need is to give them drinks and biscuits.'

'I'll make some scones.'

'You're in favour. I never get them,' Jeffreys grumbled.

'You're never at home.'

Alice turned and opened the gate. Jeffreys aimed a light, flat-handed blow on her left buttock. She disregarded the plebeian gesture and rushed for the door.

'Good night, friend,' Jeffreys called. He loved life at this moment.

At about seven on the next evening, as Sam was loitering over his preparations for his trip down to the Oak and his last meeting with Jack Brentnall, the phone rang. John Jeffreys spoke, but his voice sounded reduced, hoarse.

'Mr Martin?'

'Yes.'

'John Jeffreys. I thought I'd better ring you. We've had some bad news.' He paused, for effect, or to give Sam a slight opportunity to brace himself. 'It's about Hilda, Hilda St John. In America, you know.'

'Yes.' Sam waited.

'She's dead. She died. We heard this afternoon. Her daughter rang.'

'When was it?'

'Yesterday, or the day before. I couldn't quite make out. It was a shock.'

'Was it expected?'

'Well, again I'm not sure. As far as we could understand, she'd been ill, or off colour, most of the time she'd been over there. That's why she didn't come back. We expected her home before Christmas.'

'What did she die of?'

'Again we don't know. She was in hospital. Alice took the call. She thinks it was some internal trouble. They'd operated. For cancer.'

'Is Alice upset?'

'Yes.' Jeffreys drew in a large breath, audible over the phone. 'We both are. We've known them a long time. Alice was at school with Hilda. They were good friends. Very close. Got on well. I liked her. Not that she was everybody's cup of tea. She could be sharp. I think she'd been overshadowed by the Admiral in their earlier days. We didn't know them then. He was a big, fine handsome man. And yet he finished up not knowing where he was or what he was doing. Life can be a bastard.'

They listened, both, to penetrate the silence between them.

'We shall miss her,' Jeffreys continued. 'I used to try to do a bit for her when I could. Little jobs about the house. She appreciated my company as well as the do-it-yourself. She could talk well if she knew you. The Admiral didn't share much with her when they were young. According to her if she'd made a suggestion, he'd ignore it, and deliberately.'

'She had her own back at the end of her life.'

'But she looked after him properly. Never held it against him. And she needed patience. Incontinence and all the rest. And sometimes it looked as if he acted as he did out of sheer bloody-mindedness. I don't suppose that was so. It would be the dementia, but . . . She just soldiered on. I admired her. He was a commanding figure when he was in his prime, and to be reduced to . . .' He blew breath out. 'But she saw to him, his needs. I liked to talk to her. I admired her. She was a good woman.'

Sam seemed to recall that Alice had hinted that there was more than admiration between the two. Jeffreys himself was a tall man, strong, confident, healthy. Had the sexual relation developed while the Admiral mastered life at the height of his powers, or had it begun with his decline? Sam felt shame to be thinking thus. He could not even remember clearly that Alice had suggested any such thing, that the suspicion wasn't a mere gloss of his own on some innocent remark. He kept Jeffreys waiting.

'Let me know,' Sam started gruffly, 'if there's anything I can do. I'm sorry to hear this. It's come as a shock to me, so it will be a tremendous blow . . .' His voice, phlegmy, petered out. He cleared his throat.

'I will,' Jeffreys said.

'I don't suppose Alice will want to come up tomorrow?'

'Oh, I don't know. I have to be away. It might do her good to have company. She loves children.'

'Yes. She was really good with them last time. Full of ideas. I shall be pleased to see her, but if she doesn't feel like coming, tell her to give me a ring. We'll struggle along.'

'I expect she'll come.'

'Good.'

'It's always a shock when somebody like that dies on you. When you're not expecting.' He smiled, but half hid the expression with a dumbing hand over the mouthpiece. 'I'm not sure that Alice altogether liked Hilda. They went about together and all the rest, but never quite hit it off.'

'Why was that?'

'Don't know. Hilda was senior to her at school and might have tried it on with her in some way. I don't know. I'm talking without my book.' Sam heard a door close over the phone. 'Right, here's Alice. I've just told Sam about Hilda. Do you want a word with him?' She must have shaken her head. 'No? Right, then, Sam, Goodbye.'

Sam finished dressing. He was relieved that he had arranged to go out, for otherwise he would have hunched glooming in his chair. He'd had no very favourable impression of Hilda St John.

He remembered the afternoon he'd sat with her just after her husband's death. That was his only real contact. He recalled the sour face, the awkwardness, the silences. But the woman had lived, made her mark on the village, and was not old. She should have clung on to life, as he had. He donned his overcoat with some alacrity.

At the pub he ordered beer and told the landlord the news. Jack Brentnall was not yet down.

'They'd told the Jeffreys?' the landlord asked.

'Yes. And John rang me.'

'She was very friendly with Mrs J. Otherwise there won't be too many tears shed.'

'Not popular, then?'

'You could say so.' The landlord busied himself with one of the little bar-chores that allowed conversation to continue. 'A *grande dame*.' He smirked at his French. 'There are quite a few well-to-do people in this village, and most of them are reasonable, don't expect you to kow-tow to them.'

'She did.'

'I won't exactly say that. I don't know what she did want. But her manner gave the impression that she was a cut above everybody else, and that you ought to recognize that.'

'I didn't know her well,' Sam said, guardedly.

'Neither did I. She didn't come in here. The Admiral was something to do with naval intelligence. That was when I first arrived. I'd seen nothing of him for a year or more before the funeral.'

'Did either of them come from hereabouts?' Sam asked.

'No idea.'

The landlord inspected, then straightened his trays of sparkling glasses. Sam made for his table to await Jack Brentnall.

When Jack sidled in the two men greeted each other effusively. Sam mentioned Mrs St John's death, and in return his friend told how a letter had been forwarded to him with the news of the death of a former pupil, a professor of mathematics in an Australian university. They both sketched the characters of the dead people, but without emphasis, not expecting too much interest from the other person.

It was not until Sam asked his friend whether he was ready for next morning's departure that he realized he'd been sitting at this table for twenty minutes and felt thoroughly depressed. Brentnall was prepared, it appeared.

'I always pack the night before, so that all I have to do next day is carry my cases down to the car, and set off. I do not like last-minute rush. It's perhaps the fact that I'm getting older, but I do not want to be panicked. I shall be sorry to go this time, though that is not usually so. Anything interesting that happens to me is likely to happen at home. But this Christmas I have met you, and walked out in lanes, by fields and the sea, instead of suburban streets. And, I think I can say this without fear of contradiction, our minds have, let me use a slang word from my youth, clicked. They fitted. We found we could talk easily. I go away from our chats with my brain alive and alert, as it hasn't been for years. I'd often think of something next day, and then say to myself, "I must mention that next time I see Sam Martin. He'd be interested in this, or what would he make of that?" And tomorrow morning I shall look out of my bedroom here and see the trees that have been subtly altered by our exchanges and know that in a few minutes I shall go downstairs and be on my way home.'

Sam looked at the smart man in his blazer and matching tie with the thick hair, nicely sprayed into a silver work of art, and wondered what these fascinating subjects were which they had discussed. Any brilliance or esoteric interest must lie in Jack's brain, not in the topics themselves.

Jack, he realized, was talking again about the death of Hilda St John. He listened with apathetic half-attention. She had somehow affected the character of the village, made it a place worth observing. Jack's nephew, the landlord, respected her though he'd barely spoken to her, and she had not once crossed the threshold of his premises. Apparently stopping his uncle on his way down this evening he had passed on the news and said, 'I don't know how Margaret will take this. It's as if some important landmark has been taken away.' The wife, Margaret, did know her a bit more intimately.

'And,' Brentnall went on in full flow, 'if she has this effect on people really on the edge of her life, what will it be on those to whom she was close?'

'Who are they?'

'Your friend, Mrs Jeffreys. And, by the way, my nephew was very impressed that they came in the other night to talk to us. It hadn't happened before. The likes of Mrs St John and Mrs Jeffreys have an aura about them. They are something in themselves. Beyond us.'

'A lord's daughter,' Sam said.

'Who?'

'Mrs St John.'

'It does not surprise me. And . . . and . . . She's gone, died.'

'A long way off.'

'Yes, that's it.' Brentnall appeared excited. 'That's what I like about you. You exactly hit the target with your phrase. A long way off. That's the tragedy.'

Sam could see no great virtue in what he'd said. A trite observation couched in dull words with few implications. Brentnall rattled on, laying down the law, about beauty and exactitude. This great English lady had died thousands of miles from home in America, the brash super-power in the world. They could have learnt from her.

'She didn't die amongst cannibals,' Sam objected.

'Ah. You won't allow me to exaggerate. Not by a hair's breadth. Good for you, Sam Martin.'

He sounded as fervid as before. The man was not himself. Perhaps the imminent break between them had stirred him so that he did not think rationally. Sam wondered why he was not moved in this way. They'd shake hands tonight and when he and Alice and the Craig family came into the pub for lunch tomorrow Jack would be gone, well along his way home, to the place where he was known, a respected if, occasionally, a ridiculous figure. It was quite possible that they would never meet again. Sam scratched his face, and listened to his companion now in full spate about some mathematical genius called Gauss.

Sam grew quieter by the minute. When, half an hour later, they said goodbye, Jack not only shook hands, but slapped his companion's shoulders, pulled him into himself to be hugged. Tears brimmed in the man's eyes. The flushed face, the convulsive movements of the wrinkled, strong, age-spotted hands expressed overwhelming feeling that Sam neither shared nor understood.

'When are you down here next?' Sam asked.

'Easter. The spring. Thereabouts.'

'Let me know.'

'I will. Come and spend a few days with me.'

196

'We'll see,' Sam said. The thought of whole days in Jack's company did not appeal.

'I hate parting. It's like a little death.'

'Who said that?'

'I did.' Brentnall smiled. 'I'll come outside and say goodbye in the car-park.'

They did so. Again they shook hands. Jack held on to his friend's, gently. He appeared idiotic in his jaunty cap and club scarf.

'At our age,' he said, 'one's never sure that we'll meet again.'

'Don't let it cross your mind. You feel well, don't you? Nowhere near snuffing it? I tell you, we're among the lucky ones.'

'Yes,' Jack answered. 'That's so.' He shook Sam's hand harder, drew himself up, threw his shoulders back.

"'If we do meet again, why, we shall smile.
If not, why then this parting was well made."

That's Brutus in *Julius Caesar*.'

'Good,' Sam said, removing his hand. 'Goodbye, then.' He walked out from the shadow into the glare of the floodlights, and crossing the park reached the road. He stepped slightly painfully over the iron-chain railings which were hung higher than he had bargained for. There he looked back expecting to find Brentnall still in his histrionic pose, but he had disappeared indoors. Sam laughed. On cold nights the old schoolmaster did not loiter in the open. Some sense remained.

As he walked down the dark road Sam considered this final meeting. Brentnall had played his expected part. He was used to schools, though he must have been retired for a few years, closed communities where he was a person of consequence. He could walk into a dramatic society rehearsal, and act out a line or two. In his youth he'd made amateur appearances, 'graced the boards', and did not allow his pupils or colleagues to forget it. Tonight he had spouted *Julius Caesar*, and had expected Sam to receive it appreciatively. Alice had been exactly right. A funny little man. Vain. And yet there had been a seriousness about him. His loneliness had perhaps dictated his exaggeration. Sam could not recall any topics of conversation he had raised that deserved, or anything near, the praise Brentnall had lavished on them. That

197

did not matter. Sam felt pleased to be so commended, even if wrongly. But he had filled in some dragging time profitably for a solitary man, and that was worth the effort. His spirits rose. He ought, he chided himself, to be thinking of Hilda St John's death and its effect on Alice. He'd face that tomorrow, after a night's sleep.

He lengthened his stride for a few steps, then dropped back to his old man's trot. Not a shuffle yet. He hummed tunelessly, happy with himself in spite of cold wind, some beer, bad news. If Brentnall wrote, he decided, he would reply.

XV

Sam was up early, ready for the Craig family.

At about nine Alice appeared, kissed him, accepted a cup of tea, but before she drank it inspected the house.

'I'll get the coffee things out,' she said, 'then we shan't waste the Craigs' time. Mrs Craig, Karen, is pregnant, and will be grateful if everything's laid on for her. And I tell you what. Ring up the landlord at the Royal Oak, and tell him at what time we'll be coming in for lunch. That'll make sure there are no mistakes.'

Sam had not foreseen errors, but did as he was told.

He spoke to Margaret, the landlord's wife, who promised they'd be ready for his party at twelve fifteen. She gave him details of the menu. He took a note. She said children's meals could be arranged in next to no time. He thanked her and asked if Jack Brentnall had left. She seemed slightly fazed by the name.

'Oh, Uncle John,' she said. 'Yes. He left at nine, exactly as he'd intended. He'd been no trouble at all. He is very independent.' He'd lived on his own for some years now; his wife had died before he retired. He had a son, but they saw each other rarely. There had been a daughter, but she had died as a child, as the result, she thought, of a medical accident. 'Yes,' Margaret said, 'it must have been very sad for them, but it was before I knew the family. He's Len's relative. His father's elder brother.'

Alice sat Sam down.

'John told you about Hilda, didn't he?' she began.

'Yes. He didn't seem to have any of the details.'

'No. We know very little, but my guess is that she's been ill most of the time she's been out there at her daughter's. I don't think she's been right since Clement died. She was always complaining about her health, but this time she was probably right and there was something seriously amiss.'

'What?'

'I don't know. Cancer. Some breakdown of the system.'

199

'And her husband's death triggered that?'

'No, I didn't say so. It made a large difference to the pattern of her life. When Clement first retired, they were happy enough. He'd had enough of whatever he was doing in the Navy. Intelligence. Something to do with dirty-tricks as far as I could gather from Hilda. I don't know whether it was the nature of his work that he disliked, or whether he thought it a waste of national time and money. Anyhow he was glad to come out. He could travel whenever he liked, and he used to read an enormous amount, and do mathematical puzzles, and write to academic people about them. He was never so settled. He made no demands on her. The home was her place. She arranged things without consulting him, and as long as he had a day or two's notice he'd fall in with her plans. She loved it. She bossed him and bullied him and he didn't seem to notice. And then he began to be ill. Memory went, and will. He hung about the house, without anything to occupy him. He was out of his normal mind very quickly. I have read that people who think and read and use their brains a great deal tend to go more slowly down into dementia, but it wasn't so in his case. And his mental decline was matched by physical failure. He just wanted to sit, and before too long that was all he could do.'

'It must have been hard on his wife.'

'Again I'm not sure. She had to make a radical change, but she was always capable of that. She arranged help; they were not short of money, and she worked hard at looking after him. She kept him away from people, so that there was no embarrassment either to her or him or anybody else.'

'She didn't hold it against him?' Sam asked.

'How could she? He couldn't help it.'

'People don't always act rationally.'

Alice looked up sharply, like an animal in fear.

'No, they don't,' she said. 'It got on her nerves, and she complained to one or two friends who knew the truth about Clement's illness, but she did her duty by him. And this was remarkable because they weren't, I used to think, altogether suited in the first place.'

'In what way?'

'Hilda wanted to be at the front of the picture, the object of everyone's interest. A naval officer's wife is a kind of widow, left on her own, but without the time to establish herself in

200

people's eyes. And when Clement came back on leave, he was the one guests wanted to meet. And though he loved her, I'm sure,' her tense smile denied it, 'he wasn't exactly, well, effusive. Very handsome and all that, but rather cold.'

'Like her?' Sam said.

'I would have said not,' Alice corrected him, 'in the first place. She needed affection, and shows of affection. Later, perhaps, she fitted her persona to the total picture, and so she had the reputation for stand-offishness. She wanted people to praise her, and touch her, and love her.'

'She didn't look elsewhere for the right sort of admiration?' he asked.

Alice glared at him, but answered quietly enough,

'No. Not to the best of my knowledge, no.'

They heard the sound of the Craigs' car in the drive, the children's voices. Alice rushed the empty tea-cups away to the kitchen. The two were at the front door before the visitors rang the bell.

The children were in high spirits to be let out of the car. Edward Craig said he'd prefer to stand for a while if they didn't mind. Karen looked beautiful in her pregnancy, a full goddess with a human, delicate face and tired eyes.

'We started at the crack of dawn,' she said.

'When are we going to the sea?' Ben interrupted.

'Drinks first,' Alice said, 'and biscuits.'

'Any chocolate?' Ben asked.

'Ben,' his sister warned.

'Come and help me find them,' Alice said. 'We'll see then what we've saved for you.'

She led the children out. Sam could hear Ben asking her if she lived all the time in this bungalow. Karen, serene now, said she felt remarkably well, never better. The last week in February was the doctor's date, and she'd be glad if the child came on time.

'I'm so much slower,' she said, 'but I really do feel well. And people give me a hand. Emma's marvellous really. She's like a grown-up. I'm not sure that I want that. But she'll love the baby. She was great with Ben, and now that she's older . . .'

Edward Craig stood, monarch of all he surveyed, with his back to them, hands deep in trouser-pockets looking over the books in Sam's shelves. He carried an air of authority with him, the headmaster, and this seemed even more pronounced when he took a pair of spectacles from its case, and polished the lenses with a pensive panache, before donning them to examine some title more closely.

'Some interesting stuff here,' he said over his shoulder, not expecting a reply.

'You ought to ask permission before you go poking round people's bookshelves,' Karen chided.

'I'm sure Mr Martin won't mind.'

'You carry on,' Sam said. 'Saves me dusting.'

'Do you read much?'

'A fair amount. I go into Hunstanton to the library. I don't read very seriously, though.'

'You've a good row of D.H. Lawrence, I see,' Edward from the bookshelves.

'Yes. My mother knew him, slightly. He was a student when she was at college. She was just a year or so younger than he was.'

'What was he like?'

'She didn't say much. They'd no idea he'd be famous. He was one of the clever boys, she said.'

'Fond of the girls?' Edward inquired.

'Didn't know or say. She didn't live in his part of the world. It was only later that she bought his books. I think she was a bit shocked by his reputation. But she acquired these. They were there when I was a boy.'

'Out of reach, I hope?'

'Your mother was a teacher?' Karen asked.

'Yes. She married just before the 1914-18 War. I was born during that war.'

'Do you remember any of it?'

'No, not really, though we played English and Germans as boys.'

The children came thumping in with Alice, Ben squealing with delight. Alice ushered them out to the kitchen for glasses of lemonade, the boy still nearly incoherent.

'You two drink out here,' Alice was heard commanding. 'We've got special stools, but you, Ben, will have to be careful, and sit like a grown-up.'

'I can,' Ben claimed. 'I can, I can.'

Alice brought in tea and coffee for the visitors.

'Are they being a nuisance?' Karen asked.

'No. Good as gold.'

The children crept in when they had finished their drinks and cleared their plate of biscuits. They looked to Alice for permission before entering. She offered them an adult biscuit. Emma stood by Sam's chair; she looked very like her mother.

'How long shall we be on the beach?' Karen asked.

'Not much more than an hour, there and back. I ordered our table at the Oak for twelve fifteen sharp.'

'Do you mind if I don't come down with you?' Karen sounded plaintive. 'If you're not going to be long, I think I'd be better off sitting here.'

'Are you all right?' Edward asked at once.

'Yes, perfectly, but a rest here looking out at Mr Martin's garden or his pictures or his books will do me more good than traipsing about in the cold.'

Sam made her comfortable before the sea-going party set off in Edward's car.

'Will the car park be open?' he asked.

'Yes, but unguarded.'

Sam sat at the back between the children. He sang to them.

> 'Oh, I do like to be beside the seaside,
> I do like to be beside the sea.'

To his surprise they did not know the song, but in the minute or two at her disposal Emma did her best to join in. Alice sang in deep contralto, dwarfing the other voices. Once out of the parked and locked car, the children ran ahead, Ben shrilly shouting, 'The sea, the sea.' Alice kept close to them, and the two men walked behind.

'Is Karen well?' Sam asked.

'Yes, but she gets tired. She's always on the go. An hour in an armchair will be a luxury beyond telling. We get help with the housework at home, but I feel guilty. I have to put in such long days at school, and then quite often I'm out again in the evening. The demands these days on a headmaster are getting quite beyond reason. I know I'm new to the job, and making my mark, and I expect I shall learn the short-cuts in time, but it seems a pity that it has to be at Karen's expense, and especially at this time.'

'I thought she looked well.'

'So she is. But I don't want her run off her feet. She's like a good many teachers, or ex-teachers, too conscientious by half. And she never complains. She's one in a thousand.'

'How about the school? Are any of the teachers outstandingly good or bad?'

'Nobody is really hopeless, and two are really good. Both are young, and one's like me absolutely new, started last September.' Suddenly he laughed and lowered his voice. 'She's already connected with me in a lewd rhyme.'

'How do you know?'

'I saw it on a Cable box near the school. They have flat-tops which are tempting to all our budding scribblers. I suppose we must be grateful for small mercies. You're surprised, aren't you, that such obscenities exist in infant and junior schools?'

'Not at all. We had 'em seventy-five years ago.'

'In those innocent days?' Craig said. To Sam's slight disappointment Edward did not repeat the lubricious lines. He felt he should not ask for further enlightenment.

The children ran along the dull beach, threw two highly-coloured balls which Alice had brought down in her bag. It blew cold, and the sand spread dark brown, even black, between the long, cold, silver streaks of the sea-pools.

'The tide's out,' Sam said. 'The wind must have urged it very high in the night.'

The sky arched icy, streaked with wind-shredded clouds. The larger of the children's balls skidded towards Sam who attempted to control it and failed, merely diverting it. He trotted after it happily enough, aimed a kick at it which did not connect, tried again, sent it looping in the air.

'Well played, sir,' Craig shouted. Ben howled with pleasure and chased the ball. He fell, but rose smilingly to his feet. Alice called him over, cleaned his knees and his jacket and set him on his way again. The children bounded ahead. Alice kept close behind, organized games when their invention flagged: catch, piggy-in-the-middle, miniature golf with Sam's stick.

'She's good with them,' Edward said. 'I wouldn't have guessed it.'

'Why not?'

'Her appearance and posh voice. Her clothes are very expensive.'

'Are they?'

'They jolly well are.'

Sam wondered how Edward Craig could be so confident on the topic.

'She looks like the lady bountiful, a member of the squirearchy, patronizing lesser mortals.'

'She was trained as a professional musician,' Sam said, by no means pleased with Craig's comments. 'A pianist.'

'You surprise me. And yet one never knows. I'd got her pigeon-holed, and judging purely, or impurely from appearance. Quite wrong. I'd have her on my staff at any time. Though I don't suppose we could afford her.'

They watched Alice standing high on the beach organizing a race which the children had demanded. She had marked out the course, had determined the handicap, had stood at the finish to judge the result, had started them, twice falsely, in a stentorian voice. Emma won because Ben, arms flailing, had fallen over again. All seemed satisfied beyond reason.

The five strolled a little further along the flatness of the shore, more soberly now until Sam, tapping his wrist-watch, said they should turn about otherwise they might be late for lunch.

'Some might need cleaning up,' Edward said.

'Me,' Ben answered, excited still if subdued.

'We'll all breathe the sea air,' Edward ordered, a headmaster intervening in the PE lesson. He stood facing out to sea, hands on his chest. Such was his charisma that the others lined up beside him. 'All ready? Deep breathing, begin.' In their different fashions they aped his example. 'Again, one, two, three, in. Hold it. Slowly out.' He looked his troop over. 'Again.' This time he spread his arms to ensure unanimous benefit. 'And again.'

The children laughed, playing pouter-pigeons.

'You don't get air like this where we live,' Edward said. 'It's like wine.'

'If you drink wine, you get drunk,' Emma solemnly warned them.

'Not with this. Oh, no.'

They completed the exercises and walked on, the children skipping ahead.

'It's cold,' Sam said to Alice.

'I'm hot,' she said.

'You've been busy.'

Back in the bungalow, Karen took the children to the

bathroom whence they emerged with brushed, shining hair. The wind had coloured their cheeks. Exactly on time they set out for lunch.

'You're the first,' Margaret the landlady called, switching on lights, ushering them to an already prepared table.

'And the best,' the landlord seconded.

'Of course.'

They ordered drinks and lunch. Karen gave precise directions about the meals for Ben and Emma. While they waited Alice played 'I spy' with the children. Ben had roughly grasped the principles of the game. When that petered out, Sam took them round the pictures and explained what was happening in the prints of eighteenth-century agricultural life. Ben particularly liked the plough-horses. Sam did his best to compare modern processes with those depicted.

'There were no tractors,' he pronounced. Ben's face fell.

'I prefer a horse any day,' Emma said.

'They don't make good noises.' Ben gave a quite startling loud imitation of a tractor.

'He's mad on motors,' Emma glossed the performance.

'I've six tractors,' Ben said.

Edward walked the walls with Sam and the children. Alice and Karen talked quietly across the table. Once they clasped hands, both left and right, but Sam had no idea why. They seemed to be talking about the theatre. The landlady hovered, like a gracious hostess, unobtrusively, waiting on their wishes. Once she cornered Sam to tell him how much Uncle John had enjoyed his company.

'It made his holiday. He doesn't know how to occupy himself. He retired and then his wife died and it left him with an empty life. School had been his be-all and end-all. When he finished he meant to spend some time on Aunt Eileen, but it didn't happen that way.'

'No.' Sam nodded solemnly.

'He's a typical schoolmaster,' Margaret said. 'He loves to talk. But young people don't want to listen, and the old want nothing except to complain. But you were different. A man of parts. Never at a loose end. Always with something in mind.'

'Not true,' Sam said.

'That's how it seemed to him. And you let him talk. That was the secret.'

Margaret touched his arm, turning him back towards his friends.

The meal was excellent; children both ate heartily, the real test, Alice claimed. Sam insisted, overruling Edward, on settling the bill. They had ten minutes in the field outside where Emma and Ben took to the swings. The father whirled Emma up so high she squealed. Ben, under Alice's care, shouted to equal, to out-soar his sister. Alice played it sensibly. All were satisfied, smiling in the winter's long grass.

'It's been a marvellous day,' Karen told Sam.

'I've enjoyed every minute. Those two keep you on your toes. And soon it will be three.'

'That's it.'

'Is all well at home? Between you and Edward?'

'As near perfect as could be. He really puts in a lot of time with the children.' The two watched the youngsters swinging and their minders encouraging adventure. 'Sometimes he seems very quiet, wrapped up inside himself and I know he's thinking about next term's inspection.'

'Is he worried?'

'He wants to do well.'

'And will he?'

'Yes. He will. And the inspection will do the school a power of good. He thought it unfair, at first, that it should come so early in his time as headmaster, but now he sees it as an advantage bringing a complacent school to its senses. They do what he asks of them twice as willingly, he says, now they know they'll be judged from outside.'

'Good. And the lady?'

'We've heard nothing more. She sent a Christmas card.'

'Nothing from the anonymous letter-writers.'

'No. He spoke to the staff. I wasn't sure that was wise, but he held a final staff meeting about preparation for the inspection, and that was the last item. He'd do it well. And make them believe he knew who'd sent the letters. It would all be short. And frightening.'

'Well done, Edward.'

Karen laughed. The world seemed good, even on this cold afternoon.

Kisses abounded and the Craigs clambered into the car, all smiles. Edward did not hang about; within half a minute the car had reversed from the park and was out of earshot. Alice and Sam stood, at a loss.

'Are you coming back for a cup of coffee?' Sam asked.

'Yes, thanks. I'll just call in at home for a second.'

They walked the road, silenced.

'Shan't be long,' Alice said as she opened her own gate. 'Get the kettle on.'

Sam's bungalow seemed empty, shabby in the winter light. Inside it radiated warmth, but seemed lifeless. A ruck in the carpet, a cushion out of place in the back of the chair where Karen had sat, two or three pencils on the table, a screwed-up drawing, six empty cups and glasses on the draining board were the only vestiges of that noisy half-hour with the family. Sam washed up, fetched out two coffee cups, put on the percolator, squared up the biscuit tin and waited for Alice.

She did not keep him long. She rattled the front door which he'd left unlocked and walked in.

'It's cold,' she announced.

'Coffee's ready,' he answered. 'How about a slug of whisky with it?'

'Good idea. It's warm in here.'

They settled to their drinks. He had poured out more whisky than he'd intended. They praised the Craig family succinctly, but sat with hands round their cups.

'You look tired,' Alice said.

'Yes, I suppose I am. I didn't sleep well last night.'

'Why was that?'

'Usual bladder trouble had me up a time or two, and I was worrying, I guess, whether all would go well today. I'm not used to visitors. Any change of pattern and I'm doing my nut. That's one of the disadvantages of old age or living on your own.'

'They weren't difficult,' she said.

'No. Very good. And Karen had an hour or two's rest.'

'Edward's rather quiet, don't you think?'

'Yes. But he knows his mind.'

Sam raised his whisky glass.

'Your health,' he proposed. 'He'd like you on his staff, he said. To terrorize the inspectors they were having in next term.'

'And yours.' She drank. 'That's good.'

'Warms the cockles.'

Again they sat in reverie.

When they had finished the coffee she carried away the cups. While she was out he'd added more whisky to their glasses.

'You'll have me tiddly,' Alice said. That was not her sort of word, he thought. They talked for a little about Edward Craig, Jack Brentnall and schoolteachers. They could not make their minds up. 'I expect they're different,' Alice concluded, 'from those in my day. A few pretty, young women and the rest stiff-backed, middle-aged and old, maiden ladies.' The two laughed. Sam described his chemistry teacher, a man fit to run the country. They were now warm and Sam closed his eyes comfortably.

'You're nodding off,' Alice warned. 'Why don't you go to bed for an hour?'

'I can't do that.'

'Why not? It's miserable outside. Off you go. Sharp. Pyjamas on. Doctor's orders. And I'll join you.'

His eyes opened wide.

'In my bed?'

'Where else? Some people. Away you go.'

He could not believe his ears. He swayed out to the bathroom, emptied his bladder, washed his hands. Rather uneasily he examined his face in the mirror. It seemed peaky, mottled, aged, apprehensive, not much like his mental picture of himself, but thinner, bloodless, some other old man. He found his way to the bedroom, undressed, put on pyjamas, clambered into bed. The sheets struck cold; he sat up again, turned on the electric blanket, and slithered back, bedclothes up to his chin. Somewhere he'd read that the electric field set up by heaters or radio-sets affected the body. Not a bad thing in his case. It could only bring an improvement. A thought struck. He ought to have drawn the curtains. Sluggishly reluctant, he lowered his feet to the floor, padded over and drew the blinds. The room was darker but not significantly so. He made sure he had completed the task properly, so that no window-cleaner, passing stranger, person on the scrounge could peer in. He caught sight of his bare feet and hurried back into bed. This time he covered his face completely. As he lay there, a great shudder rippled across his back. The strength of the movement surprised him; it seemed to reduce him to the thinness of a skeleton, with each bone sensitive, capable of intense feeling. He waited for the next tide; it did not come.

Outside he could hear nothing of Alice. He lay quite still.

209

The door clicked open. He glanced up from beneath the sheet. Alice advanced, holding her clothes folded in front of her. She placed them with rapid ease on an empty chair. She was stark naked.

'Look out there,' she called.

She lifted the bedcovers and forced herself in quickly but heavily beside him.

'There we are,' she said. 'I'm not very warm.' She tried a cold foot on one of his. Again the shudder in his back flayed him. She turned, put an arm across him and drew him into her. They lay together; he felt her softness.

He turned, held her, awkwardly at first, to him. He kissed her; her lips tasted of whisky; his fingers explored her. She pulled down his pyjama trousers.

'I'm afraid,' he said.

'Of what?' Her fingers played magically over him.

'I shan't be able to do anything. Sexually. To you. I'm too old.'

'You're not supposed to,' she said. That voice had a strength, which comforted. It came from the Alice he had heard in the street, the lady of status, not the warm and naked woman he handled so delicately. 'We're in here for a rest after a morning of child-minding.' His fingers tentatively explored her smooth-nesses, her depths. In return she played with him until he knew his world had changed. He did not now mind that he had no erection; what he had received was a kind of blessedness, a lifting from everyday torpor. The bed glowed with a warmth of benignity. She stretched and drew him to her. He was no longer ashamed of his skinny legs, his small hard paunch, his painful joints.

His spirits rose as he lay. The first moments of excitement expanded into elation. His passivity lacked the power, the intransigent fire of penetration but it lifted him into a state of parallel discovery; he had found new lands. He had given himself away, or been taken by her, not into herself, but by her overwhelming caresses. Exterior, but conquering, she touched him.

Once or twice he nodded off in the warmth of the engagement. Touch and the flush of heat cradled as it roused him. His comfort towered with the inevitability of the sexual climax he did not achieve, until he fell into sleep. He woke for brief seconds from

210

time to time to enjoy those arms encircling him, that body powerfully soft against his own nakedness. He had no idea for how long he slept, but was awakened by Alice's voice.

'You can't stay there all day,' she warned. 'You won't be able to sleep tonight.'

She stood by the side of his bed, fully dressed, broadly smiling, but secretly, as if she knew something he did not. Her hair had been recently combed, and shone. Her clothes were uncreased, bright as if she was wearing them for the first time.

'I've brought you a cup of tea,' she said.

He dragged himself upright with reluctance at first, then with a sudden start of joy. Sam sat, expectant, and received the cup. He sipped. She moved round to the other side of the bed and straightened the covers, then drew one of the curtains.

'Have you got yourself a cup?' he asked, sipping.

'Yes, thank you.'

He put out a hand to touch hers. She allowed the caress, but casually, almost as if she had not noticed it. She sat for a short time at the end of the bed, out of his reach.

'I'll go to pour mine now,' she said. 'I don't like it too strong.'

Sam finished his tea, dressed himself flinging his clothes on. He donned his socks without the usual accompaniment of groans. He noticed no aches, moved like a schoolboy, his mind in a delirium of delight. He whipped back the curtains to winter twilight.

'Another cup?' Alice asked as he appeared. She poured and they sat opposite. He in his exhilaration could not understand why she made no outward show. This afternoon she had bestowed a huge favour on him, but she occupied a chair by the kitchen table as if she had just dropped in on some humdrum occasion and had accepted a cup of tea before she moved on to her next dull duty. He felt in awe of her, of her composure. This was not the naked woman who had stripped him and lulled him asleep by her embrace.

'Did you go to sleep?' he asked.

'Yes. I had half an hour, and felt all the better for it.'

'How long did I have?'

'Well over an hour,' she said. 'You must have been tired.'

She cleared away the crockery to the kitchen but returned immediately to announce that she must go. She made haste to the hall, taking her coat from its hanger. She put it on, buttoned it, briefly examined the effect in the mirror, and turned to wish him goodbye. Now he rushed towards her, clasped and kissed her mouth. She stood her ground, not averting her face, but soon grabbing him by the biceps released herself. She unlocked the door, and let herself out without fuss. As she walked away along the front garden path she raised her gloved left hand, almost triumphantly, but without turning round.

Sam breathed deeply, gathering his wits, stared ravished. He existed there in the foyer of the bungalow, unthinking, a new man, recreated. When he had shuffled off towards the kitchen to wash the few pots, he watched the water run from the hot tap as if it was some miracle. Outside it grew dark as he walked round the rooms, unable to sit, to contain himself. He straightened his bed again, the bed, the holy place.

He began to prepare for his evening meal. Now he seemed no longer on the edge of the world, waiting for things to happen to other people. He was part of the action. That it had been unexpected put it lightly. Alice's behaviour seemed out of character. She had been friendly before, and that in itself had seemed surprising. What was so interesting about him that had caught her attention? She had a husband, a family, influential friends, talents, and yet she had bothered to draw him under her influence so that they met, worked together for short periods, exchanged ideas, however casually, were more than nodding acquaintances. That had brightened the flatness of his life, but what had happened this afternoon loomed huge, of a different nature. Friend had become wife, kindly gestures had become sacrifice, oblation, sacrament.

Sam had doubts, as always.

Perhaps her impulsive action could be put down to whisky. It seemed possible. And what of John Jeffreys, her husband? What would he have said? Would he have guessed that his wife was capable of this imprudent action? With an impotent, shrivelled, old man without the wit to cultivate even his own interests? A nobody with nothing to say, who now could barely be entrusted with the simplest task without supervision? Such thoughts would not cross Jeffreys' confident mind. He'd have no suspicion that Sam Martin, the nondescript, aged neighbour, could become a serious rival. This impossibility went against nature, as if an earthquake erased the quiet village.

But what if, for some reason, Alice had decided, and this

212

afternoon had declared her decision, to throw over the traces, discard her husband, and take up, marry him? Sam would not countenance that idea, could not. He had the money to provide for Alice; quite probably he was much richer than John. If he married her, it might well prove too much. The extent of Sam's life perhaps depended on insipid days skulking away from excitement so that if he wed her it could kill, obliterate him, and the hours of flaring happiness would be scythed pitilessly short. He did not want to die; that would happen soon enough. What he wanted was something equivalent to this afternoon's episode, something short and comfortable, not too often, abnormal, in secret and without consequences except his subsequent happiness and the vague hope that something like it would happen again. It depended on Alice. Sam had no idea what she'd do.

He filled the kettle.

In the next weeks he baffled himself with these ideas. Alice's husband, freshly returned from his London excursion, pleased beyond measure with his performance, had proposed that he and his wife should immediately fly out to the Mediterranean, to Majorca. Someone he'd met had offered them a villa, at a ridiculously low rent, for a month 'out of the 'flu zone'. Sam met Alice only once, such was the Jeffreys' hurry to get abroad, when she instructed him about looking after their house. An occasional postcard brought news of no importance and some further small task. Going round the place he'd found an insignificant, framed photograph of the house which he'd taken back home determined to make into a larger watercolour for them. By the first week in February, a deadline he'd set himself so that the picture would be framed and ready for hanging on their return, he had completed two versions, both eminently satisfactory. They now stood side by side in his work room, awaiting the Jeffreys' return and choice. Both shone, summer in winter.

The holiday-makers were in no hurry. At the end of their four weeks' absence Alice rang to say that they intended to stay for another ten days. Their landlord had offered them the time free of charge. 'I'd sooner have responsible tenants in than nobody,' he'd said to Alice. 'It maintains the house in good order.' John had muttered to her that it didn't matter if their own house dropped to pieces in England. Sam reassured her that both her house and that of the late St Johns' were in excellent order, kept warm by judicious use of central heating, and both given a whole day's thorough cleaning each week by the 'help'. He would see to the further payments of the cleaning women until their return, when they could 'square up. No trouble.'

He inquired, tentatively, if she was looking forward to home.

It appeared that she was not, and, in fact, when she and John returned they spent three days with their daughter and her family in London. By that time, Alice opined, the weather in Norfolk should be beginning to warm up. She asked briefly after his health, warned him not to overdo things, nor get cold. He did not mention the completed pictures. He hoped to surprise her.

In the early evening before the Jeffreys' return, Edward Craig rang to announce the safe arrival of the new baby, a girl, Madeleine Jane. Mother and child, in hospital, were doing well. Karen's mother had come down from Lancashire to look after Ben and Emma, who had welcomed with dancing glee their new sister. Edward professed himself up to the eyes in work preparing for the inspection next half-term, but said he was 'ready for anything' now.

'Three-two to the Ladies,' Sam said. 'A good score.'

'I wouldn't mind another child,' Edward said seriously.

'What does Karen say?'

'I'll have to ask her.'

Sam took out from the wardrobe the gifts for older siblings as well as for the new arrival to put in the first post the next morning. These had been packed since before Christmas under Alice's supervision.

'Won't it matter about the gender of the baby?' he had asked.

'No. All unisex for a start.'

They had laughed. It cheered him beyond measure that the Craigs were now five and not four.

He decided that he would walk down to the pub in celebration. Something had to be done. He took care with his appearance, showering then running the shaver over his face, and looking out a clean shirt and tie. He polished his shoes, deriving satisfaction from the short, hard brush-strokes. He put on his best top-coat instead of the usual anoraks. He'd greet Miss M.J. Craig, wet her bottom with propriety. Jack Brentnall would have approved.

At the Royal Oak the landlord's wife served him. She would not, if he didn't mind, join him in a drink. She seemed preoccupied.

'I'm celebrating a new baby,' he said.

'A grandchild?'

'No. A friend's baby. The family who came in for lunch just after Christmas, the Craigs.'

'Oh, yes. I remember them. They had a little girl who spoke just like an adult. I thought to myself, "My word, she's clever. She's going to make her mark in the world."'

Margaret slipped away. Sam sat down. The place was practically empty. Very soon the door opened and the landlord came across.

'Evening, Mr Martin.'

'Evening, Len.'

'How are we then?'

'I can't grumble.'

'It doesn't do any good.'

A pause developed. Sam wondered whether he should announce Madeleine's birth a second time. While he pondered this the landlord drew himself up to a kind of uneasy attention.

'I'm afraid,' he said, and stopped, 'I'm afraid I've some bad news for you.'

'Oh?'

'My uncle. John Brentnall.' He waited for some acknowledgement or sign that the name was recognized. He received no answer. Sam sat looking down at his glass of ale and the thumb and middle finger placed lightly on either side of the base of the glass. When finally he looked up, the landlord said in a husky voice, 'He died yesterday morning.' They kept silence. 'We don't know yet when the funeral is.'

Sam shook his head in disbelief.

'Was it unexpected?' he forced himself to ask.

'Yes. To us it was. He'd had one heart attack, that we know of, and angina, but this must have been major. His cleaning woman sent for an ambulance, and they came very quickly with paramedics and all the up-to-date machines, but it was too late.'

'Did he suffer much?'

'I shouldn't think so. He'd just had his breakfast and was sitting at the table reading the paper. Mrs Fairhurst was in the kitchen. She hadn't been in long. She heard him call out to her, and he told her to ring 999 and say it was a heart attack. When she came back he was sitting on the floor leaning against a settee, legs bent up. That's the best way apparently. He'd know. He was sweating and a ghastly colour and breathing heavily, but he

215

could speak. Then he went into a coma. The ambulance wasn't many minutes, and they tried all sorts to resuscitate him, but he was dead by the time he got to hospital if not before.'

'I'm sorry,' Sam said. 'I liked him.'

'Yes, a nice man. We've only got to know him well in these last few years. I was a bit scared of him as a boy.'

Margaret, the wife, had now joined her husband and stood to support him as a carrier of ill tidings.

'Yes. Very independent. Loved to give you a hand. And the amount he knew. He surprised us on more than one occasion, didn't he, Margaret, with information he came out with?'

'I liked him,' Sam said.

'He liked you. One of the old sort, he said. He was greatly looking forward to seeing you again. A man you could talk to. That was his verdict.'

Sam nodded.

A small crush of customers, six, eight perhaps, noisily pushed in. Len and Margaret turned about, lined up behind the bar. Sam sipped his ale. A tear trickled down his face from his left eye. He did not wipe it away. His throat clogged, so that he was glad not to talk. His arms hung leaden. For minutes he sat without moving. The party at the bar shouted cheerfully, but he'd no idea what they said. They spoke as they passed his table. He managed a grunted reply.

Tomorrow, he thought, his mind moving in uncontrollable jerks, the Jeffreys would appear, brown, and huge, bursting with life. He'd be glad to see them, but he would not be himself. Jack Brentnall had gone. It was not the end of the world. He hadn't known the man long enough. Since he'd gone away, they'd exchanged two postcards, each. He wasn't altogether sure he approved of him, but it would affect his meeting with John and Alice. His eye caught the picture on an advertisement for a local printer. A Degas dancer. It was at this table that he and Brentnall had last sat together. Jack had been opposite and must have seen it, the rectangle of shiny white paper, the bright colours, the girl dancing her way out of the old year and into the new. Sam sipped his beer. His eyes brimmed. This time he dashed at them with a clean handkerchief. He did not fear his own death, but that of others flung the transience of the world hard into his face. He lifted his glass for the last time. Truly he expected too much. He breathed deeply filling his lungs against misfortune. He stood, walked across, placed his glass on the bar. He'd forgotten the Craigs. One gap made another.

'Good night, Len,' he called. The landlord hurried in from the other room.

'You going, Mr Martin? Are you sure you're all right?' He appeared concerned.

'Thank you. I think so.' He nodded as vigorously as he could. 'I'm a bit tired. Getting near the head of the queue.'

'Never mind. Spring's just round the corner.'

The landlord accompanied him to the door.

Sam stepped out into the cold night.

'Let me know when the funeral is,' he said.